SUBMISSION

By the same author:

EMMA'S SECRET WORLD
EMMA ENSLAVED
EMMA'S SECRET DIARIES

EMMA'S SUBMISSION

Hilary James

This book is a work of fiction.
In real life, make sure you practise safe sex.

First published in 1996 by
Nexus
332 Ladbroke Grove
London W10 5AH

Typeset by TW Typesetting, Plymouth, Devon

Printed and bound by
BPC Paperbacks Ltd, Aylesbury, Bucks

ISBN 0 352 33108 9

Contents

This, the fourth book in the Emma series, continues the erotic adventures of a young married woman in the world of lesbian love and domination. Ursula, Emma's Mistress, demands complete obedience and makes sure that she gets it. This time, Ursula has some new experiments to try out on her unsuspecting girls . . .

1

Enter the Baroness

It all began as a harmless platonic friendship. She was a Baroness and, of course, Emma loved a title. Emma had accepted an invitation to a big dinner party given at the Dorchesters' London house at The Boltons. She had an idea it was going to be an unusual fun party as Maximillian Friend had been invited, having just completed a rather shocking nude of Lady Dorchester – 'Annie' to her friends.

Emma had told her unsuspecting husband that Ursula wanted her to help at a late evening showing at her gallery. In fact, Emma was keeping away from Ursula who, to her relief, recently seemed either to have been abroad, or busy getting her new London house ready.

Emma had ignored Ursula's angry letters and peremptory phone calls. Previously, as a confirmed masochist, she had adored being under Ursula's strict control, being her helpless slave and never knowing what was going to happen next. It had all been so exciting – even if had also been very painful at times.

But now it was time to move on. Emma had really had enough of Ursula and her exhausting ways. She was, she kept telling herself, free and independent, and a married woman to boot – even if her husband was often abroad for months at a time. Moreover, she had her own friends who greatly admired her vivacious and bubbly personality whereas Ursula just enjoyed putting her down and denigrating her.

No. It was time to make a clean break from her demanding Mistress. It was true, of course, that Ursula was a vengeful and demanding woman. But what harm, Emma asked herself, could she really do to her? And anyway, the feeling of freedom, of being able to do what she wanted and see whom she wanted, was so wonderful that she soon forgot all about her worries over Ursula.

But Emma was completely taken aback, and dismayed, to see Ursula at the party. She was with a very beautiful young woman from Eastern Europe, who spoke little or no English or French. Ursula had introduced her as her 'niece'.

The girl's role seemed merely to look decorative, to attend constantly on Ursula like a lady-in-waiting, and to look adoringly at her. It was a role that she evidently found thrilling.

Emma could not help feeling jealous, remembering how often Ursula had used her in the same role. She, too, had been taken by Ursula to parties as her 'niece', sometimes with another of her 'nieces', simply to be shown off – having been instructed to look adoringly at her Mistress and not to speak one word to anyone.

She, too, had found it thrilling to be treated publicly almost like a slave. But now she had grown out of all that. Ursula had no hold on her these days.

Emma avoided Ursula but could not help overhearing how one of her collection of very valuable pictures, all gems of modern art, had been stolen. Ursula was going round the party saying that she suspected that one of her set had organised their theft, and that she would move heaven and earth to get it back.

Serve her right, thought Emma. Quite apart from selling her own pictures, Ursula had always used her contacts in the art world to acquire paintings cheaply and sell them at a considerable profit in order to finance her acquisition and subsequent subjugation of beautiful young women like Emma herself.

The dinner was excellent and Emma was impressed by the liveried male servants. But everyone was on edge to know just what sort of amusement Annie would have arranged for after dinner. Sometimes it was games but this time, rather intriguingly, she had erected a little cinema screen in the ballroom.

The atmosphere was very jolly as the guests took their seats. To her delight, Emma found herself sitting on a little gold seat next to the Baroness. On her other side was Martin Klein, who was well known in theatrical circles. Behind her, eyeing her with a baleful stare, was Ursula, whose 'niece' was sitting dutifully at her feet, resting her head on Ursula's thigh like a little dog, whilst Ursula, talking to her neighbour, absent-mindedly stroked her hair.

Few people at the party knew of the previously turbulent relationship Emma and Ursula had shared. Suffice to say, however, that at first Emma felt she really ought to be very careful how she behaved. But then her new-found confidence returned. Ursula was just something out of her past; it was the future that mattered. So, tossing her hair in a gesture of independence, she turned her back on Ursula and ignored her.

Emma was feeling unusually excited that evening. Several of the men and women had complimented her on her appearance and when she took a look at herself in the long mirror in the hall, she also thought that she was looking particularly attractive. Her long, silky blonde hair was pinned up in a sophisticated, almost Edwardian style, her blue eyes were sparkling between long, carefully painted lashes, and her provocatively pouting scarlet lips contrasted with the perfect complexion of her cheeks. Two sparkling earrings, heirlooms from her husband's family, completed the picture.

Then, looking down, Emma could not help admiring her short, blue taffeta off-the-shoulder evening dress. Her intriguing cleavage was further enhanced by a black opal hanging from a chain around her neck. The only criticism she could make was she would have liked her waist to be as slim as it used to be. The trouble was that since becoming free of Ursula's discipline, she simply could not resist nibbling delicious chocolates and sweets. But all in all, she decided, she was a very pretty and intelligent-looking young woman.

* * *

During dinner, she found the Baroness the most amusing person at the party, but whenever she laughed aloud at her jokes she felt under the table someone - she knew who - jealously stick their high heels into her little feet, making her want to cry out in pain.

The Baroness was dark-haired and very *soignée*. She had a very cultured and well-bred look with strong, dominant-looking features.

Emma could not quite understand why there was a tension between the Baroness and Ursula - or did she, perhaps, understand only too well? Certainly, they were both dominant women, and equally certainly no one had given Emma permission to make eyes at the Baroness!

The lights went out in the ballroom and the guests sat still on their seats while some music played. As the credits rolled, Emma realised that it was a naughty French film that they were going to see.

Although her French was limited, she could see that even her little knowledge would not really be necessary as this was a film about lesbian love with the most explicit sex scenes.

You could have heard a pin drop in the ballroom, Emma thought. It seemed the men were loving it, too. Emma could see that 'Old Bollocks' Roustead was actually playing with himself whilst Annie, who was well-known in London for her little dalliances with the fairer sex, had a young woman on her knee. To some of the guests it may have looked as if it was her daughter or her niece but Emma had seen the same girl before with you know who! Goodness, she thought, surely Ursula was not now hiring out her girls to other women?

Emma was longing for the Baroness to look her way, or even perhaps to put a hand on her skirt – but nothing happened.

As she watched the bondage scenes, she began to get very excited. Would anyone notice, she wondered, if she moved her hand up under her dress? In the end she simply could not stop herself and slowly slipped her right hand up under the taffeta, so as to put her little finger into her already wet panties.

As she used her fingers to good effect, she could feel her breasts swell and she was getting more excited with every second. She was horrified lest Ursula would notice, but luckily Ursula was too preoccupied with watching Annie and her girl. The girl had once been one of Ursula's 'specials' and Emma could see the proprietary way that Ursula was watching her. Then, suddenly, she felt someone lean over her.

'Stop it, you naughty girl!' came a soft whisper.

Emma felt utterly ashamed. It was the Baroness! Will she despise me, she wondered. Will she ever talk to me again? Emma glanced nervously up at her. The Baroness was looking cool and detached – watching the film in a rather bemused way as if somewhat bored. And yet, in spite of her embarrassed and frustrated state, Emma could not help feeling attracted to her.

She remembered how she had seen the Baroness once before. Ursula had taken her to Maximillian's one evening. She was strangely aloof and Emma longed to know if Maximillian was painting her portrait, or having an affair with her or . . . what?

Emma had not dared to open her mouth, or even sit down but the others had made polite conversation and had taken tea. Then, after tea, Ursula had left the room for a few minutes and Maximillian had asked Emma if she would like to see his latest canvases. Emma had been thrilled for she had heard that usually he did not let anyone see his pictures – even after they had been finished.

'Stefanie,' he had asked the Baroness, 'do you want to see how it's progressing?'

'No, no,' the Baroness had replied, rather aloofly.

'Very well. Come, Emma,' Maximillian beckoned.

Emma had followed him up an old rickety staircase to a small and very untidy room with canvases lying around everywhere. There was a couch, and an old iron bedstead in the room and on the bedstead a young woman lay asleep.

But that was not all that was shocking, for then Emma saw the canvas. It was a full frontal, almost pornographic, painting of the Baroness in a recumbent pose on the couch with an apple sitting on her beauty lips and the young woman licking the apple.

So, Emma had thought, there is more to the Baroness than she had originally imagined. She tried not to gasp or to show any sign of shock but she did find it difficult to express words of artistic appreciation. She heard herself murmur some trite compliments but that was all. As she did not want to wake up the young girl they soon went back downstairs.

The Baroness showed no sign of embarrassment; she just went on smoking a small cigar and ignoring everyone, including Maximillian. What could this triangular situation be all about? thought Emma.

Emma had left them then, but she had thought long and hard about the Baroness and had even fantasised about meeting her again.

Therefore, it was a wonderful surprise when she saw her again at the party.

2

An Erotic Lunch and an Embarrassing Interrogation

Baroness Stefan von Altman, or Stefanie to her friends, was dark and gorgeous. She was Italian by birth, but she seemed to be able to converse in any language. Everybody adored her. She was cool, charming and sophisticated; everything that Emma aspired to.

A week had gone by without Emma hearing a word from her - she had given Stefanie her telephone number and told her to ring at any time. 'You must come and stay,' Emma had said, hoping she would really say 'no', for she could not quite see the Baroness at her home in the country. Poor Emma was without Ursula, and even without Henry, her long standing lover, who was half in her mind and half forgotten. Since he had remarried, Emma had seen little of Henry even though they had shared some wonderfully exciting times together in the past.

So it was that she could not banish the hauntingly attractive Stefanie from her mind and was desperately longing for her to make contact. She was constantly imagining their next meeting in her mind's eye, as one always does in such cases, and deciding how she would make herself even more attractive.

She recalled the Baroness's features; the tiny mole on her ear, which in most people would have been a flaw but, on the Baroness, was rather attractive. She recalled her walk: her little girl steps, almost like a little run, and the serenely forceful impact of her personality.

Finally she decided she could wait no longer. She would

ring the Baroness herself. She dialled the number only to hear an answering machine. Emma put the phone down without leaving a message.

Emma had already got into a terribly agitated state of excitement. She was now beginning to build up to a frenzy – a feeling she simply had to see the Baroness and just had to touch her.

She rang five times that evening and eventually caught her at home, but by then Emma was cross and had forgotten what she was going to say. However, she need not have worried as Stefanie was very friendly.

'Oh, Emma darling!' she exclaimed. 'How nice to hear you. Are you coming to London? How is Ursula? You haven't seen her? Well, do come and have lunch at the Boltons. How about next Tuesday?'

'Oh, yes!' said Emma, although she had other plans.

'Lovely!' said Stefanie, and abruptly hung up. Clearly she was not one for long, girlish chats.

Emma was over the moon except for the fact that the Baroness seemed to know Ursula well. She desperately hoped she had not heard about their relationship. The last thing she wanted was to have to talk about Ursula or Henry. She wanted to escape from their clutches and their overpowering manipulative ways. Oh, how she wished she had never met Ursula!

Tuesday came very quickly. Emma caught an early train to London so as to have time for a facial in Harrods' beauty salon and have her hair done. At noon she took a taxi to the Boltons, arriving at twelve thirty and feeling very good. A slim, boyish, Italian youth opened the door and showed Emma into a wonderful room decorated with mirrors. It was not garish, however, despite the gilding and ormolu.

Lying on a *chaise longue* at the end of the room, was Stefanie, looking effortlessly beautiful, her long legs stretched out in front of her. There was a little chair beside her, almost facing her, and she beckoned Emma to sit down. In the background classical music was playing.

'Darling Emma! You do look pretty!' exclaimed Stefanie, uncrossing her legs and revealing just the tops of her stockings. Emma caught a glimpse of her beauty lips which were exquisitely painted. Emma was transfixed. It was incredibly exciting to know that Stefanie, a Baroness, was not wearing any knickers.

Stefanie deliberately left her legs apart and went on talking. Emma looked up at her bosom which in the portrait had appeared round and soft and, not too ample. But now, the sight of her little nipples, which seemed to be almost breaking through her organza shirt, made Emma almost burst with sheer lust.

They chatted with habitual ease, but secretly Emma was stunned by Stefanie's sleekness; she was like a jungle cat.

'So, little girl, does Ursula know you are visiting me?' enquired Stefanie.

'No! Certainly not! I'm my own mistress,' protested Emma. 'I don't have to ask Ursula's permission to do anything. Those days are over. I can go where I like!'

'Hmm!' smirked the Baroness, leaning back against the cushions, a faint smile on her face. Suddenly, she pulled Emma towards her by her long hair.

'Get your head down!' she said, pushing Emma's head down between her beautiful legs.

My goodness, thought Emma, as her lips met Stefanie's secret place, she's literally melting! She drank Stefanie's wonderful juices and felt herself almost exploding with desire. Then, just as Emma thought the Baroness was going to turn her attentions to her, she heard her ring a little bell.

Embarrassed, Emma raised her head, and saw coming into the room the same youth who had ushered her in. Perhaps, she thought, he was older than he looked.

'Yes, Baroness?' he said.

'Dear Gianni, I'm ready for you now and little Emma is going to be our guest.'

Emma was stunned.

'Gianni, take Emma upstairs. Put her naked in the chair looking into the large mirror. And Emma, I don't want you to turn round.'

Emma climbed the stairs behind Gianni. In fact she had to run to keep up. Then, deftly, he took off her clothes.

Emma, to her embarrassment, heard herself groan with excitement under his touch. But he barely looked at her and she was left sitting on the chair facing the mirror with her back to a four poster bed.

Fifteen minutes of excited anticipation slowly passed, while she just looked into the mirror, admiring her reflection. What she saw was not merely a pretty young woman but also a very eager and aroused one. Oh, how much longer was she going to be kept waiting?

Then, in the mirror, she saw Stefanie, naked, with Gianni crawling equally naked after her. He was on a lead with a studded leather dog collar strapped round his neck.

Emma did not dare to turn round. She saw the youth slither on to the bed after the Baroness. Again, Emma was stunned, and wondered what was to come next. She could hear Stefanie moaning, panting and letting out sudden shrill cries and yelps. Astonished, she saw that the youth was as hairless and smooth between the legs as Ursula used to keep Emma. As a sign of her new-found independence she had let the blonde hair between her legs grow again. However, this youth had been completely depilated!

Depilated or not, there was nothing wrong with the boy. She saw him with his manhood poised go on top of his Mistress and then penetrate the now wildly writhing and beautiful Stefanie.

For some minutes there was a creaking crescendo of bed springs. Emma could not stop playing with herself but she still did not dare to turn around. She could feel herself coming with them and was longing to join in. Gianni was now also gripping and sucking Stefanie's nipples.

'Let me join you!' she screamed.

'Yes,' she heard the Baroness reply, to her amazement. 'But you must make yourself useful.'

Emma climbed in beside Stefanie. Even though Gianni was still inside the Baroness, it was still terribly exciting for Emma. She crushed her mouth on Stefanie's soft and beautiful breast and her tongue played with the nipple. Emma's body was on fire; she longed for Gianni to come into her. She arched her body and, tense but abandoned, she waited.

She could see Stefanie doing the same, then collapsing with exhaustion. The Baroness had obviously climaxed.

Gianni, being a mere youth with a slim, athletic body, was still firing on all cylinders. He pulled himself out of Stefanie and before Emma could move, she felt him inside her, pushing, thrusting and holding her down with his hands. Then he suddenly cried out.

Emma could feel his seed, like hot gushing water, inside her. Then he was off her, gone to shower, and Emma curled up beside Stefanie. The two satiated women stroked one another. It was a marvellous feeling and they fell asleep like two small children.

Emma woke up later to find Stefanie already dressed.

'What about a late lunch, Emma?' she was saying. But Emma had drifted off to sleep again.

Finally, Emma drowsily awoke from her trance. Where was she? She could hardly move. She always adored to sleep after love and experience the wonderful tranquillity. Men usually want to jump up immediately afterwards which spoils it all, whereas women join together, stay together, stroke one another, whisper little words together. It's like an ointment. Then they fall asleep, enraptured, in one another's arms.

Emma had always loved this side of her relationship with women and had found it more satisfying than with men. Men tend to treat making love like having a game of squash - something to be followed by a quick rub down or a bath - and then they are ready to go out hunting or back to the office or whatever.

Slowly, Emma stretched out her hand for Stefanie's but it was not there. She looked up to the ceiling; it was covered in mirrors and she could see a delightful reflection of herself - the pink cheeks and her hair, more golden than usual, falling over the pillows. She looked more beautiful after making love, as did most women.

Her face was still covered with Stefanie's juices and she could still feel a tingle between her legs. As she lay there, still half way between sleeping and waking, she could feel herself getting excited again. Then she heard a voice calling.

'Darling, lunch! Hurry up. It's almost four o'clock. Do you want to eat or not?'

Emma jumped out of bed. Quickly, she showered and put on one of Stefanie's wraps. To have put on her own clothes might have given the signal that she had another appointment, whereas she was secretly hoping to go back to bed again after lunch.

Emma wandered into the elegant Smallbone kitchen, where lunch for two was set out on the table. Lovely table mats, Portmerion plates, freesias in a crystal vase and a bottle of Hock completed the spread. The sun was streaming in and everything seemed bright and fresh.

Stefanie looked stunning. She was dressed in a Dona Karina all-in-one leisure suit which showed off her slim body to magnificent effect. Not an inch of fat was to be seen.

'Well, darling Emma, you've deserved a good lunch. Gianni has prepared a salad for us and the clever boy bought some meat and cheese at Justin de Blanc's. Isn't he a darling?' The Baroness laughed. 'His mother is one of my greatest friends. She didn't know what to do with him. He didn't want to join the famous family factory so she sent him to me to learn English. Of course I told his mother I could, maybe, also teach him some other things as well. Dieter was simply furious. He enrolled him at the Institute and said he must go there every day but, of course, he sometimes comes back for lunch with me, particularly if I have friends like you coming!'

She glanced at Emma. 'And, my dear, Gianni whispered that he rather liked you. He's going through a phase of adoring older women. Of course, by keeping him depilated I make sure he's too embarrassed to go running after younger girls! And anyway I like it! So, darling, I'm making hay while the sun shines, and I suggest you do too!' The Baroness paused. 'In fact, Emma darling, you could possibly do me a favour by entertaining Dieter for me. Take him away for a bit while I enjoy Gianni.'

Emma made a face. She did not particularly want to get involved with Stefanie's husband. He was rather a dictatorial type who had always reminded Emma of Adolf

Hitler. He had a job at an embassy and was furious that he was not the ambassador. He kept telling everyone how wonderful his family was which, of course, did not earn him any marks back at the embassy.

'But Emma,' continued Stefanie, 'what's all this I hear about you and that Ursula woman? People say that you are her slave and that she treats you like dirt.'

Emma went scarlet. Why did that awful Ursula have to spoil everything? Who had she talked to and what did Stefanie really know? What about Emma's own reputation?

'Oh yes,' Stefanie went on mockingly, 'we all know she treats you like a servant and of course there are all the rumours about her cages, her baby pens, her young nieces, her –'

'Stop, Stefanie,' cried Emma. 'Oh please stop. I hate Ursula! I hate her! I can't stand her!' Emma was in a state. Tears began to fall. She had now realised that the world of Stefanie was much more to her liking and that it would also help to kill off the ghost of Ursula. She knew she could have a really happy and contented relationship with somebody like Stefanie. It would enable her finally to break away from Ursula – and Henry, despite her magnetic attraction to them both.

You cannot fake magnetism, Emma had decided. Why should one's body tingle and open and melt like a peach when a particular man or woman touches you, and yet hundreds of others leave you cold?

And now she was feeling madly attracted to Stefanie. She almost asked her to put her hand on her nipples during lunch. However, Stefanie was being cool and calculating. She wanted Emma to take her husband off her hands and pestered Emma about Ursula. In fact, Stefanie knew all about Ursula from Maximillian. He had regaled her with stories of Ursula's amazing exploits with younger women whilst he painted her picture and Emma's name had, of course, been mentioned quite a lot.

'So, Emma, when are you going to see Ursula again?' persisted Stefanie.

'Oh, please be quiet, Stefanie. Let's forget about Ursula.'

But Stefanie was not going to let up. She shook Emma by the shoulders. 'Now tell me the truth, you little bitch.'

'Well, let's go upstairs,' cried Emma. 'It's easier to talk in bed.'

They climbed the stairs rapidly. Emma threw off her wrap and Stefanie was also soon naked.

'Lick me, you bitch! she ordered. Lick me the way Ursula had you trained to lick in Paris! Oh yes, I know all about you, all right.'

Emma started to whimper. Stefanie picked her belt up off the floor and gave Emma a sharp wallop. 'Stop your silly little tears. You're a grown up woman. Now tell me the truth about Ursula.'

'Oh, please, please, I can't. I just can't.'

Stefanie lost all patience. 'You little bitch! You stupid cow! Stop acting like a little schoolgirl with me or you'll pay for it!' She left the room for several minutes while Emma continued to sob. Emma was determined not to confess everything to Stefanie.

Suddenly Stefanie appeared with a whip. She lashed Emma on her bare buttocks then turned her over and gave her six more strokes across her legs.

Emma was wailing and miserable. Then, just as she was trying to pull herself together, she heard footsteps and Gianni appeared.

Oh, the shock, the horror. Oh, the sheer humiliation of it all! There she was, naked, with marks on her body, her face contorted with crying, her beautiful make-up running down her face and her formerly lovely blonde hair all untidy. She looked a total mess. And Gianni and Stefanie were laughing at her.

There was a sudden hush. Gianni put his fingers to his lips and announced that he could hear a car outside. It must be Dieter!

'Fly to your room, Gianni. I must quickly do my face – and you, Emma, get dressed and tidy yourself and be downstairs in twenty minutes to meet Dieter. And remember, darling, you are to make eyes at the old bore. Flatter him. Laugh at his jokes and entice him to make a plan to meet you. And do it or I'll tell Ursula all about your unfaithful ways!'

Emma was in a turmoil. She wanted to run away. She did not want Dieter; she wanted Stefanie. She was feeling muddled and unhappy - and insulted about Dieter. Why should she do what Stefanie wanted? But, my God, supposing she does tell Ursula! That was something she just could not risk.

Emma washed and dressed hurriedly, realising that she had no alternative but to please Stefanie and do what she required. She had better just get on with it.

3

Used!

Stefanie rang Emma to say that Dieter would be away on Friday as would darling Gianni. When she enquired as to whether Emma would like to come and keep her company at supper, Emma was delighted; this was what she had been longing for.

On Friday evening they quickly had supper and then retired to the Baroness's room. 'Emma darling,' said the Baroness, 'I've been shopping and you really must see some of the Valentio Collection I bought. Shall I give you a fashion show?'

'Oh, yes,' cried Emma, clapping her hands with excitement. At this stage she would have done anything to please Stefanie.

Emma watched as the Baroness glided in, showing off first a rather tweedy suit and then a ball gown. But it was the playclothes that fascinated Emma: 'teasers' the Baroness called them. She modelled a see-through black lace teddy followed by an all-in-one cat suit. Emma was electrified. Stefanie held her gaze as they looked at each other. A warm creeping tingle of desire came over Emma and her loins glowed with excitement. What delirious happiness it was to feel once again that thrilling sensation. Ursula had always told her that she would only feel it with her and Emma had almost believed her.

Stefanie pranced about acting like a cat and purring. Then she crawled near Emma. 'Get your clothes off, darling!' she ordered.

Emma obeyed immediately. Already Stefanie had started to play with herself. Now she zipped the catsuit open to reveal her glistening body. Her hand was over her beauty bud.

'Hurry, Emma Get down on your knees. Now lick, my beautiful little girl. Lick your Mistress!'

At first Emma licked her smooth thighs; they were like silk and without a hair. It was so much easier to lick a woman, Emma thought, as bits of hair did not keep falling in one's mouth. Then she moved up towards the warm tender little place between Stefanie's legs: her 'little haven' as she called her own. Stefanie was moist and on fire. She held Emma by the hair.

'Lick! Lick!' she called out. 'Lick faster, my darling!'

Emma was doing her best. Stefanie's beauty bud was different from Ursula's, which was huge. Hers was small for a tall woman like the Baroness. Emma had expected that it would be bigger but, like her breasts, everything about Stefanie was neatness itself.

Stefanie's long, strong torso began to heave and shudder. She was crying out. She moved towards her bed and stretched herself out on it.

'Kneel by the bed, Emma, and use your hands and mouth!' Stefanie's voice had become urgent and harsh. Her long legs were stretched out and she continued to make loud and incoherent sounds. Her breathing gradually grew louder and faster and Emma could see that her pupils were dilated. It was an exciting moment for Emma to feel that she could make this wonderful woman become so turned on by just using her mouth was thrilling. It was even more thrilling when a sudden scream announced that Stefanie had climaxed in Emma's mouth.

Meanwhile, poor Emma had been begging to be allowed to climb in beside her to moan and shudder with her, to squeeze her ripe nipples and have her own fondled. But then, all of a sudden, Stefanie sat up. 'That's enough now, little bitch!' she spat.

'But, but,' stammered Emma. 'Please . . .'

Stop your nonsense at once!'

Emma could not believe it. Why should anyone want to stop just when the fun was starting?

'Now, Emma, come and sit on the bed beside me and bring me my wrap. If you're cold you can borrow my silk dressing gown; it's just over there.'

Emma felt so frustrated. She began to feel so inadequate. Was Stefanie – or should she now start calling her, more respectfully, the Baroness? – bored by her love-making?

The Baroness said nothing. She remained extremely matter of fact as if nothing had happened. She was obviously a woman who could control her own arousal; something Emma had always found very difficult. Ursula, who enjoyed keeping her girls frustrated, used to tell her teasingly that she must learn to do so.

'It's merely,' Ursula used to say, 'a question of mind over matter,' adding that Emma would have to learn to train her body to obey, as she had learnt to train her appetite. Ursula would then smile, knowing perfectly well that with Emma's sensuous nature she would never learn to do so of her own free will.

'It's just a habit,' Ursula would say to Emma, 'to have three meals a day. Dogs get used to eating only once a day and so, similarly, you're going to get used to only being allowed to climax as a special reward – and only when I say so.'

Like Ursula's other girls, Emma had to please her Mistress every day. She kept them all on tenterhooks by keeping them aroused but only rarely allowing them any relief – perhaps once a month or, if they were very lucky, once a fortnight. The result for Emma had been a continuous and terrible frustration mixed with wild hopes of being allowed – at last – to reach a climax when Ursula next sent for her. It was a frustration that had gnawed at Emma's mind by day and by night.

It had been a frustration that was rigorously enforced, even when she was at home, by Ursula's daily telephone calls, by threats of terrifying thrashings and sometimes by a special chastity belt, or purity belt as Ursula preferred to call it, since it prevented a girl touching herself even with a little finger, never mind a dildo or a vibrator. Even the telephone reports, four times a day, first thing in the morning, at midday, in the evening and last thing at night, had heightened the frustration. Not only did she have to report her natural functions and confirm her continuing purity, she also had to confess in detail her desperate longing to be alowed to climax and give a colourful account of her fantasies.

If Ursula was out or too busy to take her call, Emma still had to make the reports onto Ursula's answering machine, or, more humiliatingly, to her foreign maid, who used to insist, in a heavy accent, on Emma giving her every detail and then writing it all down to give to Ursula later.

This awful, and yet wildly exciting, frustration had been one of the worst aspects of Emma's relationship with Ursula. And now the Baroness seemed to be repeating it!

The Baroness laughed. 'After all, darling Dieter does pay for everything. Just look at my lifestyle. If you're good, you can share some of it too!'

Then her mood changed. 'Now, Emma, I want you to tell me all about your night with my darling husband, Dieter. Come on, Emma, I want to hear all about it, every word. He liked you a lot so you must have been a good little girl. And you're going to see him again, I hope. Ursula won't mind you seeing Dieter and of course you and I can also have great fun – as long as you please Dieter.'

'Oh, Stefanie, please no . . .' begged Emma.

'I don't like you calling me Stefanie, Emma. You must show more respect. You must call me Baroness. Now come on and tell me everything.'

Emma turned white – the memory of her evening with Dieter was so ghastly. She could now understand why the Baroness was keen to provide someone else for him. Outwardly he looked distinguished and initially Emma had thought that they would have some intelligent conversation or a civilised meal out together whilst the Baroness and Gianni enjoyed themselves.

'So, Emma, tell me. How did you spend your little evening? Make Stefanie happy, tell her all!'

Emma wondered whether the Baroness knew how ghastly Dieter really was. She knew several husbands who were awful to their mistresses but were quite placid and compassionate with their wives. Would Stefanie be disgusted?

She was pondering on this thought when she suddenly felt the Baroness's hand smack her hard across the face.

'Come on, Emma. Tell me, did he force himself on you?'

It was worse than that, Emma thought, but remained stoically silent.

'I'm going to get my cane, Emma, and you will be beaten until you tell me everything,' she said.

Emma could see that the Baroness was getting a real sexual high – her eyes were glinting, as if she was on drugs; her breasts were swelling and Emma could see that, under her wrap, she was touching herself.

'So Emma, if he didn't rape you, then perhaps you just had a romantic evening?'

Romantic! Emma started to squirm at the thought of Dieter. She had put all memories of that horrible night out of her mind. She saw that the Baroness was being sarcastic.

'All right, Emma! So it's going to be the cane!' The Baroness got up and went towards a cupboard.

'No, no! I'll tell you. What he really enjoyed most was watching me on the loo. This gave him a terrific kick. He told me that he adored watching girls spend a penny, especially in the open, and that you used to let him watch you. He said that you had stopped but that you had promised you would supply him with a few naughty girls.'

'And,' laughed the Baroness, 'as I knew you were one of Ursula's girls, I reckoned you would know all about that sort of thing and –'

'Oh stop it, you horrible woman,' Emma suddenly shouted. 'I hate you, Stefanie. You knew all about him and yet you deliberately sent me to the slaughter while you were enjoying yourself with Gianni!'

'Don't be such a silly little girl, Emma,' replied the Baroness angrily. 'I told you he pays for all this and that you can share it. Have you never heard of mind over matter? All you had to do was to take down your knickers. That sounds pretty harmless to me!'

She began to roar with laughter. Rather to her own surprise, Emma began to laugh too. 'I suppose I was being rather silly,' she admitted.

'Of course you were, little girl. So what else happened?'

'Well, I had to indulge his little fad three times but instead of doing it in the loo, he made me do it in a bowl in the middle of the floor, squatting over it with my skirt up and my panties down around my ankes.'

'And then?'

'Then he spent a penny between my legs, aiming his stream at my beauty bud before pushing me into the shower where he forced himself inside me.'

The Baroness laughed even more. 'So, Emma, now you know how much nicer it is to be with me! Come on, get the vibrator out of my drawer and I'll show you how to use it on me.' She forced Emma's hand, holding the vibrator, to move over her body. She was in a very aroused state. Clearly, hearing what Dieter had done to Emma had made her very excited. Before Emma could ask her any questions, she began to cry out. 'Oh, how wonderful! Oh, go on!'

Suddenly her body collapsed in a heap. Emma was left again with no pleasure but she hoped that the Baroness would later relent and certainly would not ask her to see the dreaded Dieter again. Indeed, she had decided that if the Baroness would only see her on condition that she amused Dieter, then she would give her up.

That night, Emma tossed and turned in a restless and frustrated half sleep. Furtively, she tried to touch herself, but she was caught and stopped by an angry Baroness.

'I'm getting my cane, Emma,' she had said, getting out of bed, going to the cupboard and pulling out a long whippy cane with a crooked handle. 'And if I catch you touching yourself again, then you'll get six strokes. And just to remind you, you're going to grip the handle of the cane with your teeth all night so that it hangs down between your breasts and between your legs. Just remember, Emma, mind over matter!'

Oh, that same awful expression of Ursula's! Poor Emma was terrified and utterly dissatisfied sexually.

In the middle of the night the Baroness removed the handle of the cane, seized Emma's hair and pulled her down between her legs.

'Lick! Lick properly, or you'll get the cane!' she cried hoarsely, giving a sharp tap to Emma's buttocks.

Then, satiated, the Baroness had, without a word, replaced the handle of the cane in Emma's mouth, leaving her once again aroused and even more frustrated. But worse was to follow, for the Baroness had then squeezed Emma's nipples with experienced fingers for several minutes; something which had aroused Emma yet further.

Then the Baroness lay back, ready to fall asleep again. 'Oh, it's so exciting feeling relaxed and sated with a frustrated little girl lying aroused and helpless alongside me not daring to touch herself,' she had laughed.

Oh how Emma had hated her! But again gripping the cane tightly in her teeth, she had not dared to beg or even say a word. She knew that she was just being used by the Baroness. She felt she was just her little performing animal, doing its tricks for both Dieter and the Baroness nothing more.

To make it worse, the Baroness was keeping Gianni for herself. She was dashing off with him the following morning to go racing and then to stay with friends near Sandown. She had not suggested that Emma should join them.

At last, still gripping the cane in her mouth, Emma fell asleep, only to be woken next morning by a smiling and fully dressed Stefanie.

'You've been a good girl,' she said removing the cane, 'but now it's time to say goodbye. And, darling, don't forget, you look after Dieter and I'll look after you. And, if you don't, then Ursula's going to be told all about it.'

Emma felt miserable. This was all very unsatisfactory and unsatisfying. Once again she felt she had just been used. On the train home she felt little tears coming. Why, oh why, did everyone just use Emma for their own pleasure? Well, she wasn't going to continue allowing them to use her like this. And she would jolly well say so, next time either the Baron or the Baroness phoned. She'd show them! And to hell with her threat to tell Ursula about it all. She was no longer Ursula's helpless plaything!

But it was not the Baroness who phoned two days later, nor the Baron, nor even Ursula. Someone unexpected was also after Emma's delightful little body.

4

Gianni

Emma jumped as the telephone suddenly rang. She had been day-dreaming about the Baroness and thinking that, all things considered, she wasn't nearly as cruel as Ursula. So why didn't she give her a ring?

Was this the Baroness herself ringing? she wondered as she picked up the receiver. But it was a man's voice she heard: a young man's voice, speaking excitedly in a foreign accent.

'Emma? Is that you? It's Gianni.'

'Gianni! What are you doing ringing me? Do you have a message for me from the Baroness?'

'Yes. I mean no. Listen . . . I want to see you!'

'Oh,' gasped Emma. 'But the Baroness?'

'That's why I'm ringing you. They're both away for several days. We could have such fun together, Emma, darling. I love you! So please do come quickly!'

Emma hardly knew whether to laugh or cry as Gianni went on telling her that he loved her and that he just longed to see her and that this was their chance. Well, she thought, he is a very good looking young man – and very virile too. It might indeed be great fun to go up and see him.

It would certainly be a good opportunity for her to finally exorcise the memory of Ursula, and to throw off the strange hold that she had over her. An eighteen year old toy boy! Well that really would be one in the eye for Ursula – not that she would ever hear about it; she'd make certain of that. But it would give her the resolve to rebuff Ursula the next time she tried to lure her into her lair.

The fact was she was fed up with the way Ursula was always trying to brainwash her into agreeing that she hated men and was, really and truly, a lesbian.

'You're one of us now,' Ursula used to say.

But she knew it wasn't true. She just enjoyed a good time and found Ursula's way of life, and dominating ways, very exciting. But so too would be a submissive young Italian toy boy!

'Yes, darling Gianni,' she heard herself murmur as if in a dream. 'I'd love to come and see you again. I'll come up this afternoon and we can spend a couple of days together.'

Oh there's really nothing like a virile young man! thought Emma for the umpteenth time as, yet again, Gianni brought her to a height of ecstasy. They had spent almost a whole day in bed together in the Baroness's bedroom. It had been magnificent. No wonder the Baroness kept this boy for her personal use. He was insatiable, as only a highly-sexed boy can be. He had taken her in every possible way; backwards, frontwards, upside down, kneeling like a dog; she had lost count of all the different ways.

And now, exhausted, they lay sleeping like young lovers should, in each other's arms, when suddenly the door of the bedroom burst open and there, standing on the threshold, was the furious figure of the Baroness herself!

Emma and Gianni huddled up under the sheets as Stefanie railed and stormed in a purple rage.

5

Abducted!

It was two weeks later and Emma, busy in her husband's isolated 17th-century rectory, had almost forgotten the dreadful scene with the Baroness and her final threat to tell Ursula everything.

Anyway, she thought, what could Ursula do about it? After all, Emma was a married woman - even if her husband was away abroad. She could do what she liked. It was none of Ursula's business!

Indeed, while her husband, John, was away, Emma had thrown herself into doing up the pretty house and its delightful garden. The garden was so lovely and the countryside so entrancing that Emma soon forgot all about the Baroness and even about Ursula. London seemed a long way away.

She had been alone in the house for the day when suddenly she heard the front door bell ring. She looked out of the window and saw, parked in the drive, an odd-looking, extra long estate car with black opaque windows. How strange, she thought. It looked rather like one of those car ambulances you saw on the Continent except that it was not painted white with a red cross and the word 'Ambulance' all over it, but was simply a plain and unobtrusive black car.

Two burly-looking men in white paramedic's uniforms were unloading a stretcher from the back under the supervision of a middle-aged woman wearing a short, white doctor's coat and holding what looked like a medical bag.

They must be lost and have come to the wrong place, she thought, as she ran down the stairs to open the door.

'Miss Emma?' asked a huge black man of about 30, in a

deep tone of voice. He spoke with a strange French accent. He was dressed in a black tie and coat and black striped trousers. He was also wearing white gloves which contrasted sharply with his black skin.

Goodness, thought Emma, he must be somebody's butler. But his face had a sinister look about it and his bloodshot eyes gleamed cruelly. Normally, Emma liked black men but this chap seemed rather frightening. Behind him stood the lady doctor and the two men in white suits bearing the stretcher.

'Yes,' replied Emma in some confusion. 'But what –'

'Don't worry, we've just come to take you away for your treatment,' said the butler in a deep voice with a strange half French and half Caribbean accent. Then, with a sinister smile, he pushed his way past her into the hall.

'Treatment!' cried Emma. 'What treatment? I'm not due for any treatment. There must be some mistake. You've come to the wrong house.'

The men with the stretcher were already placing it on the hall table. Horrified, she saw that behind them the woman doctor, a rather grim-faced woman, had opened her case and was preparing a syringe.

'No, there's no mistake,' said the woman doctor, in a strong German accent. The white-coated men had put down their stretcher and were laying out some straps attached to its sides. I'm Doctor Anna, one of Ursula's friends. She's made arrangements for you to have some special treatment.'

Ursula! Ursula had sent these awful people! And this was the same cruel lady doctor whom Ursula had previously used, without consulting Emma, to send a note to her husband certifying that she was not fit to carry out her conjugal duties.

'No!' she screamed, backing up against the wall. 'No! My husband '

'Ursula has already contacted your husband in the Pacific,' replied Doctor Anna, calmly. 'She told him that I said you need a long rest. He was only too happy to let us look after you for a few months while he's away.'

A few months! Oh my God!

'Oh, no!' cried Emma, again in desperation. 'I'll scream and the cleaning lady will hear. The police will come and arrest you all, and . . .'

The large black butler just laughed. 'We know there's no one in the house except you. We've been watching it.'

The two white-coated men had now finished preparing the stretcher.

'But the house . . . What will happen?'

'Don't you worry, little girl!' replied the German woman, speaking as if she was reassuring a child. 'Just relax. Everything has been taken care of. Ursula has hired a reliable house-keeper to look after everything while you're away.'

'But the mail, my letters, the bills . . .'

'The house-keeper will be forwarding them to Ursula to deal with. You'll have nothing to worry about, child. Your Mistress will take care of everything until your husband returns. Just relax and leave everything to her and you won't have a care in the world. Now just go and lie down on the stretcher.'

'But my clothes! I must pack.' Perhaps, she thought desperately, this might give her the chance to telephone for help.

'Miss de Vere say you not need any clothes where we're taking you,' said the big black man with a horrible grin.

'Oh!' The two big white-coated men were now coming towards her, one on either side.

'Everything is going to be all right.' Again came the hypnotic voice of the doctor. 'Just lie down on the stretcher like a good little girl and you'll soon be back with Ursula, your beloved Mistress. You'll love that won't you?'

Oh no! thought Emma. I want my freedom. But the doctor's voice was so persuasive. Perhaps she would be happy back with Ursula, after all. Anyway there seemed nothing she could do about it. And it was all rather exciting being carried off like this. And, at least, life with Ursula was never dull.

'Aren't you proud that your Mistress has arranged to

take you back into her care? You know you're longing to be looked after by your Mistress again,' the hypnotic voice went on, echoing her own secret thoughts. 'She'll take complete care of you and you won't have to worry about anything at all. You'll just be able to concentrate on serving your beloved Mistress. You'll love that, won't you, little girl?'

Emma found herself nodding, almost eagerly. Indeed, how exciting it all sounded! And how wonderful to think that Ursula cared so much about her and wanted her back.

'That's better! Now just lie down on the stretcher, like a good little girl,' came the same hypnotic voice. The doctor pointed to the syringe in her hand. 'Or I'll have to use this and you won't like that, will you?'

Emma eyed the syringe nervously and hastily lay down on the stretcher. Quickly, the straps were fastened. Within seconds she was quite helpless, strapped to the stretcher with her legs bound together and her arms secured at her sides. The big butler nodded to the two men and they picked up the stretcher and carried it to the car. They placed it on a rack. Emma saw that the doctor was there too, looking down at her.

'What are you going to do to me?' cried Emma, suddenly frightened again. 'Where are you taking me?'

The doctor merely smiled. 'No more talking,' she said in her hypnotic voice, again picking up her syringe, 'or I shall have to use this! Now be a good girl. We're taking you to a new place, a very exciting place, where Ursula's arranged some lovely little surprises for you.'

Emma caught her breath, half in fear and half in excited anticipation.

'Now, would you like to have a sleeping pill for the journey? It will make the journey much more comfortable and then you can sleep soundly and wake up in your new surroundings.'

She held out some pills enticingly. Emma nodded, and the doctor popped them into her mouth and gave her a little sip of water.

'Now I'll leave you to have a nice little sleep,' said the

doctor. She drew the curtains over the windows. Emma could not now see out. Then the doctor pointed at the frightening-looking butler, who was sitting opposite her on a stretcher. 'Sabhu will be staying with you, so you'll be all right.'

Emma looked wonderingly at him. What a name! Not at all like the innocent young elephant boy who was his namesake.

'Sabhu looks after Ursula's girls now,' explained the doctor, 'and he comes from Haiti.'

Haiti! thought Emma. Surely that's the island in the Caribbean, where they speak French. No wonder he has an odd accent. But what did the doctor mean about him looking after Ursula's girls? He's a man! A black man from Haiti looking after Ursula's girls! She knew all about the black eunuchs who controlled girls in Moorish harems. But this was England and Sabhu, with his deep voice, was clearly no eunuch.

The doctor followed the other men out of the back of the car. The rear door was slammed shut. Emma heard them climb into the front of the vehicle. She heard the engine start up and then they drove off.

Emma looked at the sinister Haitian.

'You just have a good sleep,' he muttered, adding with a laugh, 'You'll be seeing a lot more of me, now.'

Emma lay there, helpless, as the big converted estate car drove quietly on. She wondered what was going to happen to her. She thought about Ursula, about Doctor Anna and about this huge Haitian brute, Sabhu.

Soon she began to feel drowsy . . .

6

A Nasty Awakening

Slowly, Emma awoke from a deep sleep.

She remembered that she had been taken to Ursula's and how terrifying, and yet exciting, she had found the prospect. Was she already in her Mistress's bed? Soft music was playing. Oh how lovely! she thought. Then she stirred, sensing that all was not well.

She opened her eyes and blinked. Then she raised her head and looked around in amazement. She had been lying curled up on a thick rubber mat in a little alcove. She was in a cage with brick walls at the back and sides, and iron bars across the front and top.

The cage was not high enough to stand up in, being only four feet deep, and approximately four feet wide. Then she saw that it also only measured about four feet from the bars at the front, making the cage seem even smaller. She looked down and saw that under the mat were even more iron bars. It really was a cage!

The cage was lit up by a bright light in the corner. It was protected by a locked metal shield, but there was no sign of a switch.

On one wall of the small alcove was a mirror and, below it, a shelf containing a hairbrush, a comb, lipstick, eye make-up and a bottle of Chanel Number 5. Neatly folded on the thick rubber flooring was a heavy grey blanket. Hanging from the bars on the front of the cage was a drinking bowl and a metal feeding trough to which a simple wooden spoon was attached by a short chain. Both the bowl and the trough could, she realised, be filled from outside through the bars of the cage - like those of cages used to hold wild animals.

She looked down at herself. She remembered that when the estate car had driven up to her house, she had been wearing slacks and a blouse. Now, she saw she was just wearing a simple short sleeveless cape made of blue velvet. It only came down to her hips, leaving her buttocks and intimacies exposed.

She saw that the cape was well cut and made of a heavy, good-quality material that was warm and would not get crushed in the cage. It was fastened down the front by a line of brass buttons and secured round the throat by a strong leather strap.

She tried to struggle to her knees. There was a clinking noise from her hands under the cloak. She pushed up the front of the cloak and saw that her wrists had been chained together and so too had her ankles. Iron manacles, locked around each wrist and ankle, were joined by two short lengths of heavy chain.

Horrified, she tried to cry out. But she found she had also been gagged! She looked in the mirror and saw a shiny black leather gag had been fastened over her mouth. Inside the gag there was something that pressed down on her tongue, making it quite impossible for her to even whisper.

She felt underneath the cape and realised that under it she was naked. She must have been stripped while unconscious. Who by? she wondered, uneasily. Surely not by that huge Haitian butler?

Then she remembered what the lady doctor, Doctor Anna, had said about the Haitian butler now looking after Ursula's girls. Oh no, not him! Nervously she pulled the cloak tightly round her naked body.

Hesitantly, she felt down below the front of the cape. All the soft little hair that she had begun to grow again on her mound and beauty lips, as a sign of her independence, had been removed. She was now completely hairless again. But who had depilated her? That awful Haitian? She blushed at the thought. Then, looking down at the thick cloak, she saw that the figure '4' had been prominently embroidered on the breast. There was also some initials embroidered under it rather like an owner's initials on a race-horse's rug.

She peered down and gave an excited shiver of apprehension as she made out the initials 'U de V' - Ursula de Vere! Goodness, Ursula was certainly making sure that Emma realised that she was back in her Mistress's power. Emma peered through the bars and saw what seemed to be an attic room with a sloping beamed ceiling. Her cage seemed to be raised two or three feet off the ground, perhaps so as to make it easier to see into. Then she noticed that the rubber mat sloped down slightly towards a barred sluice in the floor of her cage. Through the sluice she could see iron bars and below them a metal collecting tray. She blushed as she realised its purpose.

The walls of the attic, like those of her cage, glistened with shiny white gloss paint and looked as spotless as a well-kept kennel. There were radiators to keep the room warm and an extractor fan to remove smells. There was a loudspeaker on one wall from which the relaxing music was coming.

There were two small windows which let in light and air but they were both heavily barred and the windows themselves were of frosted glass which prevented anyone from seeing out - or in!

There were also metal bars on the solid-looking door. It had a strong lock and she saw, on the wall by the door, a modern electronic lock control device with a row of buttons.

Goodness, she thought, security is certainly tight here. Even if she should ever manage to get out of her cage and get hold of the key to the door, she would still not be able to get out of the attic unless she also knew the combination to the electronic lock.

She noticed a strange-looking circular metal apparatus in one corner of the room. It was fitted with several nozzles pointing inwards. With a shock of surprise Emma remembered that she had seen something identical in the changing rooms of the swimming pool at the Gleneagles Hotel, where she had once stayed during a short trip to Scotland with Henry. It was a shower. A girl could be put into it, she realised, and even if she were manacled she would still be showered whether she liked it or not.

In another corner was a large sluice, such as you see in the annexe of a hospital ward. Security might be strict here, but clearly so too was cleanliness.

Between the shower and the sluice, high up on the wall, was a small raised balcony, facing her cage. It seemed to be a short of viewing balcony, or gallery, with its own entrance and several comfortable looking chairs. Along the front of the gallery was a decorative ironwork balustrade. Emma gasped as she saw that there was also a row of iron spikes, like she had seen in a zoo. It would, she realised, serve to protect anyone in the gallery from a creature down below and also prevent any creature down below from leaping up to try and escape through the gallery.

In the middle of the room, painted on the bare varnished wooden floor, was a line of small red circles, each marked with a figure from '1' to '6'. Just beyond the line of red spots was a row of immaculately clean white china bowls, like children's pots, each also marked with a number. Along one wall was a row of cupboards and shelves containing girls' dresses, clothes and shoes. Again, each was marked with a number. She recognised her own clothes hanging in the cupboard marked '4', but there were other clothes with them which she couldn't see properly though she made out a black gymslip and ballet tutu. She saw similar gymslips and tutus hanging in the other marked cupboards.

What really astonished her was that high up the wall, facing her cage, was a small television camera. She saw that a little red light was shining on the side of the camera meaning, presumably, that it was switched on. Indeed, as she watched, the camera moved and traversed slowly to the left of her cage and then came back and pointed directly at her. Someone was watching her on a remote television screen! Was that why her cage was so brilliantly lit up? She wanted to cry out, but the gag prevented her.

Then she saw that hanging down from the ceiling was a microphone. How strange! She turned and looked around her cage. The only furniture was a solid-looking three-legged stool, standing on the rubber mat. There were no books but she saw a couple of magazines neatly stacked in a corner. There was also a pretty baby doll, dressed in rompers and a little girl's dress. It had lovely long blonde hair and appealing blue eyes. Emma picked it up and hugged it to her. It would be her friend and companion, she decided. She would call it 'Baby'.

Still hugging the doll to her with one arm, she idly picked up the magazines. They were all old copies of *Mother and Child*, full of pictures of happy and carefree young mothers and mothers-to-be. How odd, she thought. Emma scarcely knew whether to be appalled by all this or, instead, rather excited by the thought of being kept caged, manacled and gagged by her Mistress. Was it all rather sinister, like when she had been kept in a dungeon in the castle of the strange Romanian Countess? Or was it all just another exciting preamble to Ursula's passionate love-making? Certainly it was all rather thrilling!

She was lying in her cage, clasping the doll, and wondering what to make of it all, when she heard a rustling noise. It seemed to come from behind the wall of her cage. At first she thought that it must be a rat! She recoiled and gasped in horror behind her gag. But then she heard a clinking noise like that made by her manacles and then a girl's voice whispering excitedly in a strange language.

Was, Emma wondered, her cage one of a line of similar ones? Was that why the camera had traversed to its right and then come back to her? She remembered the numbered clothes cupboards. Was she in cage number '4' and were other girls in cages '1' to '3'? Was the girl whispering because of the microphone?

Suddenly the music was switched off and she heard a man's deep voice emanating from the loudspeaker. At the same time the camera moved to its right, pointing towards where she had heard the whisper.

'Number Two!'

Emma recognised the heavy French-Caribbean accent. The voice could only belong to the huge Haitian who had come into her house and abducted her. He must be here somewhere watching her on his television monitor!

She remembered, with a shiver, that he had said she would be seeing a lot of him in the future. My God! she thought; perhaps it *was* him who had stripped her naked while she was sleeping, and had then chained and gagged her and put her into this cage. Oh how shame-making! And it was presumably he who had depilated her. How doubly shame-making!

'For talking in cage without permission, Number Two,' the heavily-accented voice went on, speaking slowly as if to someone who did not understand much English. 'You now get punishment!'

She heard a little gasp, a girl's gasp, coming from behind the wall of her cage – the same place where she had heard the whispers. The hanging microphone must have picked up the girl's lowered voice.

'Yes,' the man's voice repeated slowly, 'you get punishment now!'

Suddenly the girl screamed. What on earth had made her scream? she wondered. How had she been punished? There was no sign of the horrible butler.

'And next time you get three strokes as well. Remember, three strokes!' the man's voice slowly added.

Again there was a gasp and the rattle of manacles as if the girl had raised her hands to her mouth in horror. But she did not dare to say a word in protest. The soft music started again. It was all so sinister.

Emma gripped the bars at the front of the cage. They were strong and unyielding. She saw that in the middle of the bars, down at the bottom, was a similarly barred and hinged small gate through which a girl could crawl in and out of the cage. Eagerly she shook it but to no avail. It was fastened with a heavy padlock.

She heard a scraping noise as if the girl in the next cage was moving her stool. She pressed her head against the bars to see if she could see the other cages but the bars were too close together for her to see anything. She remembered that Ursula often used to like having several young girls in her power, and occasionally older women as well. Often they came from Eastern Europe and scarcely spoke a word of English. Was she now just one of Ursula's girls? Just one of several caged girls and women? Why?

With a shock she remembered the Baroness's last words; how she had threatened to tell Ursula all about what Emma had been getting up to. Emma had been terrified at the time. She might no longer have been officially one of Ursula's girls but she knew Ursula was still extremely furious about her behaviour.

For Ursula to know that Emma was living quietly in the country with her husband was one thing, but hearing that Emma, formerly one of her own girls, was galivanting around London having affairs with Ursula's own women friends, or even worse with their husbands and toy boys, would make Ursula livid. She would be wild with jealous possessive rage.

And now Ursula had abducted her and brought her here! But where was here? There had been no attic like this in Ursula's previous London house. She remembered hearing that she had moved to a larger place. Was this where she was now?

7

Confronted by Ursula

Emma's thoughts were suddenly interrupted by the music stopping. There was the noise of a key in the lock of the door. The music, she realised, must have been switched off by a control outside the door.

There was a slight tapping sound from beyond the door; the code for the electronic lock was being inserted. Then, the door was flung open.

Emma gasped as in walked the huge Haitian, Sabhu, whom she had last seen in her own house just before she had been abducted. He was wearing the same butler's suit and the same white gloves. The formality of his dress made Emma, wearing just her little cape, feel even more naked and vulnerable.

He was looking grim and unsmiling. His bloodshot eyes looked hard and unforgiving. Horrified, she saw that he was carrying in one white-gloved hand a long, flexible riding whip with a little leather tip – like a dressage whip. His black coat was open and she saw, with a shiver, that hanging from his belt on one side was a short stiff leather strap. Also fastened to his belt was what looked like a small control box with several buttons. Emma wondered what on earth it could be.

Quickly, he strode over to Emma's cage and, without a word, he unlocked the padlock, reached into the cage and grabbed the shrinking Emma by the hair. Quickly, he dragged her out and stood her up, the chains of her wrist and ankle manacles clanking as he did so.

Emma tried to struggle against him but he was far too strong. Contemptuously ignoring her pounding little fists, he picked her up, effortlessly threw her over his shoulder and strode off towards the door.

'Put me down!' she ineffectively screamed from behind the gag. She tried to hammer with her fists against his back, and to kick him with her feet but her heavy manacles made it difficult.

'You keep still,' he grunted, 'or I'll throw you downstairs.'

Terrified, she now kept still. She looked around. She had a brief glimpse of half a dozen other cages in a row next to the one she had been in. Each was prominently numbered from '1' to '6'. As she suspected, her's was number '4'.

Two of the cages at the end of the row were empty but in the first two cages, numbered '1' and '2', each contained a young girl of about twenty, and in the one numbered '3' was a very beautiful dark-haired woman of about 40. They were all kneeling up, wearing the same pretty blue capes with their numbers prominently embroidered on the breast. They were each silently clasping a doll, just like Emma's own, and gripping the bars of their cages with their manacled hands.

They were all looking at Emma and smiling at her encouragingly. Despite their cages and manacles, and the obvious strict discipline, they seemed to be happy, Emma thought. She remembered how she herself had been blissfully happy at times when she had been forced to be one of Ursula's girls. Was she now going to be made to be one again? Gosh, how exciting - and yet also how terrifying. At least it was reassuring to be with other girls in the same situation.

One of the younger girls was blonde and with a shock, Emma recognised her as the pretty girl whom Ursula had taken to the Dorchesters' party. Then, before she could take in any more, she found she was being carried out of the attic room and down some stairs. She heard the door to the attic slam shut automatically. Sabhu carried her down two flights of stairs to what seemed to be the first floor. When they reached the landing he stopped. 'When I put you down,' he muttered harshly, 'you kneel down on all fours and keep quite still! Understand?'

Emma gave a little grunt from behind her gag. He put her down. She was now kneeling in her short cape with her manacled hands and bare knees on the floor. With her buttocks exposed she felt very naked and embarrassed alongside the huge, well-dressed, Haitian butler.

Slowly, she started to look around. There was a large closed door in front of them. Sabhu was impatiently tapping his long dressage whip, in an alarming way, against the palm of one white-gloved hand.

'You keep your head down,' he snarled. 'And keep your eyes on the floor.'

Frightened by the sight of the whip, Emma did what she was told. There was a long pause. What was going to happen now, she wondered. Out of the corner of her eye, she saw that Sabhu was looking at his watch. It was as if he had been told to bring Emma here at a certain time. For what seemed hours, Emma just knelt there in front of the door, gagged and too frightened to move.

Then suddenly Sabhu knocked on the door. 'Number Four, Madam,' he called out.

'Bring her in!' came a woman's cold, clear and precise voice. Emma recognised the slightly foreign, almost Russian or Slavic intonation. It was Ursula!

'You crawl behind me to Madam's feet!' said Sabhu as he opened the door. 'Keep eyes down on floor!'

Emma found herself crawling behind him across a thick carpet. Her heavy wrist and ankle manacles clinked loudly as she did so. Her eyes were fixed on the back of his black shoes. She did not dare to look around but she thought she must be in Ursula's new drawing room, perhaps on the first floor.

He stopped. 'Stay here and keep still!' he ordered harshly, and moved aside. 'Head down!'

Emma kept her eyes on the floor but could not help noticing that in front of her were now the legs of a chair and a woman's crossed legs. They were long and slim. She was wearing expensive red leather shoes with a low heel.

'Thank you, Sabhu,' she heard Ursula's cold voice from above her.

There was a long pause. Emma became increasingly frightened. Oh what a fool she had been, thinking that she could ever get away from Ursula!

'So, you ungrateful little slut!' Ursula was speaking slowly in a contemptuous tone. Emma shivered as she recognised the controlled anger. 'So, the little bitch thought that because she was a married woman she could get away with running away from me, did she? She thought she could have pleasure without my permission, did she? She thought she could rush around London, making a fool of me, did she? Well, the slut is now going to learn that she was wrong quite wrong!'

Emma wanted to say something in her own defence, but the gag prevented her from speaking. And, deep in her heart, she knew that all that Ursula had said was true. She had indeed behaved disgracefully. And she had been wrong, stupidly wrong, to think that even if she was a married woman she could ever really get away from Ursula.

She raised her head and her manacled hands in a silent gesture of submission, looking up beseechingly at Ursula. She caught a glimpse of a long black dress, and of two furious looking dark eyes.

'Head down!' screamed Sabhu.

Emma howled behind her gag as she felt him slash her with his whip across the back of her exposed calves, just above her manacled ankles. Humbly she lowered her head again, feeling like a slave kneeling humbly in front of an imperious Mistress.

'Lift her head up!' she heard Ursula say. Sabhu bent down and pulled her head up by the hair. Then he jerked it backwards, so that she was now looking straight at the terrifying figure of Ursula.

Ursula looked down at her contemptuously. Emma could not meet her eyes. Then Ursula leant forward and smacked Emma hard across the face. 'You disgusting little trollop!' she said coldly, and then smacked her hard again across the face. 'Bah!'

Sabhu released Emma's hair and Ursula, raising one

foot, kicked over the kneeling girl. Emma fell on her side amidst a clanking of her heavy manacles. For a moment she lay there, terrified at Ursula's sudden display of anger.

'Get back on all fours!' shouted Sabhu.

Quickly, Emma wriggled back up on her knees again. She caught a glimpse of a large television screen alonside Ursula's chair, transmitting a view of one of the cages upstairs with the beautiful dark-haired older woman gripping the bars.

She remembered the little television camera in the corner of the attic that pointed at the cages. So, Emma thought, Ursula could amuse herself down here in her drawing room, looking at her screen showing her caged girls upstairs.

'Head down!' shouted Sabhu.

Meekly Emma lowered her head. Her eyes were only inches from the carpet at Ursula's feet.

'And not only did you deceive me with the Baroness but you also deceived her with her toy boy,' the ice cold voice went on. 'A young man! You actually had the impudence to go to bed with a young man although you know very well that you're not allowed to have any sexual relations with any male! You're one of us now and by God you're going to remember it in future!'

Emma shivered with fear, not only at the threat but also at the furious tone in Ursula's voice. In the past it had always been rather exciting, she thought, being punished by Ursula. She had also rather enjoyed making Ursula jealous of her long-standing affair with Henry. But this time it sounded as though things were going to be different.

'And,' Ursula went on, 'you'll find several changes in the life of my girls since I moved into this house. One's going to be a nasty little surprise for you. Others you will have already seen. For instance, you've already experienced the cages upstairs in which I now keep my girls locked when I don't require them, or when they are not being exercised or shown off. And you're already wearing the heavy manacles that I now like my girls to wear.' She paused for greater effect.

'And you've met Sabhu here, who acts not only as my butler but also as my girls' overseer and trainer – like a keeper in a zoo! He's now in complete charge of my girls, enabling me to get on with my painting and my business affairs. He brings them to me, trained, docile and eager, whenever I want their services.'

A trainer! A Haitian man training white girls to please a woman! Emma's mind was reeling. And, Ursula had said, 'docile and eager'. Emma eyed Sabhu's dressage whip with renewed respect.

'You'll always call him sir, or Mr Sabhu,' Ursula continued, in her cold, contemptuous tone and Slavic accent. She had never dared to ask Ursula just where she came from. 'He'll simply call you number four. But you don't speak to him, or anyone else, without permission.'

Emma remembered hearing Number Two being caught whispering to one of the other girls and then being mysteriously punished. Goodness, she thought, discipline was certainly tight here.

'If you do want to speak, then you must put your hand up and ask permission to speak – just like girls at school with a strict Mistress. And you'd better remember always to be very polite to Mr Sabhu for he will be in complete charge of you from now on. He's responsible to me for supervising your most intimate moments so that he can give a fully comprehensive report every day on the health and exact state of each of my girls.'

Again she paused. Emma was horrified. To be supervised, intimately, by this horrible Haitian man! How awful!

'And, Emma, just bear in mind that he has the authority not only to use his strap on my girls, but also to give them up to three strokes of his whip, without reference to me. Indeed, he's so good with the whip that he does all my beatings for me now, usually as a little display in front of my friends.'

Emma could not help giving a little shiver. It was one thing to be beaten by Ursula, but quite another to be beaten by this huge powerful-looking Haitian.

'And he tells me that you had the effrontery to let your

body hair grow again although you know very well that all my girls have to keep themselves absolutely smooth – for ever! Sabhu's put you back into your proper state down there and he'll be keeping you like that – with a nice, shiny, little bald mound and pretty, smooth little beauty lips.'

Oh, how awful, thought Emma, to be controlled like that by a man: a Haitian man.

'And you've met my German lady doctor friend, Doctor Anna.'

Emma shuddered as she remembered the grim-faced middle-aged woman who had come to her house with Sabhu and had given her the sleeping pills.

'She may not be allowed to practise publicly in England,' Ursula continued in her cold voice with its foreign accent, 'but she's very useful in making my girls perform properly and in giving them certain – shall we say – rather interesting, little treatments. Sabhu keeps her fully informed about the state of their monthly cycles and general health. He even sends her regular specimens to analyse. Between them they keep a pretty close eye on my girls!'

Emma shuddered. Oh no!

'And that brings me to your punishment, Emma. It's going to be one that you'll not forget in a hurry. And, of course, it'll be Sabhu who will be thrashing you in front of me – and in front of a specially invited guest who's going to really enjoy watching you squirm! And she'll be going back to spread the word amongst our friends that you're back in my power again and no longer available to accept invitations on your own!'

Just then a bell rang – it sounded like a front door bell.

'Ah, this will be her. The maid will let her in. Now, Sabhu, take this revolting creature back upstairs and put her back in her cage again until we are ready to witness her punishment. Meanwhile, bring us some tea. And you, Emma, while you're in your cage, make yourself look as pretty as possible for your thrashing – or you'll get a double ration! And you know what I mean by pretty!'

8

Emma is Thrashed

Once again the attic was filled with the relaxing noise of soft music.

Emma knelt up in her cage and concentrated on applying make-up to her eyes above her black shiny leather gag with her manacled hands. She outlined them with black kohl to give herself the Eastern look that Ursula liked. She looked down. Her mound was now looking beautifully powdered and smooth and her beauty lips, outlined in black kohl to match her eyes, were painted red. Then she pulled back the front of her cape and checked her nipples. They too were now painted the same shade of red, and also outlined in black kohl.

She knew she was looking very exotic and normally would have felt very excited as well. But although making up like this had helped to keep her mind off her forthcoming thrashing, secretly she was absolutely terrified at the thought of Sabhu's long whip and his bulging muscles.

She started to brush her hair down over her shoulders in the style that she knew Ursula so liked to see on one of her grown up girls. Then she dabbed Chanel No. 5 around her hairline and under her chin so lavishly that it ran down between her breasts.

As she did this, she could hear the chink of the other girls' manacles as they moved about in their cages. There was no more whispering – just an ominous silence broken only by the clanking of the heavy chains.

Who were they? she wondered, and what was the strange language she had heard one of them speaking. Ursula had connections with Eastern Europe and presumably these girls had come from one of these newly liberated, but still impoverished, countries.

Who was the slightly older woman? She knew that Ursula liked young girls but also liked to dominate the occasional older woman such as me, she thought, for Emma herself was now just in her thirties. But, with her long blonde hair and her size ten figure, she could still pass as a much younger girl.

With her forthcoming beating preying on her mind, she longed to ask Sabhu how many strokes she was going to get. It was awful not knowing and being kept in suspense all this time.

Suddenly the music stopped again and the door opened. Again Sabhu strode across to her cage. 'Number Four! Kneel up!' he ordered, in the harsh voice he used when speaking to the girls in his charge.

Emma saw that he was checking her eye make-up. Satisfied, he nodded. 'Kneel right up! Legs apart.'

Emma saw that he was now checking her mound and beauty lips.

'Hand me the lipstick and press up against the bars of your cage. Head up and keep looking straight ahead.'

Nervously, Emma did what she was told. He bent down and put his white-gloved hands between the bars. Suddenly she jumped as she felt his hands on her beauty lips.

'Keep still' he ordered. 'We want you looking beautiful for your thrashing. Eyes to the front!'

Not daring to look down, she felt him hold her beauty lips apart and apply the lipstick.

Then he leant back and looked down at her. 'That's better,' he muttered. 'Now turn round and press buttocks against the bars.'

Blushing with shame, Emma did so.

'Head right down!' he grunted. 'And buttocks up.'

Poor Emma blushed even more at the thought of what she was now displaying. She felt his hands part her buttocks and again she felt the lipstick being applied.

'Very nice!' she heard him say. 'Now turn round and undo front buttons on cape!'

Biting her lips she did so.

'Pull back sides of cape and thrust breasts through bars.'

Emma had always been proud of her shapely firm breasts, but she could not help feeling humiliated as he slowly stroked them and examined the lipstick on each nipple and the surrounding black circle of kohl.

'Button up cape!' he finally ordered. Then he unlocked the little gate in the bars of her cage.

'Crawl out!' he ordered.

Feeling very apprehensive about what was going to happen, Emma crawled through the little gate on to the floor of the attic.

'Follow me downstairs on all fours!' he ordered in his sharp voice. Like a little dog, Emma hurried after him, hatred and resentment in her heart. Why, oh why, did Ursula now employ this hateful and terrifying creature? Why did she allow him to treat her as if she was just a dog?

Emma was made to stand on a large padded stool in the middle of the strikingly decorated room with its valuable antique furniture – a reflection of both the artistic nature and wealth of Ursula.

Her hands were clasped behind her neck. Her heavy blue cape covered the top of her body, leaving her buttocks and hairless mound and beauty lips quite bare. She was facing sideways toward a sofa on which two well-dressed women, Ursula and her guest, were sitting enjoying cups of tea and cucumber sandwiches.

Emma was appalled to see that the guest was none other than Stefanie – the Baroness – the very woman who, by reporting her to Ursula, had caused her abduction and now her thrashing.

As ordered, Emma was looking straight ahead. She seemed too scared to turn and look at the women. Indeed, she was petrified out of her wits.

This was partly because behind her stood the huge figure of Sabhu, a long dressage whip in his hand, and partly because she recognised the chair over which she had so often, in the past, been made to bend to receive Ursula's cane.

But there was a difference now. This time Ursula would be watching as Emma got, not the cane, but Sabhu's dressage whip!

The chair had been placed with its back facing the sofa on which the two women were seated. 'Oh my God!' thought Emma.

The dual presence of Sabhu and the chair was making her tremble with fear at the thought of her forthcoming thrashing. Try as she might, and she certainly wanted to, she was scarcely able to concentrate on listening to what the two women were saying.

'Well, Baroness,' she now heard Ursula say, 'I am very grateful to you for having sent me such a full report on what little Emma has been up to in London whilst I was away. The little liar had assured me that she would be living a quiet life in the country with her husband.'

'When in fact,' said the Baroness, 'he was also away and she was going around London making you look a complete laughing stock.'

Ursula flushed angrily. 'And perhaps,' she said, 'she made you look a pretty good fool, too, by carrying on with your young Gianni behind your back.

'Indeed,' agreed the Baroness bitterly. 'She's just a liar and a strumpet, who can't keep her hands off men.'

'And yet,' said Ursula slowly, 'she knows very well she's not allowed to have anything to do with men; not even with her booby of a husband. And so she deliberately chooses to defy me. Very well, she's now going to be punished for disobedience   a punishment that she knows she thoroughly deserves.'

Emma caught her breath. Oh what a fool she had been to think that she could ever get away from Ursula's tentacles.

'And I much appreciate being asked to come and watch her punishment,' said the Baroness with conviction. 'And that trainer of yours certainly looks as though he can lay it on pretty hard. The harder the better as far as I'm concerned.'

'Indeed!' laughed Ursula.

'Before you start, however, I really must congratulate you on her attire. That little cape sets off her naked body very well and the manacles are very fetching, as is the make-up – and she smells delicious.'

Hearing those words, Emma found herself blushing with a mixture of excited embarrassment and pride: excited embarrassment at her body being so erotically displayed to these two strict women, and pride that they found her so pleasing.

What a masochistic slut I am, she thought. I just love pleasing other people – men or women.

'Yes,' mused Ursula, 'and I find that overseas visitors also approve, when my girls are paraded before them.'

Overseas visitors! What did Ursula mean, Emma wondered. She knew that Ursula sold many of her own pictures to women visiting London. Did she also now show off her girls to them? How awful to be paraded by Sabhu, like an animal, in front of strangers.

'And I love the idea of her being gagged,' added the Baroness.

'Yes,' agreed Ursula, 'I prefer a girl to be gagged when she's going to be beaten; being unable to make excuses, she then concentrates more on thinking what a little fool she has been, and how much more obedient and submissive she'll be in future – and so the more pleasure that I and my clients will get from her.'

Emma caught her breath. How true! She hated being gagged but it would certainly make her resolve, during her beating, to be more obedient and subservient in future. But what did Ursula mean by clients getting pleasure? Surely her clients simply came to buy pictures?

'Yes,' added Ursula, 'I like my girls to be really subservient. And the interesting thing is that the more harshly I treat them the more they enjoy it. It may sound incredible but there's no doubt about it! Look at that girl, I bet she's now wet with excited anticipation at the thought of being beaten in front of us.'

Both women laughed. Emma gave a little shiver. How right Ursula was – as always – when it came to her girls.

'Well, let us see,' said Ursula. 'Sabhu. Test her!'

The big Haitian smiled and pulled a piece of pink-coloured paper from his pocket.

'My German lady doctor friend devised this,' Ursula whispered to the intrigued Baroness.

'Legs apart,' shouted Sabhu.

The two women watched, fascinated, as Sabhu bent down and slowly parted Emma's beauty lips, then drew the coloured paper along them. Then he held it up for the women to see; it was changing to a blue colour.

'Number four is extremely aroused,' he reported. 'She's wet and very slippery.'

Emma was blushing with shame.

'Well, what did I tell you? laughed Ursula.

Again Emma found herself catching her breath. How unfair they all were to treat a poor girl like this.

'Well, we might as well make a start,' said Ursula after a pause. She nodded to Sabhu.

'Number four! Bend over the chair,' he ordered.

Dumbly, her manacles clinking, Emma went over to the dreaded chair and, facing away from the two women, bent over the back. She then lowered her head and shoulders so that she could grip the arms.

Her buttocks were now sticking up in the air, and on display to Ursula and her guest. Emma blushed at the thought of the erotic view she was now presenting – thanks to the hated Sabhu's additional touches of lipstick.

Sabhu pulled Emma's cape up to her shoulders, leaving her whole back and buttocks bare. 'Legs apart!' he ordered. 'Up on toes! Slightly bend knees!'

Once again Emma blushed at the realisation of what she was displaying to Ursula and the Baroness, never mind to the terrifying Haitian butler.

There was a sudden swishing noise as Sabhu made a few practice strokes of his whip through the air, and then a crash as he brought it down on a cushion.

Emma jumped with fear. She wanted to run away, to run anywhere to get away from this terrifying whip. Her manacles tinkled as she hesitantly straightened up.

'Get back into position!' Sabhu shouted. 'Keep still! Bend over further! Further! Higher up on toes! Now grip arms of chair!'

Then he stood back several yards, looked carefully at Emma's little white bottom, and ran towards her, his whip high in the air. There was another swishing noise and this time the whip cracked down right across Emma's soft little buttocks, making her jump in the air and scream behind her gag.

'Get back into position,' snarled Sabhu.

'Of course, he's not really using all his strength,' laughed Ursula in a little whisper, 'or he'd half kill the girl. But all this play acting really does put the wind up the woman he's thrashing, even if the actual pain he's inflicting is pretty limited.'

'Yes, of course,' the Baroness answered in another whisper. 'But I suppose that with his run, his powerful muscles, and his long whip, he really makes the girl think that she's being half-killed!'

'Exactly!' laughed Ursula. 'Especially as he likes to give a girl six strokes on her bottom followed by six across her front: breasts, belly and upper thighs,' Ursula explained to the Baroness. 'That's what he calls his serious punishment – one that gives the appearance of being a proper flogging. However, I only allow him to give it to a girl who really needs to be taught a lesson – like Emma here. I'm sure you'd like her to think she's being really flogged to death, after what she did to you, deceiving you with your young toy boy.'

'Yes! yes!' replied the Baroness harshly. 'He got the thrashing of his life and so should she – or at least be terrified into thinking that she is. But, anyway, what's the alternative to your trainer's serious punishment?'

'Well, I do allow Sabhu to give a girl what he calls his standard punishment which is three strokes   two on the bottom and one on the front   to any girl without reference to me. It may not sound very much, but you must remember how strong he is. Even one stroke can reduce a girl to a snivelling wreck. That's why he has to be careful and why he also carries that strap. He uses it to punish minor infringements of the rules on a girl's hands. It still stings like hell! So you can see how the threat of a beating from Sabhu ensures that discipline here is very good. They're all as terrified of him as they are of me!'

'Yes, I'm sure,' laughed the Baroness. 'Oh by the way, is there any chance of seeing your other girls sometime?'

'Of course!' She dropped her voice so that Emma would not hear. 'After Emma's had her beating, I'll take you up to the little viewing gallery. I often take my clients up there. You'll be able to see the girls in their cages. They're an interesting new lot and already earning me a lot of money. Quite apart from rich American and European women, wealthy Middle Eastern and African women will pay anything to have a pretty, submissive, European "ladies maid". Perhaps you'll be able to introduce some new clients? I'll make it worth your while!'

'Oh!' laughed the Baroness. 'A little pin money! Well, I do see quite a few rich women passing through London.'

'And you can tell them that soon I shall have at least one girl in milk.'

'Aha! That'll intrigue them!'

'Yes, it's very popular. The clients just love it!'

'And Emma?'

'Well, we'll see!'

Emma was concentrating so hard on holding her position that she hadn't even noticed Ursula had been speaking. She was just too frightened to listen as Sabhu carefully examined the new long red weal on her buttocks. Apparently satisfied, he put a little chalk mark an inch below it.

'He likes to have a perfect ladder effect,' explained Ursula.

Indeed Sabhu now walked back again, like a fast bowler in cricket going back to start his run. Again he turned, paused, raised his whip and took careful aim, like a toreador with his sword at the moment of truth in a bullfight. It was a magnificent and erotic sight for the two spectators. Then he ran forward again, very fast, and brought the whip down exactly on the chalk mark.

Emma's screams were muffled by her gag and she was crying helplessly as the Baroness congratulated the now beaming Sabhu on his accuracy.

Sabhu noticed that Emma was trying with one manacled hand to reach back and rub her bottom to ease the pain.

'Hands to front!' he roared. 'Go on gripping arms of chair. Or that stroke not count!'

Not count, thought Emma. My God! She quickly gripped the arms of the chair again, biting her lips under her gag as she writhed with real or imagined pain. She was used to being beaten by Ursula but never had anyone thrashed her in such a terrifying and drawn out way as this.

The actual physical pain was not too bad, she now realised, and would soon wear off. But even so, she was really scared of what Sabhu might do to her. However, what was so shame-making about it all was that, despite the pain and fear, she could feel herself becoming more and more aroused at the thought of being beaten for the amusement of her Mistress and her guest.

She longed to beg for forgiveness, to cry that she would never deceive Ursula again, that she would never go to bed with a man, and not even kiss one, but gagged as she was, there was nothing she could do. She knew that she would simply have to take the full six strokes, that she had heard Ursula mention, on her soft little backside.

'Sabhu likes a woman to keep still and absorb the full pain of each stroke before getting the next one,' explained Ursula. 'It makes a better spectacle and ensures she does not quickly forget it.'

'Woman?' queried the Baroness. 'I thought you only had girls in their late teens.'

'Oh no! Emma's thirty now   scarcely a young girl. And I've a lovely 40-year-old woman now as well as two young ones. You'll see her shortly. Incidentally, I think Sabhu enjoys thrashing an older woman even more than he does a young girl!'

Sabhu had been marching around the tightly bent-over Emma, making her keep quite still even though she longed to ease the terrible pain with her hands.

Emma was terrified as she then felt him place his chalk marks on her bottom for the third stroke. But he seemed in no hurry and it was not for another long minute that he slowly and deliberately walked back across the room, raised his whip, took careful aim, and again ran very fast towards the proffered soft white bottom.

'I always think this part is the best,' laughed Ursula a few minutes later as Sabhu made the crying Emma stand up, unbuttoned the front of her cape and then took it off, leaving her standing with her breasts and belly exposed, shivering with pain and fear.

After a long pause, he made her lean backwards over the back of the chair, raising her heavily manacled hands above her now lowered head, to grip the arms of the chair again.

Emma's body was now strained backwards like a bow, with her feet parted as much as her ankle manacles permitted. Her knees were bent, and her painted beauty lips, powdered mound, soft little belly and firm breasts were all pointing up at the ceiling. Her hair was flung back over the front edge of the chair and hung down to the floor.

Sabhu fussed about making her adjust her position until it was just right. The Baroness caught her breath with excitement as Sabhu, standing over the petrified Emma, raised the long whip, took careful aim and brought it down across her breasts, on the soft tender flesh just below the nipples.

Poor Emma managed another piteous muffled scream. She was writhing and squirming as if in a state of agonised ecstasy. She longed to rub her breasts, but somehow managed to go on gripping the arms of the chair as the pain subsided.

'One of the advantages of this position,' said Ursula, 'is that the whip can properly get at the tender under-side of the breasts.'

Indeed a fresh red weal was now appearing just below the nipples on both breasts.

'He really is an artist with the whip,' exclaimed the Baroness. 'No real harm done, but plenty of induced fear.'

'Yes, and it's brilliant the way it's all done with just a flick of his strong wrist,' laughed Ursula. 'He doesn't leave a permanent mark and yet he really makes the girls wriggle! It's such a relief being able to leave him in charge of my girls, knowing that there is no way they can get round him – as they might with a white overseer.'

Ursula paused for a moment.

'Do you know, I now even leave it to him to recommend which girl, or girls, I should take to my bed, knowing that he will have told the girl just what she is to do to please me. He really does seem to know all the most exciting ways a girl can please her Mistress, and to understand how a Mistress likes to enjoy her girls.'

'You mean,' queried the Baroness, 'you can now lie back and let the girl selected by Sabhu arouse you in the way she has been trained to do by him?'

'Exactly!' Ursula again dropped her voice so that Emma would not now hear. 'And also arouse my clients!'

'Who then buy your pictures as well?'

'Well, quite often,' laughed Ursula. 'They are certainly interested in the services my girls can offer – for a substantial fee, of course. And then, being delighted with the girl's performance, they often also buy a picture or two as a memento of an unforgettable experience, for many of my pictures feature my girls half naked or exotically dressed or even manacled! And then they come back for more excitements and also tell their friends.'

'Well! That's certainly one way of beating the recession in the art world!'

'Indeed!'

'And will our little friend Emma be on offer to your clients too?'

'Shush!' laughed Ursula, keeping her voice down. 'She doesn't yet know it! Yes, she'll be on offer, just like my paintings and the other girls, just as soon as Sabhu has trained her up.'

'Trained her up?' queried the Baroness.

'Yes, you see, many of my clients don't speak much English, nor do most of my girls. So the girls are trained by

Sabhu to respond to a printed list of certain key orders which is given to the clients. In this way they don't have to waste time trying to explain to a girl what they want her to do – one simple word of command, and she does it!'

'But do they? These girls can be such contrary little bitches.'

'Oh, Sabhu makes certain that mine aren't. They're far too frightened of his whip. My girls all know that if they do not completely satisfy me, or any of my clients, then they'll get the whip from Sabhu afterwards or next morning. It's something that concentrates their minds wonderfully, and indeed all the time they are in my bed, or that of my clients, they're thinking of little else.'

Emma was again far too concerned with her pain to take in what was being said. But she saw that the Baroness was now clapping her hands with admiration.

'Wonderful!' she cried. 'But where did you find this . . . Sabhu?'

'In a circus!' laughed Ursula. 'He comes from Haiti – that's why his English is rather limited. He was an expert trainer of performing dogs and wild animals. But I thought that he was rather wasted and would make an ideal trainer of performing girls. And he has!'

'Indeed!' laughed the Baroness. 'And Sabhu – what a suitable name for an animal trainer!'

'Yes, that was his name in the circus and I kept it on to help make my girls feel more frightened of him and subservient.'

'And more like performing animals!' said the Baroness with another little laugh.

'Yes! I like him to treat the girls as if they were just animals and that's why he calls them only by their numbers.'

'But he's still a man – and they are girls. How can you be sure that . . .'

'Oh,' laughed Ursula, 'there's no risk of that! He's far too busy with Babindu, my Caribbean housekeeper, whom he much prefers to any white woman. They get on very well, and as he's a damn good overseer and trains my girls beautifully, I turn a blind eye to what they get up to.'

'Ah, well!' smiled the Baroness. 'I can see you're very lucky to have found him and kept him happy.'

'Yes, he just adores being in charge of my girls and he's also a good butler. He and Babindu make a good team. She's a good cook not that she has to cook very much for the girls; Sabhu likes to keep them on a very light diet: mainly fruit and yoghurt very cheap!'

Sabhu had now again lifted his whip. Again, like a bull-fighter preparing for the kill, he turned sideways on to the terrified girl, raised himself up on his toes, took careful aim and then brought the whip down acrosss Emma's belly noisily, but in reality not too hard, and exactly in line with her navel.

Once again the pain seemed terrible. But all that Emma was thinking was that she could not risk being awarded another stroke like that one. She just had to keep still and grit her teeth.

'It's interesting to see how much a girl can absorb on her belly,' observed Ursula nonchalantly. Indeed it was one of the standard punishments for lazy slave women in the West Indies. That's why Sabhu now so enjoys to give it to a white woman. The black man's revenge!'

The Baroness nodded. 'It's all very educative,' she murmured reflectively.

'Well, this next stroke is even more interesting. The aim is to divide the pain equally between the tender tops of the thighs and, of course, the girl's most sensitive part of her body - her beauty bud. It calls for great accuracy or the whole point of the stroke will be missed. A really good stroke, however, and the girl will think of little else for hours!'

Indeed Sabhu had again raised himself up on his toes and taken careful aim. There was a sudden crash and two long weals began to spread across poor Emma's upper thighs; slowly, the weals spread and met just above the top of her beauty lips. It had been a perfect shot.

'Now he'll repeat those three strokes again,' explained Ursula.

'Good!' laughed the now stimulated Baroness.

Sabhu stood back and bowed. Ursula and the Baroness clapped their hands enthusiastically. Poor Emma had slid to the floor and was lying there sobbing, one hand holding her breasts, the other between her legs.

'Never, never, not ever,' she was muttering to herself under her gag, 'will I ever again risk deceiving Ursula, my Mistress.'

'Now, another cup of tea, Baroness?' said Ursula politely. 'Another scone? In a few minutes Sabhu will blindfold the girl for the next little part of our little entertainment!'

9

The Bikini-belt

'Get up, Number Four,' shouted Sabhu.

But Emma just lay there sobbing.

Sabhu raised his whip.

The whip, thought the crazed Emma, the whip! With a sudden gasp she jumped up, her eyes fixed on the terrible whip. She would do anything, absolutely anything, not to experience that terrible whip again.

'Clasp your hands behind your neck!' he ordered.

Emma raised her manacled hands over her head and clasped them behind her neck. Then he dropped a little hood over her head, and tied it with a strap.

Except for some little ventilation holes, she was now in complete darkness. She could see nothing. What's going to happen now? she wondered anxiously. She tried to call out but her gag muffled her cries, making the two women laugh at her helplessness.

'I like a girl to be hooded when it's first put on her,' she heard Ursula say. 'Then she doesn't realise just what has been done to her until it's too late - for once it's on, it stays on!'

My God, what is going to be put on me? she wondered, trembling apprehensively. She longed to untie the hood and take a look, but she dare not do so.

She felt Sabhu unbutton the front of her cape and then slip it right off. He then removed her ankle manacles. She was now standing there, gagged and hooded, but otherwise stark naked.

'It's a nice little body,' she heard Ursula say, 'but I see I shall have to tell Sabhu to get it slimmed down a bit. The little slut has obviously been eating too many sweets while she thought she had escaped from me. Well, Sabhu keeps them on a very strict diet here and well exercised!'

Once again Emma trembled, but it was true; she simply could not resist sweets and she had put on a little weight.

'Another of my problems,' Ursula was saying, 'is keeping my girls pure. I just can't stand the idea of them playing with themselves or, even worse, with each other, behind my back. They exist purely and simply to give me pleasure.'

Then she momentarily dropped her voice so that Emma could not hear. 'And, of course, also to earn money for me by giving pleasure to my clients!'

'Ah,' laughed the Baroness.

'But either way I don't allow them to have any pleasure themselves except when I occasionally allow it as a special reward. I find it very exciting keeping my girls pure and frustrated,' Ursula said, before adding in a whisper, 'and my clients will pay extra for a girl guaranteed to have been kept pure for several weeks.'

'But how can you be sure?' asked the Baroness.

'Well, I've got a new toy that makes it all much easier. Sabhu's going to put it on Emma now, if you'd like to watch?'

'Oh yes, please,' cried the Baroness with an eager laugh.

'Lift up left leg!' ordered Sabhu.

Wondering what all the whispering had been about and what was happening now, Emma felt something strange and soft being drawn up over her left ankle.

'And now the other leg.'

Emma felt that she must have stepped into something something soft that was being drawn up her legs, over her knees, and over her hips. It felt strange between her legs. Her beauty lips seemed somehow isolated. She felt Sabhu draw it up tight to her waist, where he seemed to be fastening it with a belt. She heard a click in the small of her back, as if a little padlock had been closed. Then, still wondering what was happening, she felt something soft being drawn up between her breasts. It seemed to be attached to the belt around her waist. She felt something wide and stiff being loosely fastened round her neck. Then she felt Sabhu doing something in the small of her back. There was a little noise like a key being inserted in a lock, and a click as if something was being switched on.

'Belt switched on, Madam,' reported Sabhu.

'Well that's it,' she heard Ursula laugh, 'and it's switched on and working now. Would you like to see how it works?'

'Yes, please,' she heard the Baroness reply.

What on earth did they mean? Emma wondered. How can a belt be switched on? How can a belt be working? She was soon to learn the answer.

'Right!' came Ursula's voice. 'Now, Emma, you can drop your hands. I want you to try and touch yourself like a naughty girl.'

Wonderingly, Emma put her manacled hands down between her legs. She felt soft leather and then, below her mound, what seemed to be a thick rubber pad, going between her legs. It seemed to have little rubber knobs or studs on it, and at its sides were strips of velcro keeping the rubber pad tightly fastened on to the leather.

Surprised, she began to peel the velcro strips back to get to herself, and then she lifted up the rubber pad. She touched something hard and immediately felt a little electric tingle that made her quickly drop the rubber pad. She heard Ursula laugh.

'Go on, little Emma, go on! Try again!'

Nervously Emma put her hand down. She felt the velcro strips and again lifted up the rubber pad. Again she touched something and again she got a slight shock, making her cry out under her gag and take her hands away quickly.

'You see,' she heard Ursula explain, 'she can pull back the rubber pad over the grill but every time she touches it, trying to get at herself, she gets a little shock. It's only just a tingle really but, being unexpected, it's quite enough to make a girl jump!'

Yes and how awful, thought Emma, and how frustrating for the girl.

'But that's only part of what this belt will do. Watch this!' she heard Ursula laugh. 'Now, Emma, are you going to be a good girl, and obey your trainer? Kneel down and press your gag to his shoes? Well . . .?'

Emma was furious. It was often fun and rather exciting, she knew of old, being Ursula's slave and having to kiss her feet, but to have to kiss the feet of this awful Haitian man . . . No! . . . No!

'I can see you're being obstinate, Emma. I don't like that. You know very well that my girls have to be obedient and instantly do whatever they are told. Don't they, Emma? Well do it!'

Suddenly Emma felt a slight shock between her legs. It made her jump.

'Now, do what I've told you!'

There was another little shock and this time Emma fell to her knees and awkwardly began to grope around desperately with her manacled hands for the Haitian's feet. Then, equally desperately, she started to kiss them through her gag.

She heard the two women laugh. How she hated them.

'So you can see how the belt can also be used to enforce absolute obedience,' she heard Ursula say. 'It's remarkable how, thanks to modern electronics, such little batteries can generate a shock. It's only a mild one, of course, but it's strong enough to make a girl do anything rather than have another one! Now, kneel up, Emma, and look in the mirror.'

The hood was removed and Emma, still frightened lest she got another shock, looked nervously in the mirror. She gasped in astonishment. She seemed to be wearing a sort of topless Bikini made of very soft, almost elasticated, leather, like doe skin.

She saw that the black leather was very thin, and fitted her tightly – almost like another skin. It was decorated with little diamond-shaped ventilation cutouts, through which her white skin showed erotically.

Looking further down she saw a thick rubber pad that went over her beauty lips; it was indeed covered with hard little rubber knobs. She wondered why they were there. She twisted round on her knees and looked over her shoulder into the mirror. A little padlock hung down from two interlocking catches at the back of the belt. She also saw there was a little bulge in the back of the belt.

But that was not all, for, turning back and facing the mirror again, she saw that going up from the front of the belt, between her breasts, was a strip of the same thin leather. It divided in two above her naked breasts, with each strip attached to a stiff, broad leather collar that went, quite loosely, round her neck.

She gasped as she realised the collar was prettily decorated with silver studs and imitation precious stones. Just as the belt itself was fastened in the small of her back by a small padlock, so the collar was fastened at the back of her neck by another one.

On the front of the collar was a loop, like the ring on a dog collar, to which a lead, held by Sabhu, had been fastened. Indeed, she was being held on a lead like a dog.

'Bring her over here, Sabhu, so that the Baroness can see the belt better,' called out Ursula.

Sabhu gave the lead a little tug but, embarrassed and furious at the way she was being treated, Emma held back. She did not see Sabhu smile and quietly put a hand to the little control box hanging from his belt. Suddenly she got a mild shock between her legs, making her again cry out behind her gag.

Immediately, she scuttled over on her knees to Ursula. Anything, just as Ursula had said, not to get another shock! Naked, except for the terrible Bikini-belt, she knelt nervously on the floor in front of the two well dressed women sitting comfortably on the sofa.

'You now learn what to do when I order "attention!" shouted Sabhu. 'Now stand up, Number Four!'

Then, in front of the two watching women, he began slowly calling out a series of orders, each of which was accompanied by a little shock to ensure its instant compliance.

Each order, and each shock, made Emma give a little jump much to the amusement of Ursula and the Baroness. Each was an order, Emma resolved, she would always remember whenever she was commanded, in future, to come to attention!

'Head up! Higher! Eyes looking straight ahead! Shoulders back! Properly! Hands clasped behind neck! Tummy in! More! More, I said! Legs wide apart! Knees bent! And don't forget . . . Eyes looking straight ahead!'

Emma was now straining to hold her position, standing right in front of the two women, terrified of being given another shock by the watching Sabhu.

'Thank you, Sabhu' she heard Ursula say from below her. 'I think we can now see her very well.'

Emma was aware of the horrid Haitian man giving a little bow of pleasure.

'So you can see, my dear, how Sabhu breaks in the girls he trains for me, just as he used to break in the animals he used to train for the circus. There he did it partly by fear of his whip, and partly by shocks from an electric goad. Here he still uses his whip, and the goad is replaced by something more subtle – an electronic belt!'

'Brilliant!' cried the Baroness.

'Of course,' Ursula went on, 'normally, and when the girls are in the house, he just relies on the threat of his whip. But the belts provide a wonderful back-up, especially outside.'

'Oh?' said the Baroness, not quite understanding what Ursula meant.

'Yes, you see they are so much more versatile than the simple electric goads he used in the circus as they can be controlled by radio from another room, or from across the street, or from another table in a restaurant and all without anyone suspecting what is going on. No one notices his control box, but the girls can get a painful little shock. For instance, I don't like any talking when the girls are shut up in their cages. I don't want them talking about me behind my back. But Sabhu can't be there all the time.'

'So how does he stop them talking?' queried the Baroness.

'Simple! He keeps a very sensitive microphone hanging down in front of the cages so that even when he is relaxing in his own room he can hear if any of the girls start talking to each other. Of course he can also watch them, like me, on the internal television system.' She pointed to the large monitor screen. 'And using his remote control box, and without even having to move from his room, he can still give a girl a nasty surprise if he sees her misbehaving in her cage or hears her talking.'

Or even hears them whispering, thought Emma, horrified, realising what had been going on earlier upstairs, when she had heard a girl being mysteriously punished for whispering in her cage.

'So,' Ursula went on in her precise foreign accent, 'my girls feel they are always under his supervision and control. They may sometimes hate it, but they also find it very exciting, knowing that he is simply acting for me, their beloved Mistress!'

'But can a girl really give you pleasure whilst still locked into the belt?' asked the Baroness, intrigued.

'Oh, yes! That's the whole point. The belt normally remains firmly on when you take the girl to bed.'

'But . . .' the Baroness began.

'Look down,' explained Ursula, 'and you'll see that over the girl's mound and going down between her legs is a rubber pad with a line of little rubber knobs. The pad being made of rubber acts as an insulator, so that a girl's Mistress rubbing herself against the knobs won't get a shock, even if she gives one to the girl to make her wriggle harder. You can imagine these little knocks can be very exciting for a Mistress, especially if the girl is wriggling under her like mad for fear of getting another shock or being told to report to Sabhu for a thrashing. I always keep my own control box in bed with me to make sure the girls are really trying hard to please me and bring me to a satisfactory series of climaxes. But although the girl is exciting me with the rubber knobs, she herself won't feel anything unless the belt is taken off.'

'Goodness! How very subtle,' said the Baroness.

'Ah, but you haven't yet seen the really clever part.' She turned to Sabhu. 'Give me the key.'

Sabhu handed her a tiny key which she inserted into the back of the belt. There was a little humming noise. 'Put your hand on the rubber knobs,' Ursula invited the

Baroness. 'It's quite safe you won't feel the slightest shock.'

Gingerly, the Baroness reached forward. 'Good Heavens!' she exclaimed. 'They're vibrating!'

'Exactly and you can imagine the way they can excite a woman pressing down on the girl underneath her.'

'Yes, but the girl, won't she too . . .?'

'Oh no!' laughed Ursula. 'Thanks to the rubber pad, she feels nothing, nothing at all and her Mistress can still use her control box to make her wriggle, and so excite her even more. I tell you, it's sheer heaven!

'My God!' cried the Baroness in amazement. 'Where on earth did you get these belts?'

'In Australia,' replied Ursula with a laugh. 'A woman I know there imports them from a firm of innovative Chinese in Singapore. Apparently, the local Chinese millionaires like to keep their girl-friends, often including European women, locked up in these belts – but without the rubber knobs, of course. They add those specially for use with girls in the power of a woman! But you haven't yet seen the really clever thing the Chinese did when they designed the belts; the arrangements for a girl's natural functions.'

'But I don't want to get a shock,' said the Baroness.

'Oh it'll be quite all right now,' Emma heard Ursula explain. Then Ursula said something to Sabhu and Emma heard a click in the small of her back as he inserted and turned his key.

'Sabhu's just switched off the electric shock between her legs, so we won't get a shock while we have a closer look. But don't worry, he's still got his whip, so she won't dare do anything silly.'

'No, I don't expect that she would,' laughed the Baroness, as Sabhu raised his long dressage whip warningly.

'So let me show you,' Ursula began. Emma did not dare to look down but she felt Ursula's fingers between her outstretched legs. 'You've seen how the rubber pad with the little knobs over the girl's beauty lips is held down with velcro. Now, if you peel the velcro back, like this, what do you see?'

Emma was aware of the Baroness leaning forward, and giving a gasp.

'A sort of open wire mesh and, below it, a long, narrow, flexible but firm plastic grill!'

'Exactly!' said Ursula. 'And underneath the grill, like a little prisoner looking out through the bars of her cell, the imprisoned little beauty bud itself and the shorn beauty lips which are now kept tightly closed like a sea anemone!'

'Oh, how clever,' said the Baroness, clapping her hands. 'And so, if she unfastens the velcro and tries to touch herself, then she gets a shock from the wire mesh. And the plastic grill prevents the shock from being transmitted onto her beauty lips. So if the girl tries to touch herself, then it is just her fingers that feel the shock.'

'And how about the control box?' asked the Baroness.

'Ah, that gives the girl a shock under the plastic grill, on to her beauty lips – as you saw!'

'But supposing the battery is flat or switched off?'

'Then, of course, she won't get a shock from the wire mesh but nevertheless she'll soon find that she can't get even a little finger through the plastic grill.'

'But couldn't she get her fingers underneath it from the side?' asked the Baroness, still a little sceptical.

'Feel the sides of the little Bikini, my dear. Can you feel the stiff plastic rod sewn into the edge of it? A girl would never get a finger properly underneath that.'

'And how about down from the top?' queried the Baroness.

'Feel just above the grill. There's another stiff plastic rod there too, curved just above the girl's beauty bud, pressing in to the girl's mound and making it almost impossible for her to get a finger underneath it.'

'So even if the battery runs down, and there are no more shocks, she still can't get at herself?'

'Exactly!' laughed Ursula. 'It really is very ingenious.'

'But how does she spend a penny?' asked the Baroness.

'Simple. She just unfastens the rubber pad from its velcro fastenings and then, pulling up the rubber pad, she spends her little penny through the grill – and all without touching her beauty lips, or even being able to touch them. But if she's here, of course, then first of all she has to put her hand up and ask Sabhu to supervise doing it. And he being a fairly busy man, not surprisingly, will insist on them all doing it together at specified times!'

'From now on, Emma,' said Ursula in a firm tone of voice, 'you'll never be off the lead outside your cage except sometimes when Sabhu takes you out of the house for exercise. And then you'll be under the control of your belt. Isn't that right, Sabhu?'

'Indeed, Madam,' grinned Sabhu. 'This girl has lost her freedom. She now just do what she is told - and at once!'

'It's all very clever,' enthused the Baroness, 'but how about when she needs to . . .'

'No problem,' said Ursula. 'Sabhu will show you. It's not something that I like to get involved in, thank you very much; I leave all that to Sabhu. But it's interesting to see how cleverly the belt has been designed to cope with it.'

Sabhu turned to Emma, gave her lead a tug and raised his whip warningly.

'Wake up Number Four! Feet together! Hands to your side, so that manacles are hanging down below knees. Good. Now bend knees until manacles touch floor. Good. Now step over manacles and stand up again.'

Emma's hands were now linked by the manacles behind her back.

'Number Four! About turn! Feet well apart. Bend over! Head up! Look straight ahead!'

Emma's buttocks, covered by the black leather Bikini bottom with the diamond cutouts, were now right in front of the two women on the sofa. The weals of the first two strokes were partly hidden by the Bikini but those of the later strokes, being lower down, were well displayed. Ursula ran her fingers along one red line.

'A good, well placed stroke,' she murmured admiringly. 'That Haitian butler of mine can certainly lay it on hard – and accurately.'

Sabhu turned to the Baroness. 'If Madam would like to put her hands down between the girl's legs, can she feel a little slit in the Bikini? And two hard interlocking plastic shields that slide inside the leather? Can you Madam, feel their serrated edges – intended, of course, to ensure the girl's purity?'

'Yes,' cried the Baroness, 'and beneath them, there's another plastic shield that slides up. How clever!'

'Number Four! On the order "Prepare Rear!" you put hands on buttocks and pull plastic shields apart with forefingers and thumb, and with little fingers slide up inner curved piece, thus baring rear orifice.'

Oh, what a terrible belt this is, thought poor Emma, overwhelmed with wonder and embarrassment. But, she had to admit, it was also unbelievably exciting. Never had she felt so controlled, so thrillingly and completely controlled. What an extraordinary woman Ursula was, and what a wonderful Mistress!

'It's brilliant,' enthused the Baroness again, her finger pressing into the now displayed little puckered and rouged orifice, and slightly caressing it.

'Yes. And of course, although when they're here, Sabhu insists on them performing together in front of him, Emma will soon learn how to do it by herself when she's at home. And, of course, one of the clever things in the design is that the three small shields covering the girl's backside are plastic, making it easy to keep clean and hygienic.'

'Well! They certainly seem to have thought of everything,' laughed the Baroness. She appeared reluctant to remove her finger and Emma felt she was enjoying inflicting discomfort.

'And, although the serrated edges of the two side shields will deter any man, a Mistress's dildo wouldn't feel a thing if she wanted to take the girl there, as I often do. And the girl knows she'll get a thrashing if she fails to strain to keep the serrated edges back – and if there are any marks on my dildo!'

The Baroness laughed out loud, giving Emma's anus a sharp prod with a long finger nail and then, as the girl winced, trying to insert it.

'I see,' she said. 'So thanks to the grill in the front and

the serrated plastic guard pieces at the back, a girl can be safely left locked in the belt on her own, and yet kept completely pure and deliciously frustrated, for days, or even weeks, on end. And no one looking at her would ever guess.'

'Exactly!' said Ursula, adding with a little whisper, 'And, as I said, there are many rich women who will pay handsomely for a girl who's been locked into one of these belts for some time.'

'So that she's all the more frustrated and eager,' laughed the Baroness, as she caressed Emma's orifice with a gentle finger.

'And meanwhile, of course,' added Ursula with a quiet giggle as she again dropped her voice, 'thanks to the clever vibrating knobs, both my clients and I can have exquisite pleasure, too, without the belt having to come off.'

'But don't some of the women want the girl with the belt off?'

'If they do, then they have to pay far more!'

There was a little pause while the two women laughed.

'But what happens at an airport security check, if you are taking, or sending a girl abroad?'

'Oh, there's not enough metal to trigger off the alarm that's why it's made of leather and plastic.'

'Wonderful!' laughed the Baroness, finally removing the questing finger.

'So, Emma,' Ursula said, raising her voice, 'there'll be no more illicit fun and games for you from now on not even when I let you go home. And meanwhile you'll have to learn Sabhu's drill for performing to command both together with another girl and alone. Like my other girls, you're going to be trained to obey lots of simple words of command, just like performing dogs in a circus. And you're going to be kept quite pure.'

Kept pure for my Mistress! thought Emma innocently. Oh, how exciting! Perhaps despite everything life here with Ursula was going to turn out to be rather a hoot after all.

10

The Baroness Visits the Cages

The attic was now empty except for the line of silent girls in their cages. Sabhu had gone off to the privacy of his own room next door, switching on the soft music before he left.

Emma was kneeling up, silently gripping the bars of her cage with her manacled hands. The weals on her bottom still made it painful to lie down, or sit on the hard little stool. The pretty little doll was lying beside her and she would occasionally pick it up and hug it.

She could not help noticing, hanging in front of her eyes, her hated dog lead, and she longed to call out to the other women in their cages for reassurance. But she did not dare even to whisper one word. The extent of Sabhu's control over her, she realised, was terrifying.

She could still feel the Bikini-belt – indeed she felt it the whole time. She could feel it loosely round her neck and more tightly round her waist. But even more she could feel it tight over her mound and tight down either side of her beauty lips. She could feel the metal grill over her beauty bud and the stiff little plastic shields over her backside.

She had been put into chastity belts before, but never anything like this. At any second she was expecting to feel another little shock. It was a terrifying prospect – and one that had reduced her to willing and servile obedience. Her tummy was still feeling empty and weak from the effects of a dose of castor oil that Sabhu had forced down her throat when he took her back to the attic. With a horrible grin, Sabhu had made her kneel on the red spot marked '4' in the middle of the room and swallow the dose. He told her that being given a good cleaning out, to use his humiliating expression, was all part of her induction process.

She still remembered her horror as she had knelt on all fours on her spot, behind her the bowl marked '4' half full of scented water, whilst the violent dose worked away on her insides, and the awful Haitian stood over her, whip in hand. Then she could have died of shame as he had made her pull apart the plastic shields.

She was still thinking about the extraordinary control that Ursula and Sabhu had over the caged girls when the door to the viewing gallery suddenly opened, and Ursula ushered in the Baroness.

Simultaneously, the music was switched off and the door into the attic opened. In strode the sinister figure of Sabhu, his long dressage whip in his hand, a black strap and the little control box hanging from his belt.

Watched silently and apprehensively by the women in the cages, Ursula invited the Baroness to sit down on one of the comfortable chairs in the gallery.

'Show respect!' shouted Sabhu.

Emma heard a rattle of chains from the other cages. What was she supposed to do? She soon learnt.

'Number Four! Get down on all fours before your Mistress!' Sabhu shouted at her. Simultaneously she saw him press one of the buttons on the control box. Instantly she felt a little warning shock from her belt. With a little cry, Emma put her hands on to the rubber mat. But evidently that wasn't enough. She felt another shock as she heard Sabhu angrily order: 'Head to the floor!'

Hastily, she lowered her head to the rubber flooring of her cage. But still she was not showing proper respect and she received another shock.

'Push tongue out beneath the bottom bar!'

What! That would be too awful, too ridiculous, too awkward – like a caged animal begging for food.

'Go on, Number Four! Do it!'

She felt another shock. My God! This time she desperately thrust her tongue out through the gap between the bottom of the cage and the first bar.

She did indeed now feel like a caged animal begging for a titbit. She remembered what Ursula had said about Sabhu having formerly been an animal trainer, a trainer of caged performing circus animals.

Ursula was pointing to the cage marked '1'.

'This is the girl I call Bluebell,' she said, in her cold, foreign accent. 'I like to give them simple farm names!'

She nodded to Sabhu, who unlocked the large padlock on the small cage door.

'Number One! Out!' he ordered. It was clearly one of the orders in English that he had taught this foreign lady to obey – one of the orders indeed, Emma realised, that she too would quickly have to learn to obey.

Watching from behind the bars of her cage, Emma saw the girl she had seen with Ursula at the Dorchesters' party quickly crawl out of her cage and kneel down on all fours on the floor of the attic. Sabhu unhooked a lead hanging from the front of the girl's cage and, reaching down, fastened it to the ring on the front of her collar.

'To your spot – go!' he ordered, raising his whip with one hand and holding the end of the lead in the other.

The girl scuttled across the floor to the red spot marked '1'. She made a pretty picture as she knelt there, her head raised and her eyes looking straight ahead, and with her lead held by Sabhu. Under the back of her cape, her black Bikini-belt was on show with her white skin showing through the diamond shaped cutouts.

Clearly, Emma realised, this was another drill that she, too, would have to learn – or risk Sabhu's whip. Emma saw that the girl was a very young-looking blonde, of perhaps eighteen, with soft blue eyes and a trim figure. As well as the same terrifying black leather Bikini-belt, she also wore wrist and ankle manacles just like her own ones, and a similar little cloak with the number '1' embroidered on it together with the initials 'U de V'.

Under the back of the cloak she saw a little padlock in the small of the girl's back. A sudden pang of jealousy shot through Emma as she saw the girl briefly look up at the gallery and give an adoring little smile to Ursula. She knew the signs! This chit of a girl must be Ursula's favourite – even if she was under strict discipline.

'Attention!' the black trainer ordered sharply.

Quickly and nervously, her eyes on Sabhu's whip and on the control box hanging from his belt, Bluebell jumped up, clasped her manacled hands behind her neck, parted her legs, bent her knees and, putting out her tongue, once again looked straight ahead of her.

Just as I had to, thought Emma. What a fantastic discipline Sabhu instils in the girls in his charge. It was all so humiliating and there was so much to learn; so many words of command to learn to obey – and so much pain in store if she made any mistakes.

Sabhu now undid the brass buttons that kept the front of the girl's cape closed and flung one side of it over the girl's shoulders, disclosing a pert, full breast.

'This would give good milk, Madam,' he called out knowingly to the gallery, as he examined the now quivering breast, holding it with one hand as if carefully weighing it.

'The clients are always asking me for a girl in milk,' explained Ursula, lowering her voice so that Emma and the other girls down below could not hear her. 'So, Sabhu is always nagging me about it; he just wants to get bigger tips from delighted clients.'

Holding the lead, Sabhu now stood back looking at the girl and tapping his whip against the palm of his hand. The girl must have been terrified, Emma thought, as she stood there motionless.

'Shoulders back!' he shouted and then, giving her a sharp tap on her tummy with his whip, he added: 'Belly in!'

He consulted a temperature graph hanging on the front of the girl's cage and a notebook which he had taken out of his pocket, and then looked respectfully up at Ursula.

'Number One, Madam.' He might have been a circus trainer making a formal report on the animals in his care, as he went on. 'Its weight is steady. It eating up its feed, and its morning performance was satisfactory · firm and a good colour. Its liquid wastes were clear and tested negative. Temperature graph shows monthly cycle slightly advanced and it's now due to come into season in a week.'

Emma gasped in horror as she listened to the awful Haitian's embarrassing report. And how dare he refer to a pretty white girl as 'it'. How insulting! How could Ursula have given him such humiliating authority over her girls?

Ursula had always taken charge of her girls herself, on the previous occasions when Emma had been with her. She had been strict, it was true, but nothing like Sabhu. Why was she now employing this terrifying Haitian to take charge of them? What was different?

As if half in answer to her question, she heard Ursula say to the Baroness, 'You see, he's very thorough and records everything the girls do. It's a great relief for me, being able to leave so much to him and to know that he won't stand any nonsense from them either.'

Then she again lowered her voice, and Emma could not hear properly. 'And, of course, the clients are fascinated to see an uneducated Haitian in charge of these intelligent European women!'

'Yes, it's certainly pretty arousing!' laughed the Baroness.

'Of course,' Ursula went on, 'Bluebell speaks very little English and so I don't expect she understood half of what Sabhu said about her, but Emma will when he reports on her in future.'

'Good, I want that little bitch humiliated,' said the Baroness.

'Oh, she will be,' laughed Ursula. 'She certainly will be!'

Sabhu coughed discreetly and then went on with his report. 'She had been kept pure for four weeks . . .'

A whole month of enforced frustration! thought Emma in horror. A month of being locked in that awful belt!

'. . . until two nights ago when she was allowed an orgasm in her Mistress's bed.'

'Yes, she's an affectionate little creature, who has given me great pleasure,' said Ursula, and then added in a whisper that Emma could not hear, 'and she's earned me a lot of money!'

'I'm not surprised!' smiled the Baroness.

'Anyway, I took pity on her and, as a reward, sent for Sabhu to take off her belt.'

'But wasn't she horrible and hairy?'

'Oh no,' explained Ursula, 'Sabhu takes off their belts to depilate them once a week, so that under it she was still nicely soft, and having been unable to get at herself for a whole month she was really ready!'

Emma simply did not know whether to be jealous or excited. On the one hand she felt madly jealous that Ursula should have allowed any relief to this chit of a girl, especially in her own bed, but also greatly excited to hear that the dreaded belts were sometimes taken off and a girl allowed at least a little pleasure.

'But isn't there a risk that they might take the opportunity to play with themselves whilst they're being depilated?' asked the Baroness.

'Oh, no,' replied Ursula with a cruel smile. He does it with the girls standing with their wrist manacles fastened to a bar above their heads as he puts on the cream. So they can't touch themselves, even though they may be longing to do so!'

'But do you keep them caged the whole time? Isn't it rather stressful for them just waiting to being chosen by a –?'

'Oh no, on the contrary!' Ursula quickly cut in, lowering her voice so that Emma would not hear. 'Cut off from knowing what's going on in the outside world; forbidden to talk and so unable to wind themselves up; just occasionally being taken outdoors for a little fresh air and otherwise just playing with their dolls and listening to the relaxing background music – being chosen by a client is the biggest event in their daily lives!'

'Ha!' laughed the Baroness.

'Yes, they soon find themselves thinking of nothing else and of jealously planning how they, and not one of their companions, can best catch the eye of a client – and then what they should do to really please her.'

'And if they do, are they rewarded?'

'Oh yes, they earn a little sweetie! Sabhu doesn't normally allow them anything sweet tasting, so they just long for a little sweet or a little piece of chocolate or fudge. And they all know that if they please a client he'll give them one. And if they don't?'

'Then they'll get his whip!' laughed the Baroness.

'Exactly. Reward or punishment! It's based on his experience as an animal trainer – on how he used to treat the animals under his control in the circus. It's a simple system that works very well with these girls.'

'And Emma?'

'Oh, don't worry! Thanks to Sabhu's system, in no time she'll be just as frightened of his whip as these girls and just as desperate to please my clients.'

'But what about her husband? I know he's away for several months, but what about his letters and running their house?'

'Oh, I'll take care of all of that.' Ursula dropped her voice so that Emma would not hear. 'All his letters to Emma will come to me first. I don't want her being distracted from what is now her only task: being made to earn me money by pleasing my lady clients.'

'Good! That'll teach the little slut!'

'Remember, I certainly don't want my girls, including Emma, mooning over men. Sabhu doesn't allow them to even see a photograph of a man, never mind talk about a man or hear another man's voice. Don't worry, Emma will soon have enough on her mind not to think about her husband while he's away.'

'Good! Incidentally, will she have to wear these heavy manacles the whole time?' asked the Baroness. She was looking at the heavy shackles hanging down Bluebell's back as she stood obediently at attention, her hands clasped behind her neck, her eyes fixed on the wall in front of her.

'Oh yes, anyway as much as possible,' Ursula replied. Then whispering into the Baroness's ear, she added: 'Many of my clients are foreign women visiting London and it greatly excites Middle Eastern and African women, in particular, to see European women caged and in chains. They can hardly wait to get their hands on them!'

Ursula laughed and went on, 'And, of course, it also has a strong psychological effect on the girls – making them feel excitingly submissive as they realise that they are no longer free, but belong to me. It is for this very same reason that I like Sabhu to keep them always on a lead outside their cages.'

'And anyway,' Ursula said, now speaking normally, 'I, too, like to see a girl carrying heavy manacle chains on her wrists and ankles – and I like them on her in my bed, just as I like to hold a girl by her lead when she is pleasuring me.'

Again she laughed.

'Manacles, like the cages, the belt and the lead, affect a girl's whole attitude; they keep her feeling submissive and servile, which is what I like in a girl. And, funnily enough, the girls themselves secretly adore being kept manacled and caged, or on a lead. They secretly find it so exciting. They're all such masochists at heart!'

Oh, how true that was, thought the listening Emma. Of course, she resented being abducted and brought here to be caged and manacled under the control of the terrifying Sabhu, but, even so, she had to admit that it was thrilling being one of Ursula's girls again, whether she liked it or not – even though it had meant being thrashed by Sabhu. And, anyway, she knew it had been a thrashing she had well deserved.

'But, as you know, I'm a sadist and I can afford to indulge my fantasies,' Ursula continued with a laugh. 'So masochistic young women suit me fine!'

Emma looked at her manacles, at her belt, at the whip marks on her thighs, at the bars of her cages, at Sabhu and at the trembling and yet clearly excited half naked figure of Bluebell. Yes, that's exactly what Ursula was: a rich sadist, able to live out her wildest fantasies.

Ursula then dropped her voice so that Emma could not hear her.

'And, of course, they earn me a lot of money!'

'And Emma will too?'

'Oh, yes,' replied Ursula, angrily. 'She certainly will – Sabhu will see to that. But to answer your question about the manacles: yes, the manacles do have to come off sometimes – when, for instance, as a special treat, Sabhu takes the girls out for a walk, for a little fresh air, down the street or in the park.'

'But the belts stay on?'

'Oh yes. He controls them outside by their belts. They always stay on!'

'Oh, how they must hate that,' murmured the Baroness. Then she pointed up at the television camera in the corner and laughed. 'Ah, I see you have them under constant security surveillance as well.'

'Yes,' replied Ursula. 'Both Sabhu from his room, and I from downstairs, can control the camera and switch on the bright television lights in each girl's cage.'

She reflected for a moment and then went on.

'You see, originally I intended the television camera as a way of ensuring the girls did not play with themselves, but the belts are so effective in preventing that that we really don't have to worry about it now. It's still very nice to be able to keep a close eye on the girls, though.'

Again she lowered her voice.

'And, of course, it's also a useful way of giving a client a preview of the goods on offer.'

The Baroness laughed. 'And that, presumably, is the microphone you use to enforce your no talking rule,' she remarked admiringly. 'So they're under complete control in their cages even if Sabhu isn't in the same room. How exciting!'

'Indeed!' replied Ursula with a chuckle.

'Well, I'd heard you were doing up your new house but I never dreamt just how! To the casual passer-by, or even to the casual visitor, your house looks like any other well-restored Chelsea home. No one would ever guess what went on upstairs, about these cages, these girls, about Sabhu . . .'

'Indeed not! Well, let's move on . . . Sabhu, put this one back in her cage and let's have a look at the next one.'

'Number One! Into cage. Move!'

With a rattling of her heavy manacle chains, the pretty girl scuttled back into her cage, pulling her cape back around her shoulders.

11

Daisy and Cowslip On Parade

'And this one I call Daisy,' came the voice of Ursula from the gallery. 'She and Bluebell were lovers when I acquired them – and I had to quickly put a stop to that.'

She gestured to Sabhu.

'Number Two – out!'

Within moments another young blonde girl had crawled out of her cage, her manacles clanking, and was now kneeling on all fours, her head raised, on the red spot marked '2'. Sabhu was proudly holding her lead, like the owner of a winner at a dog show.

But if Emma had been shocked to see the way Bluebell had been treated, she had even a greater shock when she saw Sabhu look up at Ursula with a quizzical expression. Indeed he seemed particularly proud of this girl and Emma wondered why.

Ursula smiled and nodded. Sabhu then reached down to the kneeling girl and gripped her lovely long blonde hair. Then suddenly he pulled it all off – it was all just a wig! Emma gasped as she saw that under the wig the girl's head had been shaved. But it was more than that, she now saw. The girl's whole head was utterly hairless, and shone as if it had been polished, giving her a strangely erotic sub-human look.

Horrified, Emma remembered how Ursula had several times threatened to do the same to her, saying that it would make her look very erotic and would bind her even closer to her Mistress. Emma had indeed been so infatuated with Ursula, she had actually found the idea very exciting. But then, in the cold light of day, back at home, she had been horrified by the idea and by the idea of having to wear a wig when away from Ursula. Anyway, what would she have told her husband? She shivered as she realised that Ursula would simply have got Doctor Anna to tell him that it was for some medical reason just as in the past Ursula had, without any reference to herself, blandly got her doctor friend to tell him that she was not fit enough for any love-making.

Her thoughts were interrupted by the Baroness's voice, also coming from up in the gallery. 'How erotic and slave-like she looks with her shiny bald head. It would certainly be exciting to look down and see that working away between your legs!'

'Oh, yes,' laughed Ursula.' That's why I had her done. And you would then see her number tattooed onto the top of her head.'

'Goodness, what an exciting thought,' gasped the Baroness.

'Originally Sabhu persuaded me to let him shave her head simply to make her look more subservient and animal-like. Then, that so excited my clients that I got Doctor Anna to make a proper job of it by having her treated with special rays that kill off the hair completely. I must say that I find it very exciting and so does the girl. Don't you, Daisy?'

The carefully rehearsed words came out slowly, but Emma felt that they were still heartfelt even though Daisy had had to learn them parrot-fashion.

'I just love having a shiny head to please my Mistress,' the girl said in a strong Slavic accent, as she still knelt on all fours, her lead held by the huge Haitian. 'It's so exciting for her – and for me, too.'

Emma gave a little shiver as she heard the girl speak. She herself had been so nearly brainwashed by Ursula into feeling just the same and into begging Ursula to have her done.

'What are those dolls for?' asked the Baroness, pointing to the cages.

'Well, you see, Sabhu's so keen on them being in milk

before too long, that he's very cleverly preparing the way by first bringing out all the girls' natural maternal instincts whilst they're shut up here in their cages.'

'By just allowing them little baby dolls to play with? How clever!'

'Yes, like little girls they get really attached to them and spend hours looking after them. It's really quite sweet. And then, as a special treat, he sometimes gives them carefully chosen magazines to read, full of pictures of happy young mothers and mothers-to-be.'

'You mean he really brainwashes them?'

'Yes indeed, and of course he's greatly helped by the way the girls are kept here in this artificial environment – not allowed to talk and just being taken out of their cages for exercise, or to please me or my clients.

'So that when it happens, they'll half welcome it?'

'More than half!' laughed Ursula. 'They'll love it – and they'll love being brought into milk early.'

'And Emma?'

'Oh, doubtless Sabhu will soon have her just as eager as the others.'

What, thought Emma, pushing away her pretty little baby doll. No! No! But moments later she found herself reaching out for it again.

'And this one I call Cowslip,' said Ursula, as the beautiful, older, dark-haired, Latin and aristocratic-looking woman crawled out of her cage to kneel nervously on the red spot marked '3'. Her real name is very grand, but just being called Cowslip emphasises to her that now she's just one of my girls.'

'Yes, what a humiliating name,' said the Baroness. Then she pointed enquiringly at the woman's buttocks. Emma was shocked to see the weal marks on her bottom.

'Yes,' smiled Ursula. 'My African lady clients just love watching this one being thrashed by Sabhu. They'll pay a large fee to see a haughty-looking older woman being humiliated and beaten by a strong young Haitian - and being called Cowslip into the bargain!'

'Number Three! Attention!' roared Sabhu.

She was a tall, slender woman with good legs and prominent breasts, thrusting up under her cape.

'She's the wife of a South American millionaire, who discovered that she was having an affair with a young man here in London,' said Ursula

Then she lowered her voice so that Cowslip couldn't hear.

'In fact she'll very soon be his ex-wife. She doesn't know it, but her husband is using her affair as an excuse to divorce her and marry his pretty young secretary. He's paying me a large sum to keep her locked up so that she can't interfere with the divorce. Sabhu, of course, made her sign all the necessary papers without letting her see what she was signing. She has no idea what's happened.'

'And presumably her husband will not now give her a large financial settlement?' laughed the Baroness.

'Exactly. Instead, he pays me to keep her here. And the joke is that she herself also earns me a considerable amount of money – for she's very popular with the clients, especially, as I said, with the African women who enjoy dominating an older, but still very beautiful, reluctant white woman.

'Reluctant?' queried the Baroness.

'Yes, she'd never had a lesbian affair before, which made it all the more challenging for Sabhu to break her in to it – and exciting to watch. But, thanks to the threat of Sabhu's whip, she's learned to perform very well now and I rarely get complaints from the clients.'

'And, with her being older, I suppose Sabhu has had to be much stricter with her than with the younger girls,' said the Baroness.

'Indeed and, as a married woman, she feels the frustration of the belt and the humiliation of being manacled and caged, as well as being controlled by Sabhu, much more than they do. I've had to be very strict myself in not giving way to her constant pleading to be allowed relief.'

Emma was now startled when Sabhu unbuttoned the front of Cowslip's cape and, as he had done with the other women, threw first one side of it back over her shoulder, to reveal two slight weals across her firm left breast, then flung both sides back to reveal both breasts.

But that was not all. There were two more faint weals across her belly and another two across the tops of her thighs. She had not merely been whipped, like Emma herself; Cowslip had been given Sabhu's 'serious punishment'. But that still was not all. Each breast was tipped with a strangely elongated nipple from which a large, but thin, steel ring was hanging. And from the right ring hung a little silver name tag, like one often sees hanging from a dog collar.

'I wanted to do something to Cowslip that would, like the belt, really make her realise that she now belongs to me. So I readily agreed when Sabhu asked permission to try out his special nipple stretcher on her, and it has been a great success. So much so that I then told him to go ahead and pierce her nipples and fit them with these rings. They're made of toughened steel and the ends have been specially welded together. It's almost impossible to get them off. And the little name tag has been engraved with THE PROPERTY OF MISS URSULA DE VERE.'

Ursula paused.

'So,' she went on, 'even if she could escape from Sabhu's strict control and run away, I don't think she'd be very keen to meet her young boyfriend again; not while she's wearing those rings!'

Sabhu cupped one of her full breasts with one hand and raised it up as he had with Bluebell.

'This, too, would milk well,' he said.

'I told you that he won't rest until they're all in milk!' laughed Ursula. 'But it's an interesting point. You see, Cowslip was just a typical, well-fed, plump Latin woman when I handed her over to Sabhu. Now look at her! Thanks to Sabhu's strict feeding arrangements in the cages, she's lost two stone since being caged; and thanks to his daily morning exercise routine, she's fit and has muscled up nicely.'

'And she's kept her full breasts.'

'Not exactly. I asked Doctor Anna to give her breast

implants. The Doctor is very experienced at that too and, as you can see, it's turned out very well.' She dropped her voice again. 'And financially it's paid off very well. Her breast and nipple enlargement is another reason for her popularity. So, despite being older, she's in regular demand from the clients.'

'I'm not surprised. But would she milk well having had implants?'

'Oh, yes. Doctor Anna is quite adamant that it will make no difference. Anyway, I expect we'll soon see!'

12

Ursula Relaxes in Bed

Ursula and the Baroness left the attic accompanied by the fawning Sabhu. There was silence in the cages; none of the women were daring to say a word. Ten minutes later Sabhu came back, with, as usual, his whip in his hand. 'Buttocks!' he ordered.

Emma could hear the rattle of chains from the adjoining cages, but, being unable to see what the other girls were doing, did not understand what she was supposed to do. Suddenly she felt a sharp little shock.

'Number Four! On the order "Buttocks" you turn round and press backside against bars of cage and pull back plastic shields at back of belt to uncover backside. And keep head up and eyes on back of cage. Now move!'

Terrified of getting another shock, Emma did as ordered, her manacles clinking. Then, pulling back the outer shields and holding up the inner one, she humiliatingly pressed the now naked centre of her bottom against the cold bars. She heard Sabhu proceeding down the line of cages. She did not dare to turn around to see what he was doing.

When he was opposite her cage, he angrily shouted, 'Number Four! I said uncover backside!'

Appalled at such words being addressed to her by someone she regarded as ignorant, Emma, who had unwittingly allowed the shields to close partially, hastily pulled them back again. Seconds later she felt something slim being pushed up inside her. She tried to expel it with her muscles, but Sabhu again shouted, 'Number Four! You grip it tight!'

Keeping her eyes fixed on the wall at the back of her cage, and her bottom pressed against the bars, she heard Sabhu go to the end of the line of cages and once more start coming down back towards hers. A minute later she felt whatever it was being withdrawn. Then there was a scratching noise as he wrote something on the temperature graph hanging from the front of her cage. He had been taking her temperature. He must have been taking all their temperatures, she realised, so that he could check their monthly cycles and report them to Ursula and Doctor Anna. Oh, how shame-making for that to be done by a man!

Indeed, Emma would learn that 'Buttocks' was a routine that was repeated several times a day.

Sabhu now proceeded down the line of cages, dolloping out a little yoghurt and sliced fruit into the metal feeding troughs hanging from the bars at the front of each cage. Feeling very hungry after all that had happened, Emma picked up the spoon and dipped it into the metal trough. Immediately she felt a shock. She dropped the spoon with a scream.

'Number Four!' she heard Sabhu's now well-known shout. 'You not eat until given permission and then you eat up quickly.'

Sabhu now slowly walked up and down in front of the line of cages. He could feel the girls' eyes watching him eagerly.

'White sluts!' he suddenly shouted. Then, after the usual pause, he ordered: 'Eat!'

Emma heard the clatter of wrist manacles banging against metal troughs, of wooden spoons scraping metal, and of sloppy food being hastily gobbled. Then she too was gobbling up her feed.

She heard the noise of troughs being cleaned by little tongues. She baulked at the idea but then she remembered the awful shocks and the terrifying dressage whip. Soon, she too, was licking her trough clean.

After ordering the girls to smarten up their make-up, Sabhu had taken them out of their cages. He now had them lined up, standing at attention, on their numbered red spots, facing the line of numbered bowls. Tapping his whip menacingly, he walked slowly up the line of women, all of whom were looking straight ahead, and then down behind it, like a drill sergeant. Emma was trembling with fear. Her gaze fixed on the wall, she heard the sudden swish of the long dressage whip behind her as it landed on a thin leather Bikini - the one that was stretched tightly over the curvaceous rump of the older woman; the one whom Ursula so insultingly called Cowslip.

'Number Three!' she heard Sabhu shout. 'Buttocks clenched!'

Hastily, Emma strained to further clench her own buttocks, further straighten her shoulders and yet further pull in her tummy.

'Position number one!' he shouted. 'Move!'

Emma followed the other girls in scuttling over to the bowls, and then turning round to face Sabhu. Then, keeping her eyes fixed ahead and her knees bent, she humiliatingly stood with her ankles pushing her bowl forward, and her ankle manacles holding it back from the front.

'Prepare front!' shouted Sabhu, his whip raised.

Taking her time from the other girls, and keeping her eyes raised, Emma desperately felt with her manacled hands for the velcro strips that held the rubber-studded pad in position over her beauty lips.

'One!' ordered Sabhu.

There was a rasping noise as she and the other girls each pulled back their velcro fastenings.

'Two!'

With both hands the girls lifted up their rubber pads, thrust their beauty lips forward against the underlying plastic grill and stood stock still. It was a humiliating position.

Sabhu looked along the line of trembling European women. Oh the feeling of power! And he was being paid to do this! How many of his friends back in Haiti would have given their back teeth to be able to treat European women like this!

'Get ready,' he warned, in a harsh voice.

Emma was terrified that she might not be ready in time. But the sight of the whip which Sabhu was now impatiently tapping against his trouser leg, and of the soapy sponge he was holding ready in his other hand, speeded up her reactions considerably.

'Go!' he shouted. Then came the noise of water trickling.

Sabhu came down the line with his sponge. Emma winced as she felt the cold soapy water being squeezed through the plastic grill and on to her sensitive beauty lips.

Sabhu stood back and looked at each girl in turn. Yes, he thought, his girls were now ready to be paraded in front of their Mistress.

Ursula was sitting in a large, comfortable, chintz-covered chair in her beautifully decorated drawing room. An elaborate old French gilt chandelier hung from the ceiling, lighting up the thick fitted carpets and Persian rugs on the floor.

There were matching old-fashioned gilt candlestick holders on the walls and the curtains were made of heavy blue velvet, picked out in green. The furniture was all eighteenth century but the pictures, reflecting her own taste, were modern abstract paintings by well-known artists.

Sheathed in a long black dress, Ursula exuded an aura of sophistication and wealth as she sat, sipping a glass of vintage brandy and chatting to her black cook and housekeeper, Babindu. She had just got back from an amusing dinner party at which one of the leading gallery owners in London had offered to put on an exhibition for her.

She was delighted. If all went well and her pictures sold as well as they had in the past, then they would make a useful supplement to the considerable amount of money she was now making out of providing girls for female overseas visitors. Already the cost of doing up the house had been more than paid for   not that she was short of capital, but as a good businesswoman she liked her current expenditure to be covered by her current income.

The only fly in the ointment was the theft of that picture. But she now had an idea where it was – and how she might get it back.

She was feeling like celebrating with one or more of her girls in her bed, whilst the remainder writhed in frustration in children's cots in the alcove off her bedroom.

Sabhu led in the four women by their leads. Under their velvet capes they were all naked – except, of course, for their Bikini-belts and their heavy ankle and wrist manacles. Emma saw that numbered red spots had been stitched into the rug in front of her. She followed the others in lining up on their spots facing Ursula.

'Attention!' roared Sabhu, and all four women raised their manacled hands to behind their necks, bent their widely separated knees, put out their tongues and looked straight ahead.

Emma had noticed that the black woman standing behind Ursula's chair was Babindu, her new housekeeper. How she hated her presence! It was bad enough being paraded half naked and locked in her belt by Sabhu. But for a Caribbean woman servant also to be present was just too humiliating.

Sabhu now went down the line of silent women, unbuttoning and taking off their capes. Their breasts were now bare.

'Number!'

'One!' called out Bluebell, taking a step forward. Ursula noticed her keenness to catch her eye. It gave her an excited feeling.

'Two!' cried Daisy. She too stepped forward. A feeling of power spread through Ursula's loins as she took in this girl's anxiousness also to catch her eye. It really was very exciting having these pretty young girls competing for her attention. She remembered similar scenes in which the two girls had been paraded in front of clients – who were fascinated that the girls had formerly been lovers, but were now kept chaste for the greater pleasure of the clients themselves.

'Three!' called out Sabhu.

Once again a feeling of power surged through Ursula at the thought of having reduced this beautiful and sophisticated woman of the world to utter subservience.

There was a pause. Sabhu looked at Emma and raised his whip. She knew her number and it was obvious what she was expected to do – as was the punishment which awaited her if she did not comply.

'Four!' called out Emma in a submissive little voice as she, too, stepped forward. Ursula smiled; revenge was indeed very sweet.

'Your sluts are present and correct, Madam,' reported Sabhu, proudly.

Sluts! thought Emma. So that's how this damn Haitian thought of them. What a swine he was!

But Sabhu, like Ursula, was once again enjoying the feeling of power surging through his loins; the power of a simple and relatively uneducated Haitian over a team of European women in his charge. The fact that number three, and now number four, were slightly older women and well-educated and socially upper crust, made it all the more enjoyable. It was indeed a wonderful feeling. It was a natural feeling that was as old as the successful slave revolt against the hated European slave owners, two hundred years ago, in Haiti. How he hated and despised European women and yet here he was being paid to control and humiliate them by one of the few white women he respected!

All this was a feeling that Ursula well understood, and took advantage of. Sabhu made an excellent overseer whom she could safely leave in charge of the girls, and a clever trainer who seemed to know just what a dominant woman wants from a submissive girl.

'Shake!' ordered Sabhu, raising his whip menacingly.

Terrified of the whip, Emma simply did not know what to do. She looked at the other girls. They were shaking their breasts from side to side. How degrading!

But a sudden shout of 'Number Four! Shake!' made her too shake her breasts, much to Ursula's amusement. Sabhu's aim, she knew, was to give an idea of what it would feel like having a particular girl's breasts writhing under her own. It was a display that accentuated Cowslip's elongated nipples and nipple rings.

'Hips thrust!'

Emma saw that each girl was now thrusting her hips backwards and forwards erotically, as if trying to impress Ursula with her ability and desire to give her pleasure with the little rubber studs over her beauty lips.

'Tongues!'

Each girl was now wriggling her tongue rapidly from side to side as if trying to show her Mistress the oral thrills Sabhu had trained her to give if she were chosen.

This was a display that, on the one hand, highlighted Cowslip's natural repugnance for doing any such thing, and on the other hand, displayed the natural masochistic desire of the two younger girls to please Ursula in this way.

Ursula smiled as she saw Emma hesitate. Revenge was sweet, she decided, as she watched the girl gradually overcome her resentment at having been abducted and forced into becoming, once again, one of Ursula's girls. She continued to smile as Emma, consumed by her natural jealousy of the other girls, slowly began to wriggle her tongue, anxious to show that she too longed to be chosen to give pleasure to her Mistress. Oh, to be back in her Mistress's bed! It was a longing Emma simply could not control.

It was also, Ursula felt, a sign that Sabhu was going to be able to train Emma to become a really keen and submissive little bed companion for her clients. Although there were no clients tonight, Ursula did not yet intend to take Emma into her bed again. No, the girl must first be properly trained by Sabhu. Meanwhile she would enjoy making Emma madly jealous, as well as kept frustrated by her belt, as she listened whilst her Mistress enjoyed Bluebell and Daisy.

'Bluebell and Daisy, I think,' she said to Sabhu. 'But fasten the other two in the alcove.'

'Very good, Madam,' he replied. 'And may I suggest the crucifixion position for Daisy, for Madam's initial pleasure, and the foot position for Bluebell, bringing her up later from below the bed clothes to give further pleasure.'

'Um . . . Yes, Sabhu,' Ursula smiled, 'I think I'd like that very much. I look forward to finding them suitably secured in half an hour's time.'

Once again, she felt what a relief it was to have such an intelligent and understanding overseer for her girls. She could leave the detailed disciplining and training of her girls to him, just as she could also leave much of the detailed running of the house to her housekeeper, Babindu.

It was past midnight. Emma lay writhing with a mixture of pain, jealousy and frustration in a tiny cot in the alcove off Ursula's luxurious bedroom. The pain came from having to lie on her well thrashed bottom. The jealousy from hearing Ursula enjoying herself with the other two girls. And the frustration came from her belt.

Cowslip lay in a similar cot next to hers. To heighten their frustration, both girls had been gagged by Sabhu to prevent them from disturbing their Mistress's pleasure, and both girls' wrist manacles were fastened above their heads to the bars of their cots. Their ankle manacles were fastened well apart to the bars at the foot of their cots.

For an hour, Emma had been driven almost mad by the sounds of Ursula's love-making coming from the open door that led into her bedroom. When she and Cowslip, wearing short little nightdresses over their belts, had been led by Sabhu, holding their leads, into the alcove, she had caught a glimpse of Daisy stretched out across Ursula's bed – the same bed in which she herself had experienced such pleasure and pain in the past, in her Mistress's previous house.

As he had suggested, Sabhu had chained Daisy with her arms stretched out to the full extent of her wrist manacles and fastened to the head of the bed. A bolster under her hips threw into prominence the little rubber knobs on her belt, between her equally outstretched legs. They now glistened with a little oil, just below her tummy, so that her Mistress's pleasure would be all the greater. A little key projected from the side of her belt, ready to be switched on to make the rubber knobs vibrate enticingly.

Then, Emma had noticed the crouching figure of Bluebell kneeling down between Daisy's ankles. A chain was fastened to the ring at the front of her collar. It ran down between her breasts and her legs to the foot of the bed. It was a chain long enough to allow her to reach forward and further excite Ursula with her tongue, whilst her Mistress was taking her pleasure from the body and oiled rubber knobs of Daisy, lying beneath her. However, the chain was also short enough to keep her down, humbly, close to the foot of the bed.

Soon, Emma had fumed with jealousy, having been forced to listen to Ursula taking her pleasure from Daisy who was lying prostrate beneath her. A slight humming noise indicated that the little rubber pads were vibrating.

Gagged and chained to her cot, Emma had found it all madly frustrating. How she had longed to call out to Ursula to say that she would give her so much more pleasure than that chit of a girl, Daisy!

But it had been even worse when Ursula had called on Bluebell to lick her from behind just as she was reaching her climax. Now, furiously jealous, Emma could imagine the erotic scene which was taking place only a few feet away beyond the open door.

Ursula's visit to the alcove, after her first series of thrilling climaxes, had not made things any better. She had teased the chained and gagged Emma, describing in detail just what each of the two girls had been doing, and asking her if she would have liked to have been in each girl's place. Then she had mocked Emma's obvious – but, thanks to her belt, totally frustrated – state of arousal.

Finally she had excused herself saying, to Emma's silent fury, that she really must go back and again enjoy the two girls who, being younger than Emma, she found so much more exciting – though if Sabhu reported that Emma was making good progress with her training, then she might one day be invited to her Mistress's room.

Then, Emma had had to listen to a long drawn-out repeat performance, before Ursula had fallen asleep between the two girls. Emma, torn by jealousy and frustration, had lain awake most of the night.

13

Sabhu's Routine Morning Discipline

The next day Sabhu decided that Emma should be put through his full routine morning discipline - just like the other women in his charge. Although no clients were expected that morning, several had booked in for later in the week to watch, from the little viewing gallery in the attic, the girls being put through the first part of the humiliating morning display. Sabhu, therefore, wanted to start training Emma in what to do.

Sabhu prided himself on always putting on a good show of well-drilled European women being put through their paces - just as in the circus he would put on a good private display of his animals being put through their paces for the circus owner and invited local dignitaries.

He was now no longer dressed in black as a butler, but more like a circus lion tamer, with tightly-fitting white breeches and a smart red jacket with blue cuffs and lines of gold embroidered frogging across the chest. On his feet he wore gleaming black boots with a strap at the top. As usual he was carrying his long dressage whip. To the women in his charge, he looked even more frightening than ever - as he intended.

Sabhu quickly unchained the women from Ursula's room and its alcove and then, leaving Ursula sleeping, led them by their leads back into the attic. There he removed the gags that had ensured that Emma and Cowslip had not disturbed either their Mistress's pleasure or her beauty sleep. They all had to hang up their nightdresses and line up on their red spots. Holding their leads in one hand and his raised dressage whip in the other, he shouted out the orders which ensured that the women, half crouching over their bowls, all simultaneously spent a penny to Sabhu's embarrassing satisfaction.

This was followed by them being washed, one at a time, in the metal shower. Sabhu controlled the jets and sprayed them each with a soapy gel to make sure that they were thoroughly cleaned all over. He even ordered them to hold up the rubber pad that normally covered the little grill over their beauty lips and sprayed that too with the gel.

Emma could feel first the gel and then the jet of warm water penetrating and washing her beauty lips. Then she had to pull back the protective shields over her bottom and humiliatingly present her backside to Sabhu's soapy spray as well.

After being washed and dried they had to put on their short capes again and were then put back into their cages for a light breakfast of yoghurt and fruit. Sabhu did not allow his caged girls to put on weight, any more than he had allowed kennelled bitches at the circus to become plump. In both cases he kept them fit and trained for the prime purpose of their lives – to perform their tricks, and to order!

Then, locking the door of the attic behind him, Sabhu switched on the soft music and left the women to have a little rest. They had a busy morning ahead of them.

Curled up in her little cage, Emma reflected that she still had not spoken to the other girls. She did not even know if they spoke much English apart from having learnt to understand, like performing animals were taught to understand, the brief standardised words of command that Sabhu shouted at them. Ursula, she had noticed, spoke to the younger girls, Bluebell and Daisy, in some eastern European tongue but addressed the older Cowslip in Spanish. Although she had heard Sabhu speak reasonably fluent English to Ursula, to her he used just the same broken, basic English that he used to the other girls. Clearly, he regarded her as just another animal to be broken in and trained.

A quarter of an hour later, the music suddenly stopped and Sabhu again entered the attic. Astonished, Emma watched him sit down in front of the silent women in their cages, to a hearty breakfast with Ursula's black housekeeper, Babindu. It arrived on a tray by means of a little lift that conveniently led down to the kitchen. It looked and smelt delicious: fresh coffee, croissants, grapefruit, toast and bacon and eggs. The comparison with the girls' simple and meagre breakfast was dramatic.

Sabhu looked along the line of cages as he alternatively spread dollops of butter and black cherry jam on the fresh croissants and gobbled down large mouthfuls of crisp bacon, sausage and eggs.

The girls' eyes were fixed on what he was eating and they were licking their lips enviously – even Emma, who had of course not long been on the strict diet to which the girls were kept by Sabhu.

It was, she realised, yet another clever way the huge Haitian brainwashed the European women in his charge – making them realise just how subservient their position was. But worse was to follow; Sabhu, rising to his feet, picked up a now congealed piece of bacon from his plate and, holding it up between his forefinger and thumb, then walked slowly towards the cages. He laughed as he thought how clients watching from the gallery always loved this little scene.

Emma caught her breath, and could hear the other women doing the same. Sabhu looked along the line of women, each prisoner gripping the bars of her cage, and each silently pleading with her eyes for the precious and rare piece of bacon. Yes, he thought, he really had reduced these once proud white women to the level of animals! Suddenly he flung the piece of bacon through the bars of the cage of Cowslip, the older Argentinian woman; number three. It hit the wall at the back of her cage and fell to the floor. Although she was longing to eat this succulent morsel, she did not dare to move.

Sabhu watched her kneeling at the bars of her cage, her eyes occasionally flicking back to where the scrap of bacon was lying. She was licking her lips in eager anticipation. Oh, how the clients always enjoyed this!

'Fetch!' he ordered.

Emma heard a rattle of chains and a scuffling noise as the woman eagerly crawled back, picked up the bacon in her teeth, brought it back to the front of the cage and reluctantly dropped it on the rubber floor. Again Sabhu picked it up. Again he waved it in front of the cages with each woman eagerly eyeing it. Then he flung it again, this time into the cage of number two, Daisy. Again he kept the girl waiting before ordering her to fetch.

This time, however, he patted her cheek through the bars. 'Eat!' he ordered.

The girl picked it up off the floor and started to chew it slowly to draw out the pleasure. It may have been cold and congealed but it was the first little piece of meat that she had been allowed to eat for what seemed like days and days.

Taken out of their cages, and their capes taken off, they were again lined up on their red spots, waiting for the next order. Emma saw that Babindu was watching and laughing at the European women's evident embarrassment. Then, crouching over their bowls, once again half filled with sweet smelling rose water, they again had to perform in perfect unison to Sabhu's barked orders, this time holding back with their manacled hands the stiff plastic shields that normally covered their backsides.

After being sponged and cleaned by Sabhu, they had to stand up and hold their bowls in front of them for him to inspect their meagre offerings. He noted down the appearance of each bowl's contents and then carefully weighed them. Oh how shame-making it had been, Emma thought and how much worse it was being conducted by a man and this awful shouting Haitian man in particular.

He was like a tough drill sergeant in the army. She wondered if she would ever get used to this dreadful daily routine or indeed to being controlled and supervised by Sabhu at all?

But Emma would soon learn that the embarrassment would be even greater when they were watched from the gallery by several cruel-faced women, specially invited for a 'working breakfast'.

The humiliation would be even greater if they were African ladies, enjoying the spectacle of European women being made to perform to the orders of a Haitian overseer. No wonder Ursula was making a fortune out of her girls!

Sabhu had just finished putting the other three women back into their cages, and was locking each big padlock. He turned to his charges.

'Breasts!' he shouted.

Another word of command, another routine she must learn, thought Emma. She watched as the three women knelt up in their cages and thrust their naked breasts through the bars. They also raised their manacled wrists above their heads. Sabhu walked along the line of cages, fastening the raised manacles to one of the horizontal bars above their heads. They would not now, Emma realised, be able to interfere with whatever he was going to do to them. She saw that he was also securing each of them to the bars of their cages by two straps; one round the neck and the other round the waist. She gave a gasp as she realised that they would not now be able to withdraw their breasts they were held there firmly, thrust through the bars.

Emma was wondering why on earth Sabhu had done this, when he turned to her. 'Number Four! Into cage!' he ordered, raising his whip warningly. 'Go!'

Her eye on the whip, Emma dropped to all fours and then scuttled through the small barred door into her cage.

'Breasts!' he ordered once more. Quickly, Emma knelt up and thrust her breasts through the bars of her cage, just as she had seen the other women do. Sabhu then fastened her wrist manacles to a bar above her head and strapped her neck and waist to the bars in front of her.

Emma, too, found herself now held helplessly in position – but in position for what? She saw Sabhu go to the corner of the attic. Moments later he wheeled a little trolley up in front of the line of cages. She saw it was connected by an electric flex to a plug in the wall. She also saw on the trolley a rather strange looking piece of equipment that included an electric motor.

Then she noticed several pairs of small rubber cups, with straps, each connected to the trolley by long rubber tubes. The tubes seemed to lead back to a row of small numbered bottles.

She saw him go to each cage with a pair of the cups and, putting his hands through the bars, do something with them. When he came to Emma, she tried to shrink back but the straps held her firmly up against the bars of her cage. Mystified, she felt him put the cups onto her nipples. Then putting his hands through the bars of her cage, he secured the cups on to her breasts with another strap which went round her back. He tightened the strap.

Sabhu now stood back and looked at the four pairs of lovely breasts securely thrust forward and linked to the trolley with rubber tubes. 'Get ready,' he ordered.

Ready for what? Emma wondered, but she did not dare to say anything.

Sabhu switched on the machine and it started to make a pulsating noise as if sucking in air through the cups. At the same time, music started to come from the trolley – a distinctive, soft and soothing tune.

Emma felt her cups beginning to pulsate. She felt her nipples being alternatively sucked and squeezed.

Sabhu laughed as, horrified, she tried in vain to pull down her hands and tear off the cups. He laughed again as she then tried, again in vain, to shake them off. They were securely fastened on to her breasts, just as she herself was securely fastened to the bars of her cage.

There was nothing she could do to stop the alternate sucking and squeezing of her breasts. But, in any case, she began to wonder, did she really want to? This pulsating was very soft and gentle. It was a very exciting feeling; very exciting indeed.

Already she could feel her nipples being elongated as the cups sucked at them. She felt little shafts of delight shooting through her body. She could feel her nipples being pulled out and elongated and her whole breasts swelling.

She remembered Sabhu talking to Ursula about wanting the girls to be in milk. How exciting that would be, she thought, as she revelled in the delight coming from her breasts. Oh, how she longed for her breasts to be producing milk for Ursula too!

She looked down at the cups pulsating on her breasts. Would this machine be used to milk her? Would her milk, in little jets, flow into the bottle marked '4'? Oh, what an exciting idea! How she longed for it to come true. Was she being brainwashed, by this clever milking machine, into begging to be allowed to produce milk for her Mistress?

She could feel her nipples being sucked right out by the machine. Was this how Cowslip's nipples had been so stretched? Were hers going to be elongated too? How shameful and animal-like and yet how unbelievably exciting. Suddenly her excited thoughts were interrupted.

'Report!' shouted Sabhu, harshly. This he knew was regarded by watching clients as a high point in the display.

'Number One, sir,' came Bluebell's carefully rehearsed, and yet clearly thrilled, voice. 'I long to be able to give my milk for my Mistress.'

'Number Two, sir,' came Daisy's voice. 'Oh, sir! I'd be so thrilled to give my milk for my Mistress.'

'Number Three, sir.' It was the first time Emma had heard Cowslip's strong Latin accent. She too was obviously speaking with considerable emotion. 'Oh please sir, I too long to be able to give her my milk.'

'Number Four, sir,' Emma heard her own voice, panting with desire as if in a dream. 'I'd do anything, sir. I'd go through anything to be able to give my milk to my Mistress.'

They were all being cleverly brainwashed. Emma realised the full horror of what she'd just said. Oh no! However, the pulsating machine quickly made her brush her fears away. Instead, it made her genuinely feel that it would be the most exciting thing that had ever happened to her.

Crouching in her cage some half an hour later, Emma looked down at her nipples. When Sabhu had unfastened the cups he had, embarrassingly, rubbed a little cream into them. They still feel slightly sore but, she thought, proudly, they looked longer. Oh, how exciting!

She looked up to where Sabhu was walking up and down in front of the line of cages, alternately tapping his long dressage whip against the palm of his hand and against his leather boots.

They were signs that Emma had learnt to recognise as meaning that her terrifying overseer was impatiently waiting for something. Indeed there was an air of expectancy throughout the attic as if the women were impatiently or, more likely, anxiously waiting for news about something.

Suddenly, a telephone rang, puncturing the silence with a harsh bell. Emma heard a hiss of breath being caught from further down the line of cages – from Bluebell and Daisy, the two who had shared Ursula's bed the night before. What were they worrying about now? What was it that they seemed to be anticipating? Was this too, Emma wondered, part of the normal morning routine?

She would soon learn that when clients had spent the night in the house, enjoying one or more of the girls, this was the moment of truth.

This was when Sabhu learnt whether he was likely to be given a large tip by a client delighted with the services of a girl he had trained, or whether the client had complained to Ursula who would now order the girl to be punished.

On this occasion, of course, Ursula would be judging the performance of the girls in her own bed. Quite apart from getting her own pleasure, she also liked to check up on how Sabhu was getting the girls to perform. It was therefore an important moment for Sabhu, for Ursula could be generous if she was really pleased with a girl's performance.

Sabhu rushed over to the phone and picked up the receiver. His face darkened. 'Yes, Madam. Right. I quite understand. I don't expect she'll do it again. Thank you.'

He put down the phone and then slowly and deliberately picked up his dressage whip. Angrily, he swished it through the air several times. One of the little sluts had done him out of a good tip from Ursula. My God, she'd pay for her impudence!

He walked slowly over to where Bluebell and Daisy were kneeling in their cages, gripping the bars until their knuckles were white, their eyes fixed on the whip. He bent down and unlocked the little barred gates.

'Numbers One and Two!' he roared angrily. 'Out!'

Emma saw the two young women scuttle into the centre of the room and then kneel humbly on all fours on their numbered red spots, their heads raised and their eyes looking straight ahead.

'Raise buttocks for punishment!'

Looking terrified, both girls straightened their legs. Under their short capes, their leather-covered bottoms were facing Emma and Cowslip, still locked in their cages, and watching what was happening with bated breath.

'Higher!'

Both girls bent over more and raised their little bottoms.

'Number Two . . .' Sabhu paused. '. . . Mistress satisfied. You get little sweet.'

Daisy gave a sigh of relief. But how cruel of Sabhu, Emma thought, to have kept her right up to this moment thinking she was going to be beaten.

'Number One!' Emma saw that Bluebell was trembling. 'Mistress say you speak to her without permission to ask her to take you off chain to foot of bed . . . Three strokes!'

Horrified, Emma watched as, slowly and deliberately, Sabhu brought his whip down across the thin leather covering the now sobbing Bluebell's little bottom.

'You keep silent next time, and try harder!' shouted Sabhu as he brought the whip down for the third time. 'Numbers One and Two! Back into cages!' he then shouted, 'Go!'

Then he contemptuously threw a little chocolate into Daisy's cage and, once again locking the heavily barred door behind him, left the girls alone in the attic.

There was complete silence except for little sobs of pain from Bluebell and the noise of Daisy gently sucking her sweet as she tried to draw out the pleasure it was giving her.

Then the gentle soothing music started again.

14

In the Gymnasium

Shortly after this little scene, Sabhu reappeared. He was now dressed like a physical training instructor in white, wearing tight-fitting, long gym pants above which the muscles of his now naked, well-oiled torso gleamed menacingly. Clearly not in a mood to stand any nonsense, he quickly took the women out of their cages, clipped their leads to their collars and led them down to the basement. There they were taken into a specially-built gymnasium-cum-training room for what Emma would learn was the second part of their regular period of discipline – the exercise period.

This formed an essential part of Sabhu's training, for he liked to keep all of Ursula's girls slim, keen and fit so as to give greater enjoyment to the Mistress and her clients.

As in the attic, there was a little viewing gallery with its own door and a row of spikes below the iron balustrade. Like the first part of the morning routine up in the attic, the spectacle of half naked European women being put through their exercises by a virile young Haitian overseer was very popular with Ursula's lady clients.

Emma saw that on the walls were parallel wooden bars and that scattered around the sides of the gym were several fitness machines: bicycles, various types of weight-lifting services and a rowing machine. There was also a running machine with a controllable and fast-moving track. There were bars on the side of the apparatus with straps to which a girl's wrists could be fastened. The sweating girl could then be made, at Sabhu's whim, alternatively to sprint, then to run at a steady trot whilst she got her breath back, and then sprint like mad again.

On the floor, in the centre of the room, was a line of red numbered spots – just like those in the attic. Emma followed the example of the other girls and ran to her spot. They all stood there silently and expectantly.

Moments later the door to the little viewing gallery opened and in came Ursula, wearing a lovely peach-coloured silk negligée over her nightdress.

'Show respect!' bellowed Sabhu, just as he would do if it had been clients who had filed into the gallery.

As one, the line of women dropped to their knees and flung themselves forward, their foreheads touching the floor and their hair draped forward between their outstretched manacled hands. They made, thought Ursula, a perfect picture of feminine submission. It was one that she knew made a great impression on her clients and one that she could rely on Sabhu to produce. Even Emma was in the properly abject position and in a perfect line with her companions. Sabhu was breaking her in well!

However, she thought, he must be disappointed at her complaint about Bluebell's impudence. Perhaps she would give him his usual tip anyway. He was, after all, a vital part of her new enterprise to provide girls for rich lady visitors from overseas – a service for which, although she did not yet know it, Emma was now destined.

There were, of course, many call girl agencies for overseas male visitors but she was unique in providing a discreet service for women wanting a girl – and all under the very civilised pretext of coming to see her pictures. The combination of using her girls as models for her pictures and as submissive slave girls for her clients had been highly successful and Sabhu had played a key role.

Ursula was delighted to see three fresh weals on the back of Bluebell's thighs. Sabhu had not wasted time in punishing her. Bluebell was her favourite, but she needed to be brought to heel occasionally and nothing did this better than the judicious application of Sabhu's whip. Yes, she would give him his usual tip.

The only annoying thing that had happened to spoil her new venture was the theft of one of her collection of valuable pictures of abstract modern art. But she had a pretty shrewd idea of where it was – and of how she might get it back.

'Knees bend!' called out the big Haitian, as he put the women through their preliminary warming up exercises in front of the watching Ursula. His naked torso was shining as he stood behind the line of the already sweating women, each standing exactly on her numbered red spot.

Her eyes looking straight ahead, Emma was very aware of the cold gaze of Ursula watching the girls' every movements. She could not help wobbling a little as she strained to obey Sabhu's orders. The heavy weight of her wrist manacles, the chain now hanging down her back as she clasped her hands behind her neck, half unbalanced her.

Terrified, she heard behind her the familiar noise of Sabhu once again impatiently tapping his long dressage whip against the palm of his hand. Please God, she thought, don't let me topple over, as Daisy had just done.

'Number Four! Lower!'

Scared stiff, Emma strained to bend her knees more.

'Up!'

Oh, the relief of standing up straight again. But it was only momentary.

'Knees bend!' again came the order.

Emma had moved on to lifting weights. Sabhu blew his whistle. Immediately, Emma stopped pulling down on the shiny bar of the exhausting machine. The heavy weight of her wrist manacles had made it all so much harder work. The other girls had also stopped working on the other fitness machines. All of them were breathing heavily, trying to get their breath back before the next equally exhausting exercise.

Emma had seen Daisy being made to do a fast stint on the running machine, her ankle manacles clanking. Not satisfied with merely making her run fast, Sabhu had then slowed down the machine and with sharp little taps of his whip made her prance, ordering her to raise her knees high in the air, whilst her breasts swung wildly from side to side.

As Emma settled herself on the rowing machine, Sabhu

came and stood over her, his long dressage whip raised terrifyingly. There was another blast of the whistle and Emma, her eye on Sabhu's whip, strained to pull her oars against the heavy springs that kept them back.

Twice, seeing that this new girl was beginning to slacken off, Sabhu brought his whip down across her naked back with a fearsome crack, making her redouble her efforts until the sweat was pouring down between her breasts. Then he pointed to a dial facing Emma. An adjustable red hand on the dial showed the required number of strokes per minute, and a black hand showed actual number of full strokes the girl had completed so far that minute. 'You'd better pull your guts out, girl!' the big Haitian laughed cruelly.

Emma soon learnt that cheating by taking short strokes did not work. Unless each stroke started with the girl reaching fully forward and then pulling the oar right back against the pressure of the machine's strong springs, it did not count.

If at the end of a minute the girl had not reached the required number of strokes, a loud bell would ring to attract the attention of the overseer – and Sabhu's whip was applied across her back to stimulate her into trying harder.

Sabhu set the red hand at twenty strokes a minute.

'Number Four. You watch dial,' he ordered. 'If you not pass twenty strokes each minute, bell will ring and I will come and beat you again. You understand?'

'Yes, sir!' Emma cried, hastily fearing another stroke of the whip if she annoyed him.

Satisfied that Emma could now be left to strain away on her own, he went around the little gymnasium, looking at the other women.

Cowslip, her eye also on Sabhu's whip, was straining up and down on the weight-lifting machine, bending and straightening her knees as she did so. Bluebell was pedalling like mad on the bicycling machine, looking at the dial in front of her that showed how far she was deemed to have travelled. She was desperate to reach the 'mileage' that Sabhu demanded each girl was to achieve if she were to avoid a beating.

He gave a little laugh as he watched Daisy lift up two

heavy dumbbells and raise them high above her head, before bending her knees and lowering them to the floor again. Hard regular exercise was all part of his girls' routine – and certainly made a fine sight for watching clients.

Emma saw that Sabhu was watching Daisy closely as, terrified of the whip, she had strained and strained to raise her knees level with her hips. Then, with his whip still raised in one hand to keep her prancing, he carefully felt the girl's belly with the other hand through the thin leather of her belt.

Sabhu knew from experience that, carefully controlled, this exercise was an effective way of exercising a girl's tummy muscles to ensure that she could give increased pleasure to a client.

It was then Emma's turn on the running machine. While the other girls continued to strain using the other apparatus, she had to stand on the rubber track with her wrists fastened to the bars at the side of the machine. She saw Sabhu turn a switch and she found herself having to run fast, very fast, or else her manacled feet were dragged painfully along the track.

She found that the heavy weight of her ankle manacles made running and sprinting very hard work, but their weight made the prancing steps that Sabhu made her then do, even worse. She had to strain to raise her knees properly with every stride. She felt utterly exhausted as, with her wrists strapped helplessly to the side bars of the machine, Sabhu shouted at her emphasizing each command with a sharp tap of his dressage whip.

'Knees higher! Keep back straight! Head up! Shoulders back! Knees higher!'

My God! the sweating Emma thought, no wonder Daisy looked so slim. But how cruel!

By the end of her exhausting stint on the running machine, she felt as if she had already lost pounds and pounds.

'Change!' shouted Sabhu.

Emma rushed across the gymnasium and back to the rowing machine. Quickly, she sat down on the sliding seat and picked up the handles of the imitation oars.

15

Sabhu Takes the Girls Out

'Line up!'

Sabhu was once again dressed innocuously as a butler with a short black coat and trousers.

Ursula smiled as, obedient to Sabhu's order, the four girls lined up in front of her in the downstairs hall. Sabhu's formal attire contrasted excitingly with that of her girls.

Their wrist and ankle manacles had been removed and, for once, they were not on a lead. But any feeling of new-found freedom was reduced by the fact that over their belts they were now wearing identical black gymslips and white blouses.

They also wore old-fashioned schoolgirl hats, each made of felt with a red ribbon around it under which, except of course for Daisy, their hair now hung down their backs in two pigtails. Daisy's hat also served to hide her shiny bald head. On their feet, the girls wore identical flat heeled shoes and white socks.

Under her gymslip, Emma could feel her slightly extended nipples pressing against her blouse.

Sabhu had supervised their make-up to ensure that to a passer-by they would look like a crocodile of pretty young teenage schoolgirls being taken out for a walk by a devoted servant.

Indeed, Ursula thought, how young and sweet her girls were looking. How embarrassing it must be for them, especially for the older Cowslip and Emma. And how acutely they must feel the comparison between their dowdy school uniform and her own smart London business suit.

It was, Ursula knew, a sight that greatly tickled the

fancy of her clients. They would enjoy watching Sabhu and the so-called schoolgirls from an upstairs window, or even follow them in the street, fascinated by the sight and by the knowledge of what was really going on. Of course, going out today was really just a practice run for Emma to make sure that she knew she had to conform or else!

Sabhu's harsh voice interrupted Ursula's reverie. 'Number Four! Just you remember, all girls still under my control.'

Sabhu's hand moved to the small control box attached to his belt and now discreetly hidden under his black jacket. Instantly, Emma cried out as she felt a little shock.

'Well, Number Four?'

Emma raised her hand in the air. It had taken her several strokes of the whip to learn how to address her dreaded overseer in the only approved way.

'Yes, Number Four?'

'Permission to speak, sir?'

'Permission granted.'

'Sir, Number Four is still very much under your control . . . sir!'

'Good. Just you remember. You no try escape.'

Ursula smiled again. Emma was learning fast! Already, after only one day, there seemed to be little in common between this clearly terrified and well-disciplined young woman and the loose-living creature who had raced around London deceiving her and making her look such a fool.

Revenge was indeed sweet! It would be even sweeter soon when Emma realised that her only object in life was to earn money for her Mistress with her body.

'You walk two by two,' Sabhu was saying slowly, mainly for the benefit of Emma, for the others were evidently used to being occasionally taken out for a walk. It was an exciting change from being kept locked up in their cages.

'Numbers One and Two in front, holding hands like young girls. Numbers Three and Four behind, also holding hands. I walk behind watching you. You walk on inside of pavement. You stop when I order "Halt!" and when pavement stops. Only when I order "Cross!" you all cross road. When I order "Turn left!" front two girls turn left, when I order "Turn right!" front two girls turn right. If I order "Run!" all girls run. Any girl slow to obey or who moves without order, gets shock.'

Sabhu paused to make sure his orders had been taken in.

'And you, Number Four. You keep eyes looking at ground,' he continued. 'No looking at men and no talking – or you get shock! Remember Sabhu just behind and always watching you.'

Emma gave a little gasp of fear and Sabhu turned respectfully towards the well-dressed Ursula. 'Little girls ready for walk, Madam!' he reported.

'Carry on, Sabhu, please,' Ursula replied in a superior way. She might have been an officer on a parade, receiving a report from an NCO.

'Form up!' shouted Sabhu.

The crocodile was formed. Emma found herself behind the two younger girls. Cowslip shyly put her hand in Emma's, and risked a little smile. Neither dared to say a word.

'Open door! March out into street. Turn right!'

Emma found herself walking down a little street behind the two young girls. Several people looked at them for a moment and then turned away. Clearly their make-up as teenagers was realistic. How shocked these people would be if they knew the truth!

Nevertheless, Emma thought, how wonderful it was to be out in the fresh air again after being locked up in her cage or confined to the house. And the feeling of freedom that came from not having to wear the heavy manacles and from not being on a lead was wonderful.

Elated, Emma had not noticed that she and Cowslip had started to drop back, forgetting that Sabhu was behind them. Suddenly she jumped as she felt an admonishing little shock.

'Close up, Numbers Three and Four,' came a muttered order.

Hastily, they moved to just behind the two younger girls; the feeling of freedom over – just as Sabhu intended.

They passed two young men talking to each other and Emma hastily lowered her eyes. Men were forbidden now!

They walked past several shops with busy housewives coming and going. They all seemed so unconcerned. But what, Emma wondered, would they think if they knew that the innocent-looking crocodile of schoolgirls really consisted of grown-up women who had been made up to look like teenagers and who were being controlled electronically by a cruel Haitian overseer?

Indeed, the thought that at any second, at the slightest sign of any misbehaviour, Sabhu might give her another shock scared her stiff.

But, Emma had to admit, it was all also very exciting – as well as humiliating and terrifying. Or was it the very fact of being humiliated and terrified that made it so exciting? Life with Ursula was never dull.

Sabhu walked them round the area and back to the house again. Sabhu liked to give them a little fresh air, but not too much!

Upstairs, they were made to hang up their schoolgirl clothes and then, naked except for their Bikini-belts, they had to hold out their wrists and ankles to be manacled again, before being allowed to spend a penny together – once again in a line and in time with Sabhu's harshly barked and humiliating orders.

The girls refastened the velcro strips along the sides of their rubber pads and stood hesitantly on their spots, expecting that Sabhu would put them back into their cages again. But there was a change of plan. 'Get dressed for restaurant!' he ordered, pointing to their numbered cupboards.

What does he mean? Emma wondered. What restaurant? Evidently it was an order that the other women knew and recognised with joy. Clapping their hands with excitement, like schoolgirls who had been promised a second special outing, they rushed to their cupboards and held out their hands for Sabhu to unlock their wrist manacles. Their ankle manacles would, evidently, not be removed until later.

Emma watched in amazement as the other three women dressed themselves in identical well-cut and fashionable green and cream silk day dresses. There were matching hats, shoes and gloves and lovely silk scarves that hid the leather collars round their necks.

She saw that they were even sliding white lace, self-supporting stockings up under their ankle manacles and over their legs. They were outfits which, although identical showed them off prettily.

Soon they were brushing their hair and putting it up in a sophisticated style. Daisy was allowed to hide her shiny bald head with a lovely blonde wig. Then they started to make up and paint their fingernails, making themselves look lovely and quite irresistible in a quiet and submissive way.

With their identical outfits, hair styles, hats and shoes, they looked like a team of top class air hostesses - all anxious to please. But to please who? What was going to happen?

Initially, Sabhu seemed content for Emma to watch and learn. But then her reverie was suddenly interrupted. 'Number Four. Get dressed - at once!'

Sabhu was pointing to the wardrobe marked '4'. She saw a green and cream outfit. Hastily she put it on over her belt. It felt gorgeous. She looked in the mirror. She loved it! Then she too brushed her hair, put it up like the others and started to make up. Before long she too was looking quite lovely   and just like the other girls.

'Line up for inspection!' came the order.

Slowly and ponderously the huge Sabhu came down the line, looking closely at each trembling girl in turn. The slightest fault or imperfection and the girl had to hold out her hand for his strap and then run back to the mirror.

Finally, fastening their leads back on again under their scarves, Sabhu led them all downstairs; not this time to the front door but to a side door that Emma had not previously noticed. It led out to the garage where Ursula's long black estate car was parked.

With a shock Emma recognised it as the ambulance-like car which she had seen parked outside her house on the day she had been abducted. She saw that it had the same darkened windows through which nothing could be seen from the outside. A black friend of Sabhu's was already in the driving seat, wearing a chauffeur's hat and Ursula's monogram.

Sabhu opened the door at the back. 'In!' he ordered, raising his whip.

All four women, hampered by their ankle manacles, hastily scrambled in. Emma saw that the top two stretchers, which enabled the long car to be used as an ambulance, had been folded up against the sides forming the backs of two simple bench seats, facing each other, on which the women seated themselves on each side.

Sabhu followed them in and then locked the door before sitting down on a comfortable seat, facing backwards and situated just behind the darkened glass partition that separated the girls from the driver. The driver, having apparently opened the garage door electronically, started the engine and drove out into the street.

Nervous of speaking, Emma looked out of the tinted window.

Suddenly she saw a familiar figure. She caught her breath with excitement. It was Henry! She longed to wave, to call out, to ask them to stop the car, to get out and talk to him. But there was nothing she could do.

He hadn't even noticed the car. Her feeling of helplessness was overwhelming.

As Emma recovered from the shock, she remembered that Ursula and her friends often lunched at a certain restaurant. It was a well-known meeting place for rich lesbians.

It was, Emma thought, all rather exciting – just like the old days with Ursula. Ursula was bound to be angry with her at first but soon, she was sure, she would relax and they would be lovers again.

The big estate car stopped. The driver got out and went into the restaurant. Moments later he came back and nodded to Sabhu, who then started to take off the girls' ankle manacles.

'You remember,' he warned for Emma's benefit, for this was clearly a routine to which the other girls already knew, 'I sit at nearby table and I still give you shocks if I see you misbehave. You get up from table without permission, or talk unless Madam or her friends first speak to you, and you get shock. You here just to be seen - but not heard. Remember I watching you all the time! You understand, number four?'

'Yes, Mr Sabhu, sir,' Emma replied very respectfully.

'Now you all walk after me into restaurant. You walk in ladylike fashion. And you sit down quietly at end of Madam's table.'

He unfastened their leads. 'Come!' he ordered.

To a casual observer, the four attractive and uniformly dressed women being politely assisted out of the car, might have been just a party of off-duty airline hostesses or receptionists. No one would have guessed the degree of control and supervision to which they were secretly being subjected.

Emma found herself, as Number Four, bringing up the rear. There was a sudden hush as the four lovely and identically dressed young women entered the restaurant behind their black-suited companion. The tables were crowded, mainly with fashionably-dressed women, many obviously foreigners. They watched in astonished silence as Sabhu ushered the four gorgeous creatures towards the table at which Ursula and several of her women friends were already sitting, talking, sipping champagne and enjoying a delicious lunch.

Emma saw that several of the women in the restaurant were pointing at one or other of the girls as if comparing them. How embarrassing! Was Ursula just showing them off to all her friends in the restaurant?

She also saw that several women were pointing at her in particular and whispering to each other. By having her dressed identically to her other girls, and bringing her here to this fashionable restaurant frequented by her friends, was Ursula giving a signal to her world, her secret world, that Emma was now back in her control again - and hands off! Or was there more to it?

Anyway, being paraded in public like this, as one of Ursula's girls, was very shame-making yet also terribly exciting!

'Isn't that Emma?' one of Ursula's guests said in an astonished tone of voice as the girls nervously sat down at the empty end of the table.

'Yes,' Emma heard Ursula reply in a grim voice. 'She's back again and under Sabhu's orders. Of course, I've had her severely thrashed by him as a punishment.'

'I'm not surprised,' said another woman, 'after the way she carried on while she thought she was free.'

'I don't somehow think that she'll be doing so in future,' said Ursula with a laugh. Then she gestured towards the other women in the restaurant, many of them her clients, and others her part-time representatives of rich foreign visitors. Lowering her voice so that Emma would not hear, she added: 'The word will now get around after today and I expect there'll be quite a demand for her services!'

Her friends smiled and nodded in agreement.

'Meanwhile,' Ursula continued in a normal voice, 'she's being taught a lesson in abject obedience, aren't you, Emma?'

But Emma was too overcome with shame to reply.

'Emma! I asked you if you were being taught a lesson in abject obedience . . . Well, answer!'

'Yes, Madam,' Emma replied nervously.

'Yes *what*, Emma?' said Ursula coldly. Emma saw Ursula look across the room to where Sabhu was now sitting.

'I'm being punished and disciplined, Madam, like the naughty girl I've been,' cried Emma in haste, terrified of getting a shock.

'And do you deserve it, Emma?'

'Oh, yes, Madam,' Emma cried fervently, 'I do deserve it. I do.'

'Tell my friends why, Emma.'

'Because I was silly and tried to run away from my Mistress,' sobbed Emma, adding with genuine emotion, 'the Mistress I love!'

'And are you going to enjoy being back with her,

Emma?' Ursula's cold hypnotic voice went on. 'You're finding it all very exciting aren't you?'

'Oh, yes, Madam,' cried Emma. And the awful thing was, she knew, that she really meant it.

A waiter handed a menu to each of the girls. Emma looked at it hungrily. What a change from yoghurt and fruit! But she was to be disappointed.

'They'll all have just a plain salad,' Ursula told the waiter. 'And only mineral water to drink.'

Minutes later, a waiter brought four small plates of salad and four glasses of water to the silent girls. Clearly, they were to be seen but not heard, thought Emma sadly, and certainly not allowed to interrupt their betters or even eat the same food.

There must be several people here who she knew of old. How embarrassing it was being treated like this in front of them! But, she decided, she would put a brave face on it. She began to look around. She saw several faces she knew quite well.

However, Emma had not seen the silent signal that Ursula, with an almost imperceptible nod of her head towards Emma, had flashed to Sabhu, who was sitting by himself across the room.

Emma almost jumped out of her chair with surprise at the sudden little shock.

'Emma! Keep your eyes down on your plate,' said Ursula angrily. 'I don't like young girls looking around in a forward way like that. I like my girls to be shy and retiring.'

Terrified of getting another shock, Emma lowered her eyes and kept them down. Towards the end of the meal, Ursula turned towards Bluebell and said something in a foreign language. Emma saw the girl smile. She stood up and put her hand on Emma's shoulder as if taking charge of her. 'Come!' she said.

Angry at being given an order by a younger girl, Emma looked at Ursula.

'Yes, Emma,' said Ursula harshly, 'Bluebell's going to take you to spend a penny. Do what she says – she's the head girl. But remember, no talking to anyone or Bluebell will report you.'

Blushing with embarrassment, and resentful of being put under Bluebell's orders, Emma followed the pretty young girl to the powder room, passing the tables of several people she knew. They were looking up at her in astonishment. She longed to say something – a brief word of explanation – but she did not dare say a word.

There was no one else in the Ladies. Bluebell pointed to one of the cubicles. 'Go!' she said. Then she stopped Emma from closing the door completely and stood there.

Emma looked up at the little window. It was too small for her to climb through and anyway Bluebell would stop her. She gave a little sob of despair. There was no escape from Ursula's clutches.

'Hurry!' ordered Bluebell.

Emma lifted up her dress and sat down on the seat.

'No!' said Bluebell with an admonishing shake of her finger. She gestured to Emma to stand up. Emma remembered how Sabhu also did not allow the girls to sit down to spend a penny. Emma made a face at Bluebell. She was just an officious little bitch, showing off her authority! She had no right to put on airs – she had been beaten that morning just like the others.

But Emma stood up and bent her knees, as Sabhu had taught her to do over her bowl, undoing the velcro fastenings and holding up the rubber pad that covered the grill in her belt.

She heard other people come into the powder room but Bluebell remained looking at her through the slightly open door.

'Hurry!' she whispered angrily. 'Or I tell Sabhu!'

Terrified at the threat, Emma quickly spent a penny, dried the grill, dropped the rubber pad, closed the velcro fastenings and lowered her skirt. Then she followed Bluebell back to their table.

'Did she perform properly?' she heard Ursula ask Bluebell.

'She slow and rude!' replied Bluebell, adding something

in her own language. Was she reporting the face that Emma had made at her? Oh gosh!

'That'll be three strokes from Sabhu's whip when we get back, Emma,' said Ursula. 'I'm not going to have you being insolent to my head girl!'

Emma was about to protest, to say that it was unfair, when Ursula cut in, 'And if you say one word,' said Ursula with a deceptive little smile, 'it'll be another three for answering back and speaking without permission.'

She turned to her neighbour and continued her conversation, leaving Emma fuming, her eyes down and not daring to say a word. Occasionally she would flash a quick look of hatred at Bluebell.

Finally the meal was over. Ursula signed the bill and called Sabhu over. Emma saw her point to her. She said something to the big Haitian and held up three fingers. Oh my God! Three strokes! She saw Bluebell laugh.

Then they were led back to the car. The door shut. Sabhu fastened the girls' ankle manacles back on again. Then the engine started.

The little outing was over. As Emma looked out through the tinted window at the crowded streets, she could understand the excitement of the other girls at being occasionally taken to a smart restaurant as a change from life in the cages. It had indeed been a thrilling change. But her forthcoming punishment was preying on her mind. Nothing was said by Sabhu as he supervised the girls taking off their dresses and as he refastened their heavy wrist manacles. He put them, one by one, back in their cages. They were kneeling there naked, silently gripping the bars, their eyes on Emma.

She turned to crawl into her cage.

'No, Number Four!' shouted Sabhu.

Horrified, Emma saw that he had taken off his coat and rolled up his sleeve. In his hand was his long dressage whip. 'On your spot. Go!'

There was a rattle of Emma's ankle manacles as, with a little cry, she ran to the red spot on the floor marked '4'. She stood to attention, breathing heavily, her hands clasped behind her neck with her wrist manacles hanging down behind her. She heard Sabhu approach. She was trembling with fear.

'Bend over!'

It was a difficult position to hold with her hands clasped behind her neck.

'Thrust back buttocks!'

There was a pause. Nothing was said. Then suddenly there was a whistling sound as Sabhu brought his whip down across Emma's scarcely-covered bottom. The pain was like a line of fire across it. She managed to suppress a scream.

'Attention!'

She jumped up. The pain was acute, but somehow she managed to hold her position and look straight ahead. Sabhu walked slowly round her, tapping the dressage whip against his palm. He raised her chin with his whip and then tapped her belly. Desperately she pulled it in. She could feel the eyes of the other women on her as they gripped the bars of their cages.

'Bend over!' came the sudden order.

Twice more the whole drawn out process was repeated before a contrite Emma was finally allowed to scuttle away to her cage. As she did so, she saw the triumphant look on Bluebell's face from behind the bars of her cage.

Then, as Sabhu slammed the small barred door to her cage and locked the padlock, Emma picked up her little doll with a sob and hugged it to her breast.

16

Trained to Give Pleasure by Order

'Lick!'

Sabhu once again was dressed in his tight white gymnast's clothes, his black naked torso and strapped leather boots gleaming.

It was later that afternoon and the girls had been taken to a little room next to the gymnasium. For once there was no viewing gallery, for this was Sabhu's private training room. It was here that he trained the women to please Ursula's clients – and thus earn him a series of generous tips. But Emma, of course, still unaware of what Ursula intended to use her for, assumed that he was training them for Ursula's own pleasure.

She was kneeling on the floor at the foot of a couch on which lay two life-sized rubber dolls. One was white-skinned with blonde hair, and looked rather like Ursula herself. The other, between whose legs Emma was kneeling, was a black woman with crinkly hair just like some of Ursula's richer and more demanding clients.

Sabhu was standing over her, holding her lead taut with his left hand, and his raised dressage whip in his right hand.

Emma had had to watch as each of the three other women were quickly put through a standard routine of basic words of command. Now it was her turn to show what she had learnt.

Lined up behind her and watching, were the other women. Each was remembering her own first lessons from

Sabhu in giving a woman pleasure, and how painful and embarrassing they had been.

They had been painful because of the way that Sabhu relentlessly used his whip to make his pupils do exactly not only what he ordered, but do it with zeal and eagerness. They had been embarrassing because the teacher had not been a female who had gently shown them how to give pleasure to another woman, but a man; this harsh Haitian, who had taught them to obey a list of certain words of command that Ursula and her clients would use.

'Lick!' Sabhu repeated, and gave Emma a sharp tap with his whip across her naked back.

Hastily Emma reached out with her tongue to caress the doll's realistic black beauty lips. Sabhu dropped her lead and now reached down to check that her tongue was licking properly as he had taught her: twice slowly up and down, and then six little quick sideways movements with the tongue stretched right out.

Satisfied, he began to teach her all the other orders and to put her through the standard routine that he had devised for the greater pleasure of both Ursula and her clients.

Slowly and deliberately, he punctuated each order with a tap of his whip and checked with his free hand that she was carrying it out in the way that he considered would give the greatest pleasure and, of course, thereby earn him all the more tips from the delighted clients.

'Sideways! Faster! Slow! Up and down! Sideways again! Faster! Purse lips! Thrust inside! Right in! Rub with nose! In! Out! In! Out!'

Poor Emma was exhausted, but the whip drove her on and on. It was so unfair, she thought. She knew just how to excite Ursula without all these orders. But, she supposed, it must be very exciting for Ursula to be able to lie back and control with these standard orders whichever girl was pleasuring her. But why was she being trained on the black doll?

'Suck!'

Oh, the relief of just sucking! But it was not to last for long.

'Suck and tongue! Thrust inside!'

'Number Four! You now learn orders for using fingers and tongue together . . . Fingers!'

There was a rattle of chains as Emma brought her manacled hands up to the doll's intimacies.

'Now on the order "tongue and fingers!", you thrust tongue through fingers. Lick with tongue and tickle with fingers. Now . . . Tongue and fingers!'

Sabhu reached down to check that Emma's forefingers were correctly playing with the doll's beauty bud whilst her tongue and remaining fingers vied with each other to give pleasure elsewhere.

'Lick neck!'

Emma was now kneeling on the couch alongside the doll which Sabhu had now placed face down. Remembering what she had seen the other women do, she started to lick the back of the doll's neck in the place where she knew from old that Ursula loved. How clever of Sabhu to know that too!

'Down!'

Obediently, Emma ran her tongue slowly down the doll's spine to the crease of its buttocks.

'Up!'

Emma's tongue ran up the doll's spine again.

'Lie on back!'

Emma was now lying on her back. Sabhu picked up the rubber doll and moved its flexible legs so that it was now sitting on Emma's face. She gasped as she felt its weight. It was as heavy as a real woman. It must, she realised, be filled with water – not air.

'Lick behind!' Sabhu ordered.

How dreadful, Emma thought. But she knew it was something that Ursula loved and anyway she was far too frightened of Sabhu's whip to hesitate. Obediently, she reached up and began to stroke the doll's realistic rear orifice with her tongue. Sabhu put his hand down to check that she was doing it properly. 'Beauty bud up!' ordered Sabhu.

Emma was still lying on her back. The heavy doll was lying on her, its flexible rubber arms gripping her round the shoulders. She raised her hips to press the rubber pad and its line of little rubber knobs against the doll's beauty lips.

It was ironic being told to raise her own beauty bud whilst still wearing the belt for, of course, she could feel nothing – thanks to the plastic grill. But she realised the same order might one day be given in Ursula's bed after the horrible belt had been taken off, and then . . .

Oh, how exciting that would be! She imagined Ursula kissing her passionately and then sending for Sabhu, and telling him to unlock her belt and take it off. She imagined Ursula throwing her down on the bed and . . .

Oh, how she longed for that, just as, she realised, the other three frustrated women must also dream of Ursula having their belts removed, too. Oh, but how long would she have to wait for it?

Meanwhile, she also realised, the line of little rubber knobs could give Ursula great pleasure without the belt being taken off especially if she were wriggling under her Mistress.

Sabhu reached down and inserted the key that activated the vibrator in the rubber pad. Emma heard the humming noise but, of course, could feel nothing herself.

'Wriggle!' came the next order.

Sabhu stood to one side to watch her efforts. Then put his hand down between the doll's realistic intimacies and the rubber pad over Emma's own ones, to judge whether she was trying hard enough. He could feel the little rubber knobs vibrating away. They would certainly give great pleasure. He laughed as he thought of Emma wriggling away under a client, desperate from fear of his whip to accentuate the pleasure.

Sabhu liked to teach the women not only to move their pelvises up and down, but also to give little sideways wriggles as well. It was a combination that, together with the vibrating knobs, would give a client really exquisite physical pleasure.

Holding a wriggling girl down under her would give a client a wonderful feeling of power the mental pleasure that comes from exerting physical power over a slave.

'Backside!'

Emma raised her legs in the air, dropped her wrist manacles over her toes and rolled over on to her tummy, her hands now behind her back. Then, not knowing what to expect, she raised her buttocks as she had been taught and pulled back the main plastic shields and raised the small internal ones to expose her little orifice.

To her embarrassment, she felt Sabhu greasing her. Then her heart sank as, out of the corner of her eye, she saw that he was strapping on to the doll a hard rubber dildo complete with testicles.

She recognised it as being just like the one Ursula so often used to enjoy strapping on herself and then using on her girls – as if they were boys. She remembered that the pad that pressed against Ursula's own body lips used to have clever little rubber projections on the inside that would rub excitingly against her beauty bud, giving her great pleasure whilst the girl only suffered pain and humiliation.

She felt the weight of the doll as Sabhu laid it over her back. She felt Sabhu moving its flexible arms so that they were gripping her breasts. Then as she knelt, straining to keep the plastic shields held back, she felt Sabhu inserting the dildo between them so that it was pressing against her orifice.

'Press back!' was the next order the next in a new sequence of orders she would have to learn to obey.

Instantly, she felt Sabhu thrust the doll forward. She screamed as she felt its artificial manhood enter her. She tried to push the doll back, but instantly Sabhu's whip came down hard across her back.

'Keep pressing backside, number four!' Sabhu shouted. 'Keep shields back!'

Desperate to avoid another stroke of his whip, Emma obediently raised her little bottom to accommodate the invading manhood.

'Wriggle!' came the order. A client would now be madly aroused both mentally with the idea of taking Emma in this humiliating way, and physically with the pleasure of her beauty bud being pressed against the wriggling dildo.

Sabhu then squeezed the artificial testicles and a mixed jet of menthol and watery soap shot up inside Emma. She gave a little cry as a peculiar sensation began to build up inside her.

'Concentrate on holding the shields back,' warned Sabhu, harshly, as Emma began to wriggle and buck with discomfort. The client's pleasure would now be intense, as she rode the wildly wriggling girl.

Running through the basic standard routines was over.

Emma and Cowslip were now standing at attention on their numbered red spots and watching as Sabhu put Bluebell and Daisy through a well-tried joint routine he had devised to amuse Ursula and her clients. He now intended Cowslip and Emma to perform together as well. It was not all that different from the very successful routine which he had suggested for Ursula's bed the night before.

The life-size doll was now lying on its back.

'Routine number six!' he ordered. Emma's heart fell. Number six! There was so much to learn. But she knew she just had to concentrate and remember like the other girls had done. Sabhu's whip would see to that. But how awful to have to be taught to give such intimate feminine pleasure by number and by this revolting instructor.

'Number One, top position! Go!'

Her manacles clanking, Bluebell rushed to the couch and knelt on it. Then kneeling down, she lowered her head and began to suck avidly at one of the doll's nipples.

'Number Two, bottom position! Go!'

Daisy rushed to the bottom of the couch, knelt on the floor and, reaching up with her head and manacled hands, began fondling and sucking the doll's intimacies.

'Lick!' called out Sabhu.

There was a pause as both girls eagerly practised applying their tongues.

'Competition!'

Emma saw both girls giving a little shiver of fear. They were now avidly kissing, sucking and stroking the doll. Evidently this order meant that both girls were now free to use their hands, mouths and tongues in any way they chose, to give maximum pleasure, knowing that in real life the client would enjoy calling in Sabhu to whip the girl who had given her the least pleasure.

'Change round!'

The two girls quickly exchanged positions.

'Continue competition!'

Emma saw that they were both straining, under Sabhu's approving eye, as if to give the doll the greatest pleasure.

Suddenly a little bell rang as if Ursula, represented by the rubber doll, had rung for Sabhu.

'I think, Sabhu, that one of these girls would benefit by your attention,' Sabhu said in a very fair imitation of Ursula's sarcastic cold tone. Emma saw that the bottoms of both the kneeling girls were trembling deliciously. How much Ursula would enjoy this scene when she was playing it for real.

'You, Number Two! You not try hard enough! Two strokes!'

Emma heard Daisy give a horrified gasp.

'On spot! Bend over!'

With a shrug of her shoulders, as if saying that there was no point in arguing, Daisy stood up, ran to her spot, put her manacles over her head and clasped her hands behind her neck. Then she bent over in front of Sabhu. He raised his whip. Then he lowered it again. 'Tighter!'

With a little moan of protest, poor Daisy bent down lower and raised her leather-covered bottom. The thin leather would in any case have given her scant protection, as it had with Bluebell earlier on. This time, however, Sabhu was aiming further down; he was concentrating on the backs of her thighs, when he brought his whip down.

Daisy screamed aloud and jumped up but Sabhu was standing no nonsense. 'Bend over!' he shouted.

Only when he was satisfied that poor Daisy was in just the right position for his whip, did he bring it down again for the second stroke. Emma gave a shiver of fear; there was no escaping Sabhu's whip. Like the belts, fear of that long dressage whip would dominate her life here, she realised.

'Back in position!' Sabhu shouted.

Daisy hastily resumed her position between the doll's legs, her tongue reaching out keenly.

'Number Four!' shouted Sabhu at Emma, standing at attention, horrified, on her numbered spot. 'You watch! You learn. When Mistress or client send for two girls for her bed, they both thinking all the time that soon one will be getting my whip.'

Clients! What did he mean? Surely, thought Emma, the only clients that Ursula had were those who bought the pictures she painted. Was she now sometimes offering her girls to them as a way of persuading them to buy a picture? A sort of procuress? How awful!

'You saw Number Two get whip this morning,' went on Sabhu. 'So each girl trying hard all night to make sure she not get whip either then or next morning and here in training classes, each girl also has fear of whip, too. You understand?'

Emma nodded her head violently. Fear of the whip? Oh, yes, she understood all right!

'Yes, sir! Yes, sir!'

Sabhu smiled to himself. This new girl certainly looked scared stiff. She would train well and give the clients much mental and physical pleasure and so earn him many valuable little presents.

'Now Number Four. You now learn special performance with Number Three.' Sabhu emphasised his words by bringing his whip up against his leather boots with a crack. 'Numbers Three and Four! Arousal!'

Emma saw Cowslip step smartly forward two paces and stand rigidly at attention, her wrist manacles hanging down her back as she clasped her hands behind her neck. Nervously, Emma copied her.

'Number Three! Lick neck!'

Cowslip now came behind Emma. Suddenly she felt Cowslip's tongue running gently up and down her spine, just below her neck. Oh what a lovely feeling! It was delicious, so delicate and yet so exciting! Only a woman could give such pleasure.

As Sabhu's bloodshot eyes watched closely, the tonguing went on and on. She could feel herself becoming wet and aroused under the grill on her belt. Oh, how she longed to be able to touch herself! How cruel the belt was. And how embarrassing being aroused like this in front of Sabhu.

'Turn round!'

Emma was now facing Cowslip's back. She was panting with excitement.

'Number Four! Lick neck!'

Now Emma in turn began to excite Cowslip. Out of the corner of her eye she was watching Sabhu's whip as she leant forward and ran her tongue up and down the bottom of Cowslip's neck – just as Cowslip had done to her. Soon, she heard Cowslip giving little moaning noises.

Sabhu seemed satisfied. 'Number Three! About turn!'

The two women were now facing each other, their naked breasts almost touching as they continued to stand rigidly at attention, their leads held by Sabhu in one hand, his raised whip held in the other.

'Number Three! Caress right breast!'

Cowslip brought her manacled wrists back over her head. Then, with her left hand, she lifted up Emma's right breast and with the thumb and forefinger of her right hand she played sensuously with Emma's nipple and gently began to pull it out.

Emma caught her breath. It was so exciting! She moaned with delight.

'Number Four! Caress right breast!'

Both women were now stimulating each other's right nipples, alternatively rubbing and stretching them. Both of them were moaning with pleasure.

'Number Three! Suck!'

Emma could hardly restrain herself from crying out with the sheer thrill as Cowslip bent down and began to suck her nipple. She could feel herself becoming wetter than ever under the grill of her belt. Oh the sheer bliss! She even forgot the shame of all this being done to the order of their trainer.

'Number Three! Head up! Caress!'

They were back playing with each other's nipples again.

'Change nipples!'

Now Emma was fondling Cowslip's left nipple and Cowslip was doing the same to Emma's left one.

'Number Four! Suck!'

It was Emma's turn to bend down and, as Cowslip continued to play with her nipple, she began to suck Cowslip's. Both women were now panting hard. Both were longing to be able to touch their throbbing beauty buds, cruelly locked away behind the grills of their belts.

'Attention!'

Reluctantly, both women straightened up.

'Line up!'

All four women were now standing at attention on their spots. Their leads were hanging down in front of them, in between their naked breasts. There was the distinct scent of feminine arousal in the room; a scent accentuated by the enforced frustration.

All were so ashamed at being so obviously in such a state in front of their trainer who was walking up and down in front of them, smiling and tapping his whip against his boots.

'And you, Number Four! You now ready to be put on selection parade.' Sabhu pointed to his whip. 'Any girl not selected gets this! So you try hard. You smile and look submissive. And if you selected, then you still remember this waiting for you if you not give full pleasure or if you reported for disobedience or impudence, or just lack of zeal. Understand?'

Emma's heart was pounding. Selection parade! Was Ursula again going to choose her girls for the night? How exciting! Oh, dear God, please let her choose me this time I'll please her all right! She looked at the whip. My God, she would!

'But if you give proper pleasure, you get little sweet.'

He reached into a pocket and pulled out a chocolate. Four pairs of eyes watched as he tossed the chocolate into the air a couple of times and then put it back into his pocket.

'Yes,' he said teasingly, 'a real piece of delicious chocolate but only if you give real pleasure. So, little girls, just remember: the choice is yours chocolate or the whip!'

17

Selection Parade – and Emma Learns the Truth

From behind the closed door of Ursula's drawing room came the sudden sound of the introductory bars of the music to which Sabhu had them practice.

Sabhu raised his whip.

The four women, standing one behind the other, half naked under their capes and clasping their manacled wrists behind their necks, straightened up nervously.

Sabhu was wearing his smart 'lion tamer' uniform with gold frogging on his red tunic, white breeches and black leather riding boots. Emma wondered why. Did Ursula get an extra kick from seeing him put her girls through their paces while dressed like that?

There seemed no end to Ursula's extraordinary and exciting inventiveness. It really was very thrilling being kept here as one of her girls, but wasn't she ever going to relax and take Emma to bed? Perhaps she would tonight! Oh how thrilling!

'Prance!'

Eyeing the whip fearfully, the four women started to run on the spot, taking their time from Bluebell, their leader.

Sabhu glanced down the line of prancing women. He liked to see each one straining to raise her knees as high in the air as her clanking ankle manacles permitted. It was, he realised, hard for Emma, for she was not yet properly fit. But she soon would be and meanwhile her fear of his whip was making sure she tried her best. He certainly wasn't going to accept any excuses. 'Up!' he shouted, bringing his whip down across her backside. 'Higher!'

With a sob, poor Emma, taking her time from Cowslip who was prancing just in front of her, somehow managed to raise her knees almost as high as the older woman.

Sabhu turned to Cowslip who was prancing behind Daisy. He felt he had done very well to get a pretty, 40-year-old woman prancing so well. He had had to use his whip on her frequently during the morning exercise periods but she was now fit and sleek with hardly an ounce of fat on her – a real credit to him. And, yet, thanks to the implants, her breasts were firm and full.

He turned back to Emma. She was breathing heavily: he noticed there was a little fat to get off from around her waist. But he was confident that he'd soon get her fit and sleek, too. Emma jumped as Sabhu snapped his long dressage whip across her bouncing buttocks.

'Number Four! Higher!' he snarled. He wasn't going to let this new girl spoil the well-disciplined effect that he had so patiently trained the women to achieve.

'Left! Right! Left! Right!' he shouted, emphasising each order with a sharp tap of his whip.

Terrified, Emma was now prancing well, her breasts jiggling up and down under her cape. She could feel herself becoming wet with arousal at the thought that she was about to be paraded in front of Ursula. For the umpteenth time she prayed, Please God, let her choose me for her bed this time. I'll be a good girl and really please her!

Suddenly the door into Ursula's large drawing room was opened.

'Forward!' shouted Sabhu.

Led by Bluebell, the four women pranced round and round the room. Emma, at the end of the line, tried to keep her eyes fixed on Cowslip's back, just in front of her. She was also trying to concentrate on keeping in step and on raising her knees high enough.

Then, out of the corner of her eye, she saw Ursula, strangely dressed in a black business suit and holding a pencil and pad, sitting at one end of a long sofa with Sabhu standing proudly behind her.

But they were not alone. Sitting together on the other

end of the sofa were two large, middle-aged women. They were stern looking with short cropped hair. They both looked like lesbians, Emma thought; feminist lesbians. They were pointing to the various prancing girls and then questioning the smiling Ursula. Emma could not make out what they were saying.

Emma saw Sabhu glaring at her. Hastily, she turned her eyes away from the sofa, praying that her lapse of discipline would not later earn her Sabhu's usual three strokes.

'To your spots!' called out Sabhu.

Bluebell led the now panting women to the line of spots on the carpet. Each stopped at her spot but continued to prance.

'Halt!' At last came the order, followed by, 'Into line, left turn!'

In unison, the panting women raised their knees and stamped, turning with military precision just as Sabhu had trained them to do. They must have made an erotic sight, Emma realised.

They were now in a line facing the wall with their backsides towards Ursula and the women. Emma blushed as she realised that two strangers would now be looking at the weals on the backs of her thighs.

'Unbutton capes!'

Hastily, Emma brought her manacled wrists up over her head and unfastened the buttons. Then, moving in time with the other women, she raised her manacled wrists and again clasped her hands behind her neck.

Sabhu now stepped forward and gave a little bow to the women sitting on the sofa. Then he moved down the line of young women, throwing the left side of each woman's cape back over her shoulder, baring her left breast and her belly – and, behind, the top of one buttock, displaying more weal marks.

'About turn!'

Once again, stamping in unison, the performing prisoners turned with military precision towards the women, keeping their eyes fixed on the wall behind the sofa. Once again, Emma blushed as she realised that the weals on her left breast and across her belly would now be erotically displayed to the two strange guests.

Sabhu came down the line of women and stopped in front of Daisy. He lifted up the exposed breast which was rising and falling rapidly as she tried to get her breath back. Then he gently squeezed the nipple. Daisy gave a little gasp of pleasure.

'Well, fancy that,' said one of them in an American accent.

Sabhu bowed to the women and enquiringly repeated the process with Bluebell.

'No!' said the same woman. She pointed at Daisy. 'That sure is the one I want!'

Out of the corner of her eye, Emma saw Ursula pointing to her pad on which she had written some figures.

'As you can see,' Ursula said, 'I charge more, of course, for the two younger girls. Number three, being older, is less expensive and, as number four is not yet properly broken in, I also charge less for her. But there is a twenty per cent discount if you want two of them. The charges are, of course, for the whole night in a large bedroom with en-suite bathroom and include breakfast. The girls are guaranteed not to have been allowed near a man and to have been kept quite pure.'

Emma's mind was reeling as she slowly took in what Ursula was saying. She was being displayed and offered as if in a brothel – a brothel for women! A brothel for women? Well, there was nothing illegal about that.

Ursula's new house must be a secret and very expensive up-market brothel specialising in satisfying foreign women visitors. And Emma was now one just one of its helpless inmates!

Ursula must have had her abducted to earn money for her in her new brothel. Goodness, what a revenge! Everything was now falling into place: Sabhu, the belts, the cages, the manacles, the discipline, the drills, the odd remarks about clients, Ursula's strange whispers to the Baroness, the exhausting exercises and that awful special training in making love.

And that strange outing to the restaurant · Ursula must just have been showing off her girls and in particular her new girl, Emma, to potential clients! My God! What a life. No wonder the girls were kept locked up and helpless in those cages.

She wanted to run away, to escape, before she was locked back in her cage. But how could she, manacled as she was? She looked around desperately and promptly felt a sharp warning tap on her buttocks from Sabhu's whip. With a little sob of despair she fixed her eyes again on the wall behind the sofa.

Sabhu now came down the line again, unfastening the collar straps of their capes.

'Off capes!' he ordered.

Four capes fell to the floor. Emma blushed again at the display of her near nudity.

'Left turn! Prance! Forward!'

The orders came in rapid sequence. Emma once more found herself prancing round the room behind the other women but this time her naked bouncing breasts were on display as, of course, were the expanded ones of Cowslip with their stretched nipples and large nipple rings.

Emma could hear the two women gasp in admiration. Certainly if the display had been erotic before, now it was superbly erotic!

At last they were halted and lined up facing the sofa again, their naked breasts rising and falling after their exertions.

Emma saw Ursula hand each of the women a little plastic-coated list. 'These,' she heard Ursula say encouragingly, 'are the words of command that they have been trained to obey – instantly. If you have any problems during the night, just ring for Sabhu. Now, which of them would you like?'

'Oh, I'll take the two young ones,' Emma heard the same American voice say.

'And I'll take the two older ones,' came another American voice. 'It'll be more humiliating for them – not that they look very old, especially your pretty little Number Four!'

Emma blushed at the compliment. But it did not soothe

her inward rage. How she hated Ursula. She would rebel. Then she remembered Sabhu's morning beating of any girl who had been complained about. My God, she would do anything to avoid another beating. She would be a good girl. She really would. And she'd earn a little sweet!

Half an hour later Emma lay tied down to a bed in the large bedroom with her wrist manacles tied well apart to the head of the bed and her ankle manacles similarly fastened to the foot of the bed. Sabhu had placed a large cushion under her buttocks, thrusting up the rubber pad covering her beauty lips. She could hear a little hum from the vibrator concealed in the rubber studs. But she herself could feel nothing.

The large woman forced herself upon Emma. In one hand she held the plastic covered list of words of command. She had already tried out several of them and had been delighted with Emma's response. Now, with her other hand, she clasped Emma's small body as she alternatively rubbed her beauty lips against the excitingly vibrating rubber studs. She thrust her nipples into Emma's mouth.

'Lick behind!' she called out and Cowslip, kneeling behind her, lowered her head.

'Oh yes, you little sluts,' the large woman cried out in ecstasy. 'Oh yes!'

Sabhu, looking through a secret spyhole, smiled contentedly. He would certainly get a good tip in the morning!'

18

Emma's New Life

Emma was gripping the bars of her cage. As usual, the attic was filled with the sound of soft, relaxing music coming from the loudspeaker on the wall. It was a little time after she had learnt with horror her own ghastly fate and what Ursula now used her girls for. She was uncertain as to just how long it was since that terrible first day when she had woken to find herself caged and manacled in Ursula's new house. With no access to a calendar, she had lost track of the date and indeed each day had seemed rather like another – just as it was intended to be.

She now lived, she realised, in constant terror of Sabhu's whip. She had to admit if it was not for that, life would not be too bad. But Sabhu and his whip played an essential part in Ursula's new enterprise, just as overseers and their whips had played an essential part of life on the American slave plantations.

It was Sabhu and his whip that kept Emma and the other girls on their toes and desperate to please the clients. It was Sabhu and his whip that made Ursula's enterprise such a profitable one. He did not apply it very hard, Emma had learnt, and he left no permanent marks. But it still stung like mad! She found herself being increasingly obsessed by the fear of more strokes to come.

The strange thing was that Sabhu and his whip, and the strict routine to which the girls were subjected, made her look on her cruel and implacable Mistress with increasing respect and adoration. If only her love was returned. If only Ursula knew just how cruelly Sabhu treated them. She felt like a former favourite slave who had run away and then been recaptured and, as a punishment, had now been put to work on her Mistress's plantation under the whip of a cruel overseer.

She bitterly resented what had happened to her but was far too frightened of Sabhu to say a word. How could Ursula, her beloved Mistress, have used her in such an awful way?

It was true she had defied her Mistress and had been unfaithful to her and with a young man at that. But she had been punished for her behaviour indeed she still remembered with dread that awful whipping from Sabhu in front of the Baroness. She knew she had deserved that but not this awful fate.

She wondered what would have happened if she had never left Ursula. Would she still have been put to work, under Sabhu's whip, in Ursula's new and obviously highly profitable enterprise? She sighed sadly, for in her heart she knew that the answer was undoubtedly yes.

She remembered her first client with disgust. A girl doesn't easily forget her first paying client. But there had been numerous others since then. Every day a succession of well-dressed foreign women would come to choose a girl, or girls; sometimes for the night, sometimes just for the afternoon. Often clients who had become highly aroused by watching the girls being put through their humiliating morning routines would want a girl there and then.

For some clients Ursula would order the girls to be made to prance round her drawing room as they had for Emma's first client. Others would pay extra to come to the viewing gallery to see the girls in their cages and have them paraded one by one for her inspection, just as they had been paraded for the Baroness.

Sometimes, as when Ursula chose a girl for herself, Sabhu would order them to shake their naked breasts, thrust their belted hips to and fro, and wiggle their tongues round and round, all in a parody of giving pleasure. Sometimes, for a special client, they might be displayed dressed in their 'little girl' outfits and made up as young teenagers.

On one occasion they had even been displayed crawling in a little playpen, dressed as baby girls with dummies strapped into their mouth and wearing nappies over their Bikini-belts.

But always Sabhu was there, whip in hand, proudly showing off the state of blind obedience to which he had reduced the women in his charge.

To make sure that the women looked eager and submissive, all trying to outdo each other in catching the eye of a client, Sabhu had introduced a blackboard facing the line of cages with the girls' numbers painted on it. Every time a girl was selected by a client, a tick was placed after her number. At the end of the week the girl with the lowest number of ticks would be thrashed by Sabhu as a special spectacle for the more discerning visitors.

It would not be an ordinary thrashing but one of Sabhu's special punishments – the same as Emma had been given in front of the Baroness when she had first arrived. The terrified girls all knew what that meant: twelve strokes of his long dressage whip; six on the backside and six on the breasts, belly and thighs. They might not be very hard but they still hurt!

This weekly thrashing was itself a considerable money earner for Ursula – and moreover invariably resulted in the now well-aroused clients paying even more to take a girl to bed with them.

Like the other girls, Emma found herself gripping the bars of her cage and endlessly counting the ticks after each girl's number. It made them all become increasingly desperate to be chosen by the next client and so earn a precious tick. To further ensure that, once selected, a girl strived her utmost to please, the slighest complaint from a client resulted in the removal of the tick which she had tried so hard to earn at the selection parade.

Emma had also soon learnt that any failure to concentrate on giving the utmost pleasure to the client would also result, as well as the removal of the tick after her name, in a simple thrashing from Sabhu afterwards or next morning. What was so unfair was that sometimes a particularly cruel client would unfairly report her to Sabhu just so that she could then watch Emma being thrashed. And if Emma tried to protest, she was given double the strokes for 'insolence'.

Emma had jealously noticed that the other girls had slightly more ticks after their names. As the threat of being given a special punishment by Sabhu loomed ever closer, so Emma's jealousy also grew. She was prettier than the others! It wasn't fair not being chosen so often!

The twice daily sucking of her breasts by Sabhu's stimulating milking machine was already making them larger, but the sight of Cowslip's artificially enlarged ones still made Emma jealous. Was that why she was so often chosen? Certainly the rings on her nipples did seem to stop the cups from sucking.

Emma began to long for her own breasts to be similarly enlarged. Already she longed to be in milk! She knew it was crazy but here in the strange and artificial atmosphere of Ursula's house, such longings seemed quite normal indeed they were longings that Sabhu encouraged. She would constantly find herself instinctively holding her doll to her breasts. Although she could not see them, the other girls would be doing the same in their cages, much to the approval of the smiling Sabhu watching them on the big television monitor in his room. The day was coming!

Whether she liked it or not, Emma knew that she had now become a good little tart, earning her Mistress large sums of money, though she had no idea just how much Ursula was charging for her increasingly expert services - nor how much the grinning Sabhu was earning in tips from the delighted clients. Certainly, Emma would angrily calculate, Ursula's outgoings on food, clothing and entertainment for her girls must be minimal.

Still, to her great disappointment and chagrin, Ursula had ignored her for her own bed, apparently preferring the other girls. Not only did Emma feel desperately frustrated, and often physically repelled by the clients she had so eagerly to please, but she was also becoming increasingly jealous of the other girls; jealous of their success in sometimes being selected by clients in preference to herself; jealous of their bigger breasts and, most of all, jealous because Ursula chose them and not her.

Meanwhile Sabhu's daily strict routine continued. If Emma had been selected the previous evening by a client spending the night, Sabhu would collect her early in the morning and, holding her lead, take her back upstairs, her ankle manacles clanking, to her cage.

All the time she would be longing to ask him if the client had been pleased with her efforts and whether she was going to be thrashed. But she knew that to do so would only incur Sabhu's wrath; something she was far too frightened to risk doing. Sabhu liked to keep these once proud European women constantly scared and uncertain about when they would next get the whip.

If she was not selected by a client, then she would lie silently curled up in her little cage, watched by the television camera and still not daring even to whisper to any of the other girls who were also still in their cages. Often, her eyes would anxiously flicker back to the illuminated blackboard displaying the number of ticks that each girl had earned so far that week. Oh, if only she had tried harder to be selected! Over and over again, she would wonder why she had not caught the client's eye and would be making little plans to try to ensure that she was picked by the next client, no matter how humiliating it might be. Fear of another special punishment was never far from her thoughts.

Each day started with the awful morning routine, all performed under Sabhu's whip, and under his bloodshot, beady and watchful eyes – and of course to his command. The simultaneous performance of natural functions as well as washing, feeding, the milking machine, and the exhausting half hour in the gymnasium, all formed an essential part of Sabhu's disciplinary training.

Sometimes, as on Emma's first day, and as a special treat, they would be taken out dressed as little girls, for some fresh air.

But every day Sabhu would again put them through their paces in his special training room, making sure that they would almost instinctively obey whenever a client, holding the printed list of commands in her hand, called out an order. But most of the time, Emma, like the other girls, just knelt silently in her cage, looking at the ticks on the blackboard and nervously and longingly clasping her baby doll to her breasts.

She would never know when suddenly and unexpectedly the door to the viewing gallery would be opened to usher in a client, or when Sabhu would suddenly take them all downstairs on their leads to prance round in front of visitors.

Although the clients made appointments for specific times, the girls were deliberately not told what was going to happen; therefore, they were kept constantly on their toes.

Emma now just existed, she knew, to earn money for her Mistress, and handsome tips for Sabhu, by giving pleasure to order. Her only reward for a good performance was a little sweet – and not to get the whip!

19

The Kennels

Emma's eyes slowly cleared, as did her mind. It was night and, astonished, she saw that she was looking up at the moon. She could also see stars. She must be outside.

Indeed, the air felt fresh and there was a smell of newly cut grass but over her head were bars metal bars. She was in a sort of cage. However, she was not back in the awful attic with its line of cages; they weren't open to the stars. If she was in the open why wasn't she colder? She could feel the night air on her cheeks. She raised a hand to put it up to her face, expecting to feel the weight of the heavy wrist manacles and to hear them clinking. But her hands were free. Free! Or were they? They seemed to be encased in some sort of thick padded glove which kept her fingers tightly closed so that she could not hold anything. They looked rather like an animal's paws. How odd!

She put her gloved paw to her face. Through the thick material she could feel little but there seemed to be hair on her face. Hair growing on her face! My God! She gave a little cry of horror. Now what dreadful thing had Ursula done to her?

Her cry was strangely muted. She put her hand to her mouth. It was covered with what seemed to be a sort of muzzle. Indeed, her whole head was encased in some sort of hairy plastic cover. Inside this cover, over her head, was some sort of chain across her mouth that kept her tongue down so that she could not talk properly. There were little slits in front of her eyes.

Terrified, she tried to pull the cover off but her paw-like gloves prevented her from gripping anything. She felt a little bulge below her neck. As she touched it, it gave a realistic dog's bark. Astonished, she pressed it harder. Again came the bark but this time louder and repeated. How clever, she thought.

Immediately, other dogs' barks answered her from all around. Some, like her own bark, were squeaks like those of a bitch; others were like the deeper bark of a large dog.

Bewildered, she tried to jump up only to find that a heavy chain was fastened to a brass-studded collar round her neck. The other end was fastened to a ring in the cement floor of her cage, keeping her down on all fours. There was also something else keeping her down. She found she could not straighten her knees.

Emma's eyes slowly adjusted to the moonlight. She began to make out her body. It seemed to be tightly encased in some sort of black and white spotted imitation dog skin – like that of a Dalmatian. To make sure that it fitted tightly, there seemed to be narrow elastic strips running down the side.

Only her breasts were free and she saw, as she knelt on all fours, that they were hanging down through two cutaway holes in the dog skin, looking like rather the teats of a bitch, but much larger and more erotic.

She put her stiffly-gloved hands down and awkwardly felt a strange, curved metal bar inside the dog skin on either side of each knee. It must be these that was keeping her knees bent, she thought. They cleverly kept her permanently kneeling down on all fours or, at best, kneeling up like a begging dog. There was also some sort of padding over her knees. And what about that awful Bikini-belt? She put her paws down between her legs. She could not feel it! Instead the dog skin seemed to have been cut away between the legs and over her bottom.

She looked around. She was in a small barred kennel. She tried to crawl over to the barred side but her collar chain prevented her from reaching it. Through the bars of the cage she saw another dog-like figure. It was looking at her and growling. It really was a dog!

On the other side she could make out another figure.

This one looked more like a human being that had been put into a dog skin, just like herself. The person's head was encased in a very realistic hairy dog's head with upright ears sticking up on either side and a smooth black muzzle. Goodness! was that what she was wearing too?

Emma put her paws up to her own head. She felt similarly shaped false ears on either side of her head. Then she felt her mouth; it too was indeed covered by what seemed to be an imitation dog's muzzle.

There was now a glimmer of light on the skyline. Dawn was approaching. As the light increased, she saw that the human figure in the kennel next to hers was about her size. However, there were no breasts hanging down below it as it crawled across its cage, its collar chain clinking. It must be a youth! A male!

She saw that, like hers, the creature's dog skin fitted tightly. But whereas her skin resembled that of a short-haired Dalmatian, the other's was that of a long-haired Pomeranian with a bushy tail curled back proudly over its hindquarters. She saw that its dog skin was extra tight over the belly but there was no sign of a zip fastener. Then she gasped. There, hanging down, just as in a real dog, was a hair-covered manhood. She saw, however, that it had a very human looking pink tip that was half thrusting its way out of its dog-like hairy sheath. And, behind it, hung a sack containing two rather large testicles, again covered in hairy dog skin.

Emma tried to see the creature's face but it was totally hidden by the realistic dog's head. As she looked at it wonderingly, she saw it crawl over to the bars that separated their two kennels - evidently it was excused the ignominy of being chained by the neck to a ring in the centre of its kennel, though it did have a stout leather collar strapped round its neck. She saw it tap its chest and immediately there came a deep barking noise. The creature was trying to communicate with her! She tried to call out in return but the dog's muzzle once again muffled her voice. What should she do?

Suddenly she knew and tapped the bulge in the dog skin

below her neck. Immediately it gave a distinctive high pitched bark which was again answered by the creature. Soon they were happily barking at each other like real dogs.

Then she noticed that the dog was looking at her hanging white breasts. As he did so, his pink manhood began to thrust its way through its enveloping hairy sheath and became more and more erect. Under her head piece Emma blushed with embarrassment – but it was rather exciting being the cause of such a very male reaction.

As the light improved, she realised that she seemed to have been zipped into her dog skin, with the zip locked by a little padlock at the neck. It was all rather soft and lovely. Her headpiece had also been locked into place round the neck.

Peering through the little slits in front of her eyes, she saw that she was in a line of small, iron-barred kennels around what seemed to be a courtyard. And in nearly all the kennels there seemed to be human beings dressed up like different types of dog with different coloured dog skins. Were the other black and white spotted Dalmatians with hanging white breasts Ursula's other girls? Goodness! But then who were the others, and why were they all here? And what about this strange and randy male in the next door kennel?

Amazed and appalled at finding herself in this startling place, Emma thought back to how it had all started. It was, she imagined, a week or two after she had been first caged that Sabhu had mysteriously taken all their measurements – even those of their legs, their arms and their heads. He was, she now realised, making sure that their dog skins would fit really tightly.

She had also overheard when later Ursula had given Sabhu his instructions.

'Right! Now that the costumes are ready, tomorrow take them all to Irma's castle   use the Channel Tunnel, so that they can stay in the car and not attract attention. Doctor Anna will be coming too and she'll give each of them several sleeping pills before you get to Dover so you'll then be able to take off their wrist and ankle manacles. Then, if anyone wants to look inside the car, all they'll see is four sleepy girls wearing their cloaks under the blankets. You know what to do when you get to the castle. I'll join you there.'

Emma had seen Ursula hand the women's passports to Sabhu, including her own. Hers, she thought, must have been taken when she was abducted from her home.

Early next morning Sabhu had taken them out of their cages and made them step over their wrist manacles so that their hands were chained behind their backs, under their capes. Then he had led them downstairs and made them, one at a time, climb into the big estate car.

The narrow bunks had been pulled out and Emma had watched as each woman was made to lie down on her back. Sabhu had then covered each girl with a blanket over which went straps which held her down on the bunk. A second blanket was then tucked into the bunk, hiding the straps.

Emma found that with her hands manacled behind her back, she was quite unable to get at the restraining straps. All she could do was simply lie there helplessly.

'No talking!' warned Sabhu raising his whip menacingly. Then, as a reminder, he left his whip hanging menacingly from a hook in front of the women before closing and locking the rear door.

Sabhu had climbed into the driving seat. The large, frightening Doctor Anna had appeared and climbed up beside him. He put the control box for the women's belt down alongside him, ready for instant use if required. He glanced up into a special mirror. It gave him a clear view of the girls lying helplessly strapped in their bunks.

Sabhu and the doctor set off with their load of women.

They might have been a family setting off for a continental holiday except that the doors were locked and the windows were opaque so that no one could see in and the curtains were drawn so that the women could not see out.

After an hour, Sabhu stopped the car in a lay-by and Doctor Anna came into the back of the big estate car. Smiling encouragingly, she gave each of the helpless women some pills and a little sip of water.

Soon, Emma had begun to feel sleepy ... and had woken up here!

It must have been two or three hours after first awaking that Emma heard voices – girls' voices, speaking in what sounded like German. Then, through the door into the courtyard, came two pretty girls dressed in Bavarian peasants' costumes with low cut white blouses, black laced bodices and speckled red and black skirts. Long blonde pigtails hung down their backs. They carried dog whips.

They were laughing to each other as they unlocked Emma's kennel and that of the strange male creature next to her. One of them stepped into Emma's kennel and, still talking to her companion who was now in the other kennel, unlocked the heavy chain fastened to her collar and replaced it with a dog lead.

Giving Emma a sharp tap with her dog whip, and an incomprehensible order in German, she led her, crawling on her hands and knees, out of the kennel to where her companion was already standing, holding the lead of the other, male, creature.

The two girls led their dog-like charges through a locked grill doorway into a pretty garden. There, sitting on a terrace in front of a castle, were half a dozen well-dressed women having breakfast. And among them was Ursula!

She was sitting between two Teutonic-looking women in their fifties. Near them was Doctor Anna. Sabhu, dressed again as a butler, was standing behind them serving breakfast.

Emma heard one of the women call out, 'But, Ursula, is this Dalmatian the little bitch who gave you so much trouble? Well she looks very nice and docile now. And doesn't she make a pretty companion for my little Pomeranian hound? Doesn't he look proud alongside her! Oh look! Your Dalmatian has got my Pomeranian aroused – the naughty boy! You'll have to forgive him – he's kept so frustrated here, except for my visits of course! Yes, keeping him here in the kennels has certainly turned out to be a great success. He's developed into another obedient and satisfying . . . Oh, what is the English expression? Ah, yes . . . toy boy.'

Toy boy! The word caught Emma's attention. That randy male creature was a toy boy. A youth, kept by a rich and dominant woman, here in the kennels, sewn into a dog skin? Goodness!

'Did you say "another" toy boy?' Emma heard Ursula reply. 'How many have you got here?'

'Oh, I've the two of them: one sixteen-year-old and one seventeen-year-old – ideal ages for pleasing a woman. And they do get so randy locked up in their cages unable to play with themselves with their hands strapped into those thick padded paws!'

Randy! thought Emma, looking at the pink manhood forcing its way out of the fur covered sheath. I'll say! No wonder, poor little bastard, if he's kept shut up here!

'And only I have the keys to their kennels,' the woman went on. 'I don't trust those kennel maids. They just hose out the kennels and put the food into their dog bowls – but they can't go into their kennels, or take them out, unless I give them the key – as I have done now. And, of course, being sewn into their dog skins means that no other woman can see their faces – or their bodies. So they're mine, just mine. My randy little toy boy dogs!'

'Ah!' said Ursula with a sudden intensity, 'I know what you mean – the feeling of ownership and control, complete power!'

'Yes, you can't imagine how excited I get at the thought of coming here to see them. And then, when I arrive, I take them out for a little run and then give the keys to the kennel maid and undress and crawl into one kennel, telling her to come back in half an hour's time. And then my toy boy dog, randy as hell, can't wait to mount me. And by this time, kneeling on all fours, I'm feeling like a bitch on heat! Oh, it's so exciting as he drives into me, gripping me with his paws and barking!

The woman paused.

'Oh, the feeling of his fur on my soft skin! If he's a good boy I let him do it twice. Then it's time for me to be let out and to repeat the performance in the kennel of my other toy boy, who'll have been driven more randy than ever by watching me with his companion! Sometimes I have them put into the same kennel and let them fight over me! Either way, as I drive home, I feel utterly satiated.'

'Well!' laughed Ursula. 'If that's what turns you on. But I don't want them mounting my bitches – they're not normally allowed to have anything to do with anything male!'

'Oh, don't worry about that,' answered the woman. 'My young toy boy dogs are equally not allowed to have anything to do with young women. They've never even had real girlfriends. They're kept strictly for me - and one or two women friends of my age.'

'But where did you get them from?'

'Eastern Europe, of course. It's so poor! Their mothers were only too anxious for them to sign a contract of domestic service in return for me sending them a regular monthly remittance. And, of course, real Pomeranians come from East Germany too. So I thought it very appropriate to put them into Pomeranian dog skins.'

'But don't they revolt about being kept here and sewn into dog skins?'

'Well . . . sometimes. But I only have to threaten to stop the monthly payments to their homes, and they soon settle down again to their carefree life of ease!'

'But why keep them here? Why not employ them as page-boys in your own house?' asked Ursula.

'What! And have them making love to every pretty young servant girl? Anyway, my husband would be far too suspicious. Like many rich and successful men, he's very jealous. But he knows I'm genuinely interested in breeding dogs, and would never suspect what I really do when I come here!'

'But suppose he asked to come and see your dogs?'

'Then he would be shown my real dogs in the other kennels at the front of the castle. He'd never know that there was also a separate set of kennels for human dogs.'

'Umm. Well I don't have quite the same problem!' laughed the woman sitting on Ursula's other side. 'Like you, Ursula, I'm really only interested in girls, and I keep a pretty little bitch here. If I keep her at home as my maid, or companion, then my husband would soon make a beeline for her. Keeping her here, I can relax knowing that she's quite safe from his attentions – and can't deceive me with any young men either!'

'So my friend Irma provides a useful service with her kennels and dog skins!' smiled Ursula. 'No wonder she invited me to bring my own bitches for her annual dog show.'

Dog show! Emma caught the words. What did that mean? But she could not hear any more as the two kennel maids, with sharp taps of their dog whips, led Emma and the young toy boy back to their kennels, their exciting exercise period over.

She saw them then walking past the line of kennels, giving each human dog a little morning run. Meanwhile Ursula was continuing her conversation with the second woman. I've brought my girls over here,' she was explaining, 'because Irma thinks that some of her clients might well also be interested in coming to see more of my bitches, as they call them here, in London – and so earn her a hefty commission.'

'Oh, I think you'll find lots of new clients here,' laughed the second woman. 'I hear you provide a most stimulating service! We're not all like Sofie here who only wants toy boys! But did you know that Irma's also got another interesting side line?'

'Really?' said Ursula, her voice suddenly hardening.

'Yes,' said Sofie. 'She's copied you and gone into the art world as well – selling expensive pictures to her richer clients who keep young men or women in her kennels, with no questions asked about where the pictures came from.'

'Oh, yes?' said Ursula, putting on a rather bored voice to mask her growing excitement. 'What sort of pictures?' She had suspected all along that something like that was going on here and had been waiting for a good excuse to come and tactfully see whether her own missing picture might perhaps have passed through Irma's hands.

'Oh, mainly very modern abstracts. She sold one last month to a hugely rich African woman. I thought it was just a jumble of colour but she got a good price for it as it was by a well-known artist.'

'Oh, which one?' asked Ursula in an innocent voice.

'I think it was an American, with a name like Tolstoy or Template. No, I remember now . . . Templeton.'

'Maurice Templeton!' exclaimed Ursula, hardly able to contain her rising excitement. It was indeed one of his pictures that had mysteriously disappeared from her house after Irma's last visit.

'Anyway, the African woman was the fat and ugly wife of an African dictator. She certainly had plenty of money to spend!'

'I wonder what she did with the picture,' said Ursula in an artificially casual tone.

'Oh, I think I heard Irma saying that the woman had had it sent back to Africa on her husband's presidential plane.'

'Did she, indeed?' murmured Ursula. No wonder that it had so mysteriously disappered.

'She's probably going to be at the dog show this afternoon – I hear she rather enjoys the sight of white girls being humbled. You might even be able to tempt her over to London after the *dénouement*!'

'The *dénouement*?' queried Ursula.

'Yes, the moment of truth. After each of the various classes, stallion dogs, young bitches, brood bitches and matched pairs of bitches has been judged and the prizes awarded, the winners are auctioned for the night.'

'Oh!' laughed Ursula. 'But if one of your toy boys wins, won't you be jealous?'

'If there were any young women bidding, yes I would, but there are only older women here today. And of course I may get the chance to bid for one of the other toy boys kept here. So it's all rather exciting.'

'Yes,' added the second woman, 'and the same applies to people like me who prefer girls. If my girl wins, I'll have to offer her for auction, but if she doesn't, then I can bid for someone else's girl – like one of yours!'

'And what makes it all the more exciting,' laughed Sofie, 'is that both the girl and toy boy winners are auctioned while still in their dog skins – so you don't know exactly what you have bought.'

Ursula was deep in thought. She had entered for three classes. How could she best tempt the African woman to London?

20

The Dog Show

They were coming to the end of the last class: the matched pairs of bitches. The judge, an attractive well-dressed woman in a cream linen dress and a picture hat, holding a pencil and pad, peered down at her notes. Then she looked again at the three pairs of bitches. They made a fine sight as they knelt on all fours in the small, fenced-off and mown grass judging arena, in front of the Bavarian castle with its yellow painted walls and green shutters.

Turning to her assistant, one of the kennel maids, the judge pointed to two young women sewn into matching dog skins. Each had the number '10' pasted onto her naked hindquarters.

'Number ten: out!' called out the kennel maid in German for the benefit of the women sitting around the arena.

The bitches' owner, a stout blonde woman, looked angrily at her charges and gave a sharp jerk to the lead fastened to the middle of the chain linking their collars. Looking furious at having been eliminated, she led them crawling out of the arena to a barred dog run in which several other pairs of already eliminated pairs of bitches were waiting.

Still in the ring, Emma peered around through her tiny eye holes in her head piece. There was now only one other pair still left in the competition: a pair of pretty, long-haired red setters. Temporarily off their lead, but still chained together, they were bounding about the little arena chasing little dog biscuits that their owner was throwing to them to show off their fitness and obedience. All that could be seen of the young women inside the furry skins were their swinging breasts hanging down under them, their exposed soft little bottoms and the occasional glimpse of hairless intimacies in the cutaway part of the skins between their legs.

From the slightly olive colour of their exposed skin, Emma thought that they must either have been sunbathing both topless and bottomless or, more likely, were from the eastern Mediterranean or Middle East.

She herself was chained to Cowslip who was also locked into a Dalmatian dog skin. It must be Cowslip, she knew, because of the distinctive big rings that hung from her elongated nipples.

The judge murmured something to the kennel maid.

'Lead round!' called out the girl.

Sabhu, now dressed once again as a keeper in his circus lion-tamer outfit and with his long dressage whip in his hand, gave their lead a jerk. Obediently, Emma and Cowslip started to scamper around the little judging arena behind him. The other matched pair were led round behind them, whilst the judge watched them both closely.

'Keep buttocks well up,' muttered Sabhu, raising his whip imperceptibly – a gesture that might not have been noticed by the judge, but which certainly had been by the two crawling women.

Sabhu was anxious for his pair to impress the judge. If these two bitches won then he would also get a prize as their trainer – and a handsome tip not only from Ursula but also, with a spot of luck, from the woman who won the right to enjoy them for the night.

Ursula was also watching closely as her entries were paraded round. Already Daisy and Bluebell had come second and third in the young bitches class. Her new friend Sofie had won the stallion dog class with one of her toy boys. This previous class had been a close-run thing and the judge, unable to decide between Sofie's toy boy and another young stallion dog, had asked to see them both in action as mating dogs so to further judge their qualities.

To the delight of the spectators, the winner of the young bitch class had agreed that her bitch should be used for the contest. While her owner stood over her, the two rival dogs had been brought in one at a time to cover her.

The judge had awarded marks to each dog for licking his mate to bring her to arousal, for his dexterity in then mounting and penetrating her unaided whilst still in his dog skin, and then for the speed with which he reached his climax. It has been a remarkable demonstration of the training and virility of these young toy boys, particularly as their hindquarters had jerked to and fro, animal-like, as they covered the bitch.

The prizes for the various classes had been pretty pieces of silver that would innocently serve to decorate their Mistresses' dinner tables. But the championship cup, a magnificent silver trophy, with the names of the previous winners engraved on it, was reserved for the matched pairs class.

Ursula looked across the small grass arena to where a large African woman, dressed in a brightly coloured robe and matching head scarf, was sitting. She smiled as she saw that the eyes of Her Excellency, Madame M'tout Korema, the wife of the cruel and ruthless dictator of a certain central African republic, were still fixed on the very white bottoms and hanging breasts of Cowslip and Emma – and on their delicate pink intimacies.

Clearly, Ursula decided, her two girls had caught the black lady's eye. The first part of her plan was working well. But all now depended on the girls winning the championship so that the judge could make the announcement that Ursula had already agreed with Irma.

As Ursula watched Emma and Cowslip parade around, she cursed herself for not having told Sabhu to put a pair of big rings, like Cowslip's, through Emma's nipples, too. That would really have made them a matched pair! But she need not have worried. Suddenly the judge announced her decision. Perhaps it was indeed the very whiteness of their bottoms and hanging breasts, and the delicate shade of pinkness of their intimacies, that swayed the scales. Anyway, Emma and Cowslip had won!

Everyone crowded round Ursula, congratulating her.

But then the judge clapped her hands for silence. 'Ladies!' she called, 'The show is not yet over! The winner of the matched pairs has made a most generous gesture. Instead of the winning pair being auctioned for the night, she has suggested that the two bitches be raffled instead, and moreover has agreed that the proceeds should go to improve our kennels here.'

There was a round of applause, for not all the spectators could afford the sort of money that this pair of lovely bitches would raise at auction – especially as it was known that they were owned by the famous Ursula! Moreover, many felt, a raffle would prevent the rich African woman from using her husband's ill-gotten wealth to out-bid the other spectators to get these prize girls. Now, instead, there was a chance for them all to enjoy them.

Indeed, they had already agreed, as they whispered amongst themselves during the judging, that one only had to look at the girls' great brute of a trainer, with his whip ever ready in his hand, and on the weals on their exposed bottoms, to imagine how well trained they must be to give pleasure.

'So hurry up,' the judge went on, 'and buy your raffle tickets from our kennel maids before it's too late!'

It was an invitation that was followed up with eager laughter and alacrity. Clearly all were intrigued to see and enjoy what lay behind the dog skins and dog headpieces.

Ursula smiled as she saw that Her Excellency was buying entire strips of raffle tickets. If she won, well and good, and if she didn't then her frustration would make her even more anxious to visit Ursula's little establishment in London . . . and then . . . ah!

In any case, it was all excellent publicity.

Meanwhile, Emma was horrified. The expression on her face was hidden by her dog's headpiece as she realised what was happening. She was even more horrified to see a fat, cruel-faced African woman buying so many tickets. She had often found pretty African girls very attractive, but not this horrible creature!

The judge then clapped her hands again. 'To make the

draw even more exciting, I will now ask the bitches' owner to hand over the keys to their dog skins. Not that of their head pieces, mark you, just their dog skins.'

With a delighted laugh, Ursula tossed the keys to Sabhu who now slowly and tantalisingly unzipped first the front of Emma's dog skin and then that of Cowslip. Then, amidst cries of laughter and approval, he made them put their hands behind their backs and then eased the skins over their shoulders and down to their wrists, baring their breasts and arms.

Then he humiliatingly eased the tight skins down over their hips to their knees. Blushing with embarrassment under their head pieces, the two women were now made by Sabhu's whip to shuffle forward awkwardly toward the increasingly excited spectators. It was a highly erotic sight that produced another flurry of ticket buying. But still the judge had not finished.

'Of course, ladies, you will now be anxious to know yet more about what you are hoping to win. Well,' she waved Ursula's now famous printed list of commands, 'this is the list of words of commands that these women have been trained to obey - instantly.'

Amidst much laughter, and murmurs of astonishment and approval, she then read out extracts from the list together with a description of just what the women would do at each command. Ursula smiled to herself as there was another rush to buy tickets. There would indeed be plenty of new clients coming to London shortly - all determined to make up for their disappointment in the draw.

As for the African lady, she almost seemed to be slavering at the mouth with lust as she looked at the naked white bodies being so wantonly displayed, and heard how they had been trained to perform.

'Now ladies,' cried the judge, 'the final denouement! Have you wasted your money buying your tickets or do you desperately want to buy more?'

She nodded at Sabhu who unlocked each woman's headpiece and slowly drew them off. Gasps of astonishment and admiration greeted the sight of first Cowslip's aristocratic features and then Emma's blonde beauty. There was yet another rush to buy tickets.

Finally, the judge invited Ursula to draw the winning number.

'Pink, five four six!' she announced.

'Yes!' cried an excited and sophisticated German woman, stepping forward to claim her prize.

At least, thought Emma, I won't have to satisfy that fierce looking African woman!

Meanwhile, Ursula was smiling happily as she saw how Her Excellency was eyeing the blonde Emma and biting her lips in anger and disappointment. Clearly, the trap was well and truly sprung! And Emma was going to be the bait!

21

Back in the Cages

Emma slowly awoke. She was still feeling slightly sleepy and rather exhausted. For a moment she couldn't quite recall where she was. Was she in a hospital or at home? Her memory of recent events seemed strangely vague. All too soon she remembered that far from being in a hospital, she was again lying in a narrow bunk in the back of the big estate car with its curtained windows. She saw that she was wearing just her velvet cape.

Under her cape, she could feel her wrist manacles and their connecting length of heavy chain. She heard the rattle of a chain under the blanket; her ankles were similarly manacled. She vaguely remembered being manacled before and her delight when finding that they had finally been removed. But why had they been put back on?

Emma was now rapidly coming out of her daze. Beside her in the bunks were Ursula's other three girls. She saw that the woman driver was the awful Doctor Anna and that next to her was Sabhu, once again dressed like a chauffeur.

Sabhu's seat was not facing towards the front but had been swivelled round towards the girls. His deep black eyes were staring right through Emma as if he knew her every thought. How she hated this man with his ugly face and arrogant manner. A vague memory of being closely supervised and controlled by him made her want to be sick.

She was now fully awake again and as the car sped on she made out a sign pointing to London and, on the other side, one pointing to the M25 and to the Channel.

The Channel! The word gave her memory a jolt but, try

as she might, she could remember so little of what had happened in the last few days. She did vaguely remember swallowing some pills and later the car being driven up onto a train. But just where had she been?

She remembered a raffle and a fat African woman. But what was she now doing with the ghastly Sabhu? She seemed to remember that he went everywhere with Ursula's girls, always watching them and always ready to use his whip.

Emma could not resist making a face at him. But then she suddenly felt a little electric shock. She gave a little cry. My God, she thought, has the ambulance been struck by lightning? But, of course, it hadn't, for it just sped on. Then, when she made another face at Sabhu, she felt it again. This time it was stronger.

A moment later they went under a tunnel and she could see a mirror image of herself in the window of the car. Yes, she could see a large stiff collar around her neck and similar collars around the necks of the other girls. She saw that Sabhu was holding a small control box with numbered buttons on it. A control box! Emma suddenly remembered that it was this control box that in turn controlled that awful Bikini-belt. She remembered that, like the manacles, it had been taken off.

She put her hands down. It was back on now. That was how she had been given the shocks. But why had it been taken off? She had a hazy memory of having to wear something furry and of her intimacies and breasts being on display.

She saw the driver of the ambulance was the German woman doctor – that same wicked woman, Doctor Anna, who, she vaguely remembered, had come with Sabhu when she had been abducted. She began to remember how on that occasion the Doctor had offered her some sleeping pills so that she'd have a little snooze during the journey – and how she had not woken up until she was firmly locked up in her cage. Then she remembered how the same thing had happened when they had been taken abroad and how she had woken up in the kennels. Had she and the other girls again been put to sleep to keep them quiet during this journey – and perhaps to make them forget what had recently been happening?

Emma wondered if the other girls had felt a shock like hers. If so, they had said nothing. She tried to talk to them but again she felt a shock and saw Sabhu's horrible black eyes staring at her. He warningly put a finger to his mouth. Oh, yes, she remembered; talking was not allowed. She looked more closely at them and saw they were all still fast asleep. But now, where were they going and what was going to happen?

Emma looked out of the window once more. They must be getting near the centre of London as the traffic was building up and they were slowed down by several traffic jams. Sabhu hated traffic jams, she remembered, presumably because he was nervous lest the girls might try to jump out of the ambulance.

But the door, she remembered, was always locked and anyway she now knew better than to try to escape. Sabhu would be furious and made life dreadful if you were merely disobedient. As for trying to escape . . . well, Emma had tried once and the punishment afterwards had been horrific.

She remembered that she had learnt to be subservient and to obey. But she also remembered that she still resented the way Sabhu treated her, and sometimes this resentment spilled over and she wanted to try to kill Sabhu, or even Ursula herself.

Suddenly, the big estate car drew up outside a garage door alongside a newly-painted terraced house off the King's Road. Hazily, Emma recognised it as Ursula's new house. They were home!

Sabhu pressed a button on the dashboard of the car and the garage door slid open, closing again after the car had driven in. He now roughly woke up the other three girls, tapping them sharply on the breasts with what Emma nervously recognised as his long dressage whip.

'Wake up, you white sluts,' he shouted. 'Wake up.'

The girls sat up, their wrist manacles rattling under their capes, and looked around in surprise.

'Up!' shouted Sabhu.

It was one of the commands the girls had all been taught to obey unthinkingly. Their ankle manacles now clanking as well, they staggered out of their bunks. Their capes came down only to just below their waists and Emma saw that, like her, each had again been locked into the thin leather Bikini-belts.

'Out!' ordered Sabhu, unlocking and raising the rear door.

Still half asleep, they were scarcely able to walk but with Sabhu gripping the arms of the two younger girls, Bluebell and Daisy, and Doctor Anna holding Cowslip and Emma, they made their way into the house. Emma recognised Babindu, Ursula's Caribbean maid.

'I've got everything nice and ready upstairs for the white trash,' Emma heard her whisper to Sabhu.

Then, suddenly, Ursula appeared, all dressed up as if she had just come in from a business meeting.

'And how are my little ones?' she purred. Despite her proprietary tone, Emma found herself warming towards her. 'Are you tired after your journey? Well you know you've all done very well for your Mistress and she's very pleased with you – especially you, Emma!'

Emma was thrilled, though she did not understand why Ursula had singled her out.

Then, glancing towards Doctor Anna, she added: 'Though I don't expect they can remember very much about it, can they?'

Grimly, Doctor Anna shook her head.

'Well, they're all going to be performing in the arena in two days time,' said Ursula. 'It's a well-booked show.'

Then she added in German to the large and unattractive woman doctor: 'Before you take Daisy away with you, I'd like you to use this performance to take the first steps into getting, say, two of the remaining ones into milk as soon as possible – then I'll be able to charge double for them. Are your treatments ready? Have you enough to do them properly?'

'Oh, yes,' replied the lady doctor meaningfully. 'Oh yes!'

The girls were recovering fast and were wondering what Ursula and the Doctor were talking about. They watched as Doctor Anna carefully studied a file of copious notes and Sabhu's meticulously-kept temperature graphs. She studied several pages and then looked at Ursula.

'Of course you can use my treatment at any time but suprisingly it does seem to work best at the natural times,' she muttered in German. Then, pointing at Bluebell and Cowslip, she added: 'Tomorrow – those ones . . . yes!'

Then, pointing at Emma, she shook her head and smiled enigmatically.

'So,' laughed Ursula mysteriously, switching back into English, 'although they won't understand what's going on, my little Bluebell and Cowslip are going to be the stars of a special and very exciting performance. And then they're going to earn their Mistress a lot more money.'

Bluebell and Cowslip looked very pleased with themselves at being the centre of attention, even though they did not understand why.

'And what about me?' asked Emma petulantly, also not understanding what was going to happen, but feeling jealous at being left out. 'Why can't I earn a lot of money for my Mistress, too?'

'Oh you will, little Emma, you will,' smiled Ursula enigmatically. 'But differently, and starting tonight!'

Then, before Emma could ask what she meant, Ursula turned to Sabhu. 'I think my little girls deserve a break before you take them back upstairs again. Let's all have a little tea together to celebrate Bluebell's and Cowslip's forthcoming happy . . . well I'd better not say what!'

With a laugh, Sabhu led the four women by their leads up to Ursula's immaculate drawing room; the one that was so beautifully decorated in the French, Louis XV style.

Emma saw that the other girls were now fully awake and obviously very pleased to be back with Ursula again. Despite being manacled and kept on leads held by Sabhu, they were soon flirting with her.

Bluebell and Daisy were talking in a strange language and in whispered voices, calling her Mistress in English, as they made a lot of flirtatious gestures at her, interspersed with seductive little curtsies. Soon Cowslip, too, joined in flashing her eyes provocatively. They were all rewarded with encouraging and affectionate little pats from Ursula. Once again, ignored by Ursula, Emma felt very jealous and excluded from these flirtations.

Babindu brought in a tray of tea and cakes for Ursula and Doctor Anna. Emma found herself eyeing the tray hungrily. How long was it since she had been allowed to eat anything sweet? It felt like months!

Still holding in one hand the leads of all four girls, and his whip in the other, Sabhu went behind them. 'Kneel!' he ordered.

They all knelt down in a line in front of the now seated Ursula.

'Beg!' he ordered.

It was one of the commands they had been taught to obey instantly and, like performing animals, they raised their cupped manacled hands towards Ursula, licking their lips as they jealously watched their Mistress and the awful Doctor Anna tuck into the delicious-looking cakes.

Finally, unable to resist her girls' silently pleading eyes, Ursula put a little piece of cake, with jam and cream in the middle, into each girl's cupped hands.

Emma was thrilled. Oh what a treat! Her earlier feelings of jealousy forgotten, Emma looked up at her Mistress, her eyes brimming with tears of gratitude. Oh, how kind she really was!

'Wait!' ordered Sabhu.

Trust him to spoil things, thought Emma.

The girls were kept waiting for a full minute.

'Eat!' finally came the order.

Raising their manacled hands to their mouths, they eagerly ate the little pieces of cake. Jam! thought Emma. And real cream!

Ursula nodded to Sabhu to take the girls back to the attic. She had several telephone calls to make and much to discuss with Doctor Anna, as well as expecting an important visitor.

* * *

As soon as Sabhu had got the girls back into the attic, and had closed the electronic lock on the door, his strict regime was resumed.

Emma's heart dropped as she recognised the line of numbered cages, each with its little door invitingly open, and in front of them the line of little numbered bowls, each containing a little scented water with a flower floating prettily on it.

'On your spots!' shouted Sabhu.

Spots? Emma shook her head, her mind still misty. Suddenly she remembered it was another of the words of command she had learnt to obey – and at the double! Encouraged by a sharp stroke of Sabhu's whip across her backside, prettily exposed under her short cape, Emma rushed forward to the spot marked '4'.

Like the other girls, she raised her manacled hands and clasped them behind her neck, put out her tongue and bent her knees. Like them, she did not dare to look down and kept her eyes fixed on the wall in front of her, but she could feel the bowl between her manacled ankles and adjusted her position accordingly – just as, she remembered, she had been taught to do.

Still holding their leads in one hand, and his raised whip in the other, Sabhu was now standing in front of the line of silent women. It was time to impose a little discipline again. They had got slack.

'Bellies in,' he warned.

He went down the line of straining women, tapping each one's belly with his whip. 'Prepare!'

Each woman now lowered her manacled hands to below her short cape and, keeping her eyes fixed ahead of her, unfastened the velcro keeping the rubber pad over her intimacies.

'Up!'

Each woman now held up the rubber pad, exposing the plastic grill over her beauty lips.

'Stand by!' Sabhu raised his whip menacingly. He paused.

'Remember! All together! Three strokes for any girl who is slow!' he warned.

Oh, this was so humiliating, thought Emma. She longed to revolt against the Haitian's cruel control. But three strokes! Desperately Emma relaxed her muscles. She must be ready. She must.

'One . . . Two . . . Three . . . Perform!'

The women were blushing now, as instantly there came the noise of four fountains each prettily trickling into its own numbered bowl. Sabhu smiled contently. This was the way to teach stuck-up European women obedience and humility. Treat them like performing animals! Tomorrow he would dose them – he did not want to risk one of his little animals disgracing herself at the performance in the arena in two days time.

Locked up in her cage, later that afternoon, Emma felt very jealous when Sabhu came in and woke up Cowslip and then took her down on her lead to Ursula's bedroom. Why hadn't Ursula chosen *her* for afternoon pleasure, instead of that Latin bitch?

Her jealousy knew no bounds as she lay awake, curled up on the rubber mat of her cage, frustratingly wondering what tricks Ursula was making Cowslip perform for her. Angrily, she gripped the bars of her cage to prevent herself from pointlessly tearing at the plastic grill over her beauty bud – thereby getting a shock.

Would Ursula have switched on the hidden vibrator in the rubber pad on Cowslip's belt? Were the little vibrating rubber knobs giving Ursula exquisite pleasure at this very moment? Was Ursula now being driven to a peak of excitement as she pressed down on Cowslip? Was Cowslip's eager little tongue now delicately further exciting Ursula? Emma tossed and turned in her little cage in a frenzy of frustration and jealousy.

So it was that she was thrilled when later Sabhu came for her and led her crawling down to a large bedroom. Obviously, her Mistress, dissatisfied with Cowslip's performance had sent for her. Oh how exciting! This was her big chance!

She saw that there was a figure lying hidden on the huge

bed on her back, her feet outstretched. She was thrilled. Ursula was waiting for her! Waiting for the feel of her hot little tongue between her legs. Oh yes. She'd soon show her Mistress how much better she was than those other girls of hers.

'Remember, I waiting with whip. You get special punishment – twelve strokes if you not please,' whispered Sabhu, as he lifted up the bedclothes.

Not please? Not please Ursula? Emma gave a little laugh. Sabhu needn't worry – she would please Ursula as she'd never been pleased before!

She saw that there was a chain hanging out from beneath the bedclothes at the foot of the bed. Sabhu gestured to her to kneel down and, unfastening his own leather lead from her collar, replaced it with a chain one. Then he gestured to her to climb, as she had so often had to practice under his guidance, up under the bed clothes from the foot of the bed.

Eagerly she put her head and shoulders under the bedclothes, eagerly waiting for the tug on her lead that would tell her to creep up higher and higher, her tongue licking as she went.

'Madame,' she heard Sabhu say, 'the girl is in position and awaiting your orders. I shall wait for a moment with my whip to ensure her instant obedience.

How silly, thought Emma again. She would not have to be driven by the whip to please her beloved Mistress.

There was a tug on her lead. Emma started to crawl up the bed, hidden in the darkness under the bedclothes. Soon she found she was between two outstretched legs. She started to lick one and then the other humbly and respectfully. She heard a little moan of pleasure.

Slowly she made her way higher.

But something was wrong. This wasn't Ursula! She started to retreat down the bed but the lead held her tight.

'Beat her, Sabhu!' she heard a strange woman's heavily accented voice command. 'Use your whip!'

Emma felt the bedclothes being lifted up, exposing her bottom. She screamed as the whip came down. Hastily, she applied her tongue reaching up to where the two legs joined.

Then she saw, in the dim light under the bedclothes, that the skin she was so assiduously licking was black. She drew back in astonishment. Down came Sabhu's whip again across her backside.

'Lick it!' he ordered.

She did so and suddenly the top of the bedclothes were lifted. Keeping her tongue stroking the woman's beauty lips, Emma raised her eyes.

There, looking down at her, above a huge belly, was the cruel face of Her Excellency, Madame M'tout Korema.

Emma recoiled in horror. 'No!' she cried. 'No!'

'Oh yes, white slut! Oh yes!' answered Her Excellency with a cruel laugh. 'Beat her Sabhu. Beat her!'

Emma's Calvary had begun . . .

It was a shaken and sobbing Emma who, two hours later, was put back into her cage by a grinning Sabhu. A new fifty pound note, a tip for services well rendered, was almost burning a hole in his pocket.

He smiled as he remembered how with his whip he had driven Emma into pleasing Her Excellency in increasingly humiliating ways. It had culminated in Her Excellency taking the girl from behind with a dildo. The sobbing Emma had had to hold back the little plastic shields of her belt, just as she had been taught to do, to proffer her tight rear orifice to the grinning African lady.

Oh yes, Her Excellency would soon be back for more. And that would mean more tips for Sabhu!

22

A Visit to a Strange Gallery

Two days later, Emma was astonished to hear Ursula telling Sabhu to take off the girls' manacles and belts. She could hardly believe her ears. What was going to happen?

Ursula told him to dress them all in their matching 'little girl' smocks, matching hats and dancing shoes. She said she was going to have a portrait of them done at the gallery.

All four of them were very excited and even Ursula seemed to be affected by her girls' infectious gaiety. Although Ursula was usually very strict, it amused her at times to see her girls smiling and jealously flirting with her again just as they had on their return from the dog show.

But, Emma reflected, Sabhu was coming as well, which would spoil the fun. How she wished he were dead! How much more fun she would have with Ursula if only she could get rid of him and, preferably, the other girls as well. But Sabhu was an evil influence and so was Doctor Anna.

Ursula checked that they were properly dressed and then off they all tripped merrily down the King's Road in pairs; one pair behind the other. This time, Emma walked hand in hand with Bluebell, to whom she was becoming more and more attracted. They made a pretty sight as they skipped along, all so happy to be free of their horrible belts and heavy manacles. But they still kept a wary eye on Sabhu grimly bringing up the rear.

Carefully made up as they were, they could pass as young girls, certainly to a casual observer. Emma's own hair had grown longer and, thanks to Sabhu's strict diet, she was now getting quite thin. She wore little bows in her hair, like Bluebell and the other girls. She felt very excited. Life as one of Ursula's girls was really all a huge laugh and she knew that Ursula would be nice to her in the end. She just had to suffer in the meantime, while the other girls got all the goodies and all the attention. Even Sabhu was being nicer to them that day. Of course he paid special attention to Bluebell because she was head girl.

They arrived at the gallery where Ursula was already waiting for them. She was being very strict again. 'Now girls, customers want to see the pictures on display, not a crowd of silly schoolgirls gawking at them. So off you go stand at the back of the gallery!'

Emma was startled to see the German woman doctor sitting there at the back, smoking, a smile on her ugly face. She had a big doctor's bag with her. What on earth, wondered Emma, was she doing with that here? She saw that Layla, the girl who was apparently running the gallery, was talking to a customer. Emma would have liked to stay with her; after all she had helped Ursula on many such occasions and now knew quite a bit about the business. However, she was hardly dressed for the part and anyway Sabhu was angrily gesturing to her to join the others. He may not have had his whip in his hand but she still did not dare disobey him.

After a few minutes, to Emma's surprise, Sabhu opened a little door and ushered them through it into a storage room with paintings slotted into shelved compartments presumably all ready to be shipped abroad. Then, before she had time to take in very much, they were pushed into a darkened back room. The door was shut and locked behind them.

Suddenly, some brilliant spotlights were switched on. Emma gasped as she saw that it was not just a room, but was fitted out as a shop an old fashioned butcher's shop.

It seemed more like a small arena with a viewing balcony on one wall. It was rather like the balconies in the attic and gymnasium in Ursula's new house, except that it was larger and curtained off, with the curtains hiding it completely.

However, it was the feeling of sawdust under her little dancing shoes that really struck Emma. It brought back childhood memories of Ireland, where all butcher's shops used to have sawdust on the floors.

She remembered the fun she used to have making designs and patterns in the sawdust whilst her nanny chatted away to her lover, the assistant butcher, in his blue-ribboned boater hat. She had never minded waiting for her nanny; she had loved her so much.

But these days, and especially in London, she had never seen a butcher's shop like this. She was amazed. What was going on?

In her usual naive way, Emma suspected it was all quite innocent. Always naturally light hearted and good humoured, she entered into the spirit of everything. She smiled at Bluebell and, forgetting that she only understood a little English, was starting to tell her about her childhood days in Ireland when she heard a frightening crack of a whip. She turned and saw Sabhu coming towards her in his menacing way with his whip once again in his hand. Overcome with trepidation, she fell silent. He towered over her and tied her hands behind her back. Then he did the same to Bluebell and Cowslip.

Daisy was left free and, minutes later, much to her annoyance, Emma saw Ursula slip into the room and take Daisy off with her. What were they up to? Emma felt so jealous, but there was no time to think about that for the next minute Sabhu was fastening a wide, strong strap round her waist. Another thick leather strap was fastened round her chest just above her breasts. The two straps were joined behind her back by another, this time with a big ring in it.

She saw Sabhu pull down a chain attached to a pulley. At the end of the chain was a hook. He clicked the hook on to the ring at her back and turned the pulley. Suddenly Emma found herself being hoisted up high and then left there, suspended, like a carcass in a butcher's shop.

She felt little constriction, but being suspended in mid air, her arms, legs and breasts hanging down and her little panties exposed from behind, was at first a horribly vulnerable feeling. Underneath her was the big butcher's table and she tried in vain to reach down and rest her feet on it.

As she got used to the feeling, however, she had to admit that it was rather exciting being hung up there, dangling quite helplessly. Certainly, life with Ursula was unusual!

She heard Cowslip give a loud scream and she saw Sabhu's whip give her a wallop. She, too, evidently, was not used to being hung up. Horrified by the sight of what had happened to Emma, Cowslip kicked and screamed and tried to fight Sabhu off. But he quickly overpowered her and Emma had to listen to her pained whimpers as Sabhu gave her three more strokes of his whip as a punishment. Eventually, after more moans and tears, Cowslip joined Emma, dangling helplessly on an adjoining hook.

Then it was the turn of Bluebell. Having seen what had happened to Cowslip, she did not struggle as the heavy belt was fastened around her slim waist and the hook was attached. Moments later she, too, was hanging there, helpless. Emma could not help thinking how lovely she looked. She was getting more and more fond of the young girl.

Sabhu then amused himself by pushing them all to and fro as if they were on swings.

'Now, little girls,' he mocked, 'you all so pretty but in one way not pretty enough. Your Mistress will be back shortly with her friends and they'll want to see three beautiful little girls dangling from hooks, nicely positioned for Doctor Anna's treatment and waiting helplessly for it.

What treatment? thought Emma anxiously. And why does she need the girls to be hung up like this?

'But first I want to be sure that everything is perfect,' he said, mysteriously.

Emma saw Sabhu go off to a corner of the room and start boiling something in a saucepan. It was difficult to see properly, suspended as she was, and anyway, when Sabhu noticed her looking at him, he turned and raised his whip. 'Eyes down!' he growled.

Emma lowered her gaze submissively but out of the

corner of her eye, she saw that he kept adding something to the boiling water, as if making some sort of paste. What was he doing? It had a sweet smell, like sugar. Surely he wasn't going to use this paste on them   and in a particular place. Oh, no!

Like the other two women, she was still in her pretty smocked dress and they were all wearing pretty little lace pants. However, within seconds Sabhu pulled their little dresses up over their heads so that they could see nothing. Then he pulled down their lace pants.

Doctor Anna entered the arena and began peering at each girl in turn and pointing out to Sabhu any hairs she wanted removed. Next minute, Emma felt hot paste being ladled between her legs and over her beauty lips. She gave a little cry as she felt it beginning to burn. It was barely a week since Sabhu had last carefully depilated all the girls with tweezers but evidently this was a special occasion and he was now going to use a paste to make sure that not one little hair was visible.

Emma and the other two girls were now crying out in discomfort as he applied several coats of the hot paste. Under Doctor Anna's approving gaze he began rubbing the paste in between their beauty lips with a brush. Both ignored the girls' cries.

'You don't cry out so much,' said Doctor Anna. 'This not really hurt!'

Well it might not if you were a fat and ugly German, thought Emma, and never used depilatory creams, but she and the other girls had no protective hairs and the paste burnt like hell.

Although the girls seemed completely smooth, Sabhu went on remorselessly working the paste up into a lather on each girl.

Watched by an approving Doctor Anna, the horrible brute also started to penetrate Emma's, and the other girls', backsides with oil. Up and up went his finger. It was horrible. Why is he doing this? Emma asked herself desperately. She tried to tighten her bottom to stop him but this made him only probe deeper with his oily finger.

Then she heard Doctor Anna say something to Sabhu about getting the girls ready whilst she prepared the treatment. She heard her unlock the door and leave the room. Moments later she felt Sabhu rub some oil on to her beauty bud, massaging it carefully into erection and then slowly manoeuvring his great black hand inside her.

Emma was disgusted but powerless to prevent herself from becoming aroused. Hanging as she was with her dress over her head, she could not properly see what he was doing. Then, to her utter horror, she felt his long wet tongue expertly probing her most intimate parts.

Emma was getting wet with arousal and, hanging as she was, her moisture embarrassingly began to drop on to the sawdust, making a damp spot.

'So,' she heard Sabhu say with that horrible smirking laugh of his, 'your Mistress will see what a naughty girl you have been.'

Then his mood changed.

'How dare you get excited without my permission!'

Down came his whip making Emma cry out and wriggle helplessly as she swayed there, hanging from her hook.

But Sabhu was now enormously excited himself. He simply could not leave the girls alone and was running his hands all over their helpless bodies. The paste was still burning them but he continued to oil their bottoms, his finger going up each girl, carefully loosening their back passages. Then his slippery hands lifted their breasts and pinched their nipples.

At last, he scraped the paste off them and then rubbed in some wonderfully soft cream. After all the brutality, Emma began to relax as the cream eased the pain. Then, just as she thought her treatment was over, she felt Sabhu's huge manhood push up inside her well-prepared rear orifice. He was standing behind her, on the table, pushing her head and shoulders down so that he could drive deeper and deeper into her as she hung from her hook. It was horribly uncomfortable for her as he began to pump slowly in and out, enjoying the oily and slippery feeling.

He was now rutting like an animal. The sight of the three

women hanging there had obviously turned him on. Why should he, too, not help warm them all up for Doctor Anna's treatment?

Emma felt herself melting again as his fingers cunningly used the cream to arouse her again. Overcome with wanton desire, she began to pant and to open her legs. To her disgust she now wanted Sabhu inside her. It was a strange feeling. Although she hated him and he disgusted her, here she was hanging helplessly from a hook, her intimacies wet and longing for a hard manhood to penetrate them but properly this time, not from behind. She was displaying her availability like a mare in season or a bitch on heat.

But Sabhu, his virility intact, had moved on to Cowslip. Emma could still see nothing but she heard the older girl cry out, first in helpless protest, then in helpless delirium. Her cries mixed with Sabhu's animal-like grunts of pleasure but he seemed to be saving himself for yet further delights.

Indeed it was now the turn of Bluebell. But first, he cruelly pulled Emma's dress down so that she could see him oil and open Bluebell up, as he had with her. Emma could not help feeling jealous as she watched him driving himself up Bluebell's bottom, pushing her head down so that her body was at just the right angle for his proudly curved manhood, whilst his creamed fingers rubbed her beauty bud.

'Stop, you beast! Stop!' cried the younger girl, in vain.

Soon she too became excited. Emma could see her eyes glaze over. Her cheeks turned pink, her mouth opened, and little drops of saliva dropped out on to the sawdust. She looked as though she was going to faint, but she had reached her climax.

Sabhu stayed inside her, swaying her body so that his manhood was pumping in and out of it. It was all too much for Bluebell, and she fainted. Alarmed, Sabhu pulled himself out of her. Quickly, he lifted her off the hook and put her down on the rough butcher's table.

Emma was scared. Was Bluebell all right? She made no sound. Emma began to fear the worst. She thought of the headline news: 'Girl dead in butcher's shop'. And what about herself? She imagined the questions: 'What were you doing hanging from a butcher's hook?' And the awful examination to see if she had been interfered with. Everyone would read about it: her friends, her husband. Her nerves were shattered and she was shaking with fear.

'Bluebell, darling, are you all right?' she called out.

There was no response. Sabhu seemed terrified, too.

'Miss Ursula come back very soon!' he muttered. 'She bring party of clients who have paid to watch you little bitches being done and now one of you has passed out!'

He pushed Bluebell. There was not a sound and she was as white as a ghost. Emma began to pray. Like a good Irish girl, she always did so in times of trouble. 'Hail Mary, full of grace . . . .' She prayed as she had never prayed before. Poor Bluebell, you can't be dead.

'Get her a drink of water!' she screamed at Sabhu. 'Open her mouth and breathe into it!'

Sabhu had lost his usual arrogant self confidence. He was trembling and calling out all sorts of Caribbean voodoo cries which Emma could not understand.

'Fetch more water,' she cried, and Sabhu went off to the back of the arena which was still in darkness. It was just at that moment that Emma looked down once again nervously at Bluebell; to her astonishment she saw the girl give her a little wink. Bluebell was just pretending!

Emma longed to whisper to her but did not dare to for Sabhu was coming back with the drink of water. He poured some into Bluebell's mouth. He was being amazingly gentle. This horrible great brute must have another side to him, thought Emma.

Bluebell was responding. She moved her head and opened her eyes. Sabhu was almost crying with relief, cradling her in his arms. It was an astonishing sight this huge Haitian who had always appeared to have no feelings, to take and never to give, and to scorn the women in his charge. Yet here he was, holding Bluebell, caressing her and mumbling little words of tenderness. Emma could only stare in disbelief.

Then, suddenly, Sabhu straightened up and looked at his watch. 'The Mistress here in twenty minutes,' he roared, pointing his whip at the curtained balcony. 'Now what do I do with you lot of useless wimps?'

When the curtains were pulled back, the clients were supposed to see all three girls hanging there beautifully and ready to be warmed up for Doctor Anna's treatment even if it was only to be a pretence. It would certainly have been very erotic and the thrilled clients would doubtlessly have tipped him well.

But Bluebell was continuing her act of being ill and weak, so how could he possibly hang her up again from her butcher's hook? And Emma was still suffering from shock and fright. Only Cowslip, still blindfolded by her dress was all right; in fact she seemed still lost in the ecstasy of her climax.

Sabhu thought hard. He would have to change the plan and yet produce a display that would both satisfy the clients and also enable Doctor Anna to give the girls the full treatment she had prepared. If not, he might be sacked, and the tips he was getting were far too good for him to want to risk that happening.

Clearly, the original plan would have to be changed. Cowslip, of course, could still be given her intended treatment as she hung from her hook, but it was the sight of 'unusual couplings' that really excited the clients. That was what the Mistress had promised them and what they had paid to see.

Quickly, his fertile brain devised a new scenario. Indeed, he thought, it might even be better than the original one, especially as he remembered that there were some useful dressing up clothes here!

23

A Glimpse of Plantation Life

Sabhu now lowered Emma from her hook.

'Oh, what a relief!' cried Emma. She could not help exclaiming.

'Shut up, you white trash!' Sabhu shouted, picking up his whip. He switched on a light at the back of the arena and opened up what seemed to be a large refrigerator. Inside Emma could see all sorts of rubber dresses and masks. The outfit that he handed to Emma was one of a Barbie Doll nurse.

'You. Put this on quickly!' he shouted and then busied himself putting Bluebell into a set of baby clothes, complete with rompers and a nappy. He thrust a rubber dummy into her mouth and tied it with a ribbon behind her neck. Her hair was covered with a baby's cap and her hands were immobilised in baby gloves then tied together with a pretty blue ribbon. Only her naked breasts betrayed the fact that she was not just an outsize infant.

Evidently, thought Emma, as she struggled into the very tight rubber nurse's outfit, Cowslip was to be left as she was, hanging from a hook. Her own outfit was freezing cold, having been kept chilled to prevent the rubber from perishing. It felt horrible and clammy on Emma's soft body and clung to her almost like a second skin. It had huge false breasts which fitted over her own ones, distorting her body and making her look ridiculous – almost a figure of fun, Emma thought ruefully, like a woman on a 1930 postcard from Blackpool.

Sabhu now quickly transformed the butcher's shop into a cross between a nursery and a hospital operating theatre.

Over the table he laid a white cloth and next to it placed a playpen into which he put the helpless Bluebell. Then he looked at the now transformed Emma and grunted his approval.

'Five minutes to go!' he said, speaking slowly and carefully so that Cowslip and Bluebell could understand, and waving his whip to emphasise his instructions.

'When Mistress and clients arrive, you all look at me as if terrified out of your wits. In any case, you soon will be. You do as I say. You act part of white slaves of black Sabhu, sent here by your Mistress for special treatment. And remember – any disobedience and you get special punishment. Yes, special punishment! And very hard! Clients will like that.'

He pointed up at the still curtained-off balcony. 'You now put on special exhibition for clients and Mistress and you earn me good tips or you get thrashed. Understand?'

He paused, looking thoroughly relieved at the now trembling women. 'And you, Emma,' he said, pointing to her with his whip and speaking more quickly. 'You will play special role. I tell you what to do. You remember always, you do as I say or you get beaten. You lucky this time. You not get doctor's treatment you just help give it. Exciting for clients to see a girl having to help Doctor Anna. Understand?'

Help give the treatment? What treatment, Emma wondered. She was mystified and also horrified. What was this awful doctor going to do to her poor companions for the amusement of Ursula's friends? She would not be a party to any outrage.

'No! No!' she cried, adding bravely. 'Beat me if you like, but I won't do it. I won't, so there!'

Before she could say another word, Sabhu seized her by her hair and bent her over. She felt his whip on her bare bottom. The rubber dress was so skimpy that it only came down to the tops of her thighs, barely covering her precious beauty lips and when she moved everything was exposed, for there were no knickers with the outfit.

Sabhu raised his whip again, and again brought it down across her defenceless buttocks.

'You damn well do what I say, white slut!' he roared. Then he pushed her down on to her hands and knees. Then, standing over her, his strong calves gripping her wriggling waist, he again raised his whip. Probing the tender opening between her legs, he threatened to beat her on her most sensitive area.

'All right!' Emma screamed. 'All right! I'll do whatever you want.'

'Yes! You damn well will,' shouted Sabhu, holding her down and threatening again to give her a stroke of his whip. 'Now get up!'

Next moment the now thoroughly chastened Emma heard Ursula call out for Sabhu from beyond the locked door into the arena.

'You, Barbie Doll! Just stand at attention next to playpen,' ordered Sabhu. 'You, Cowslip, when I give order, you make crying noises and swing from your hook, and you, Bluebell, make noise with this rattle! That's better! Now stop and don't move until I tell you. I now go and tell Mistress about change of plan. You all keep quite still and no talking or you get whip!'

A few minutes later Sabhu returned, now dressed in his tight-fitting white breeches and black riding boots and wearing a military style cap. His muscular naked torso was oiled and gleaming. He was smiling confidently as he looked at his girls. Almost immediately all the lights went out, plunging them into darkness.

'Keep still,' warned Sabhu, in a whisper. 'Quite still. You not move.'

Emma saw that there was now a chink of light showing beneath the closed curtain up on the balcony. She heard the noise of a door opening up there and women's voices laughing expectantly. She heard the scraping of chairs being moved behind the curtain as they sat down. Then there was a silence broken by the voice of Ursula.

'Good evening, ladies! Welcome to my little show. I hope you will find it interesting! Now I want you to imagine that you are in a mythical land somewhere in, say,

Latin America, where slave plantations still exist owned by rich ladies who also enjoy owning young women. But here the slaves are not black but white white women and the overseers working for our lady plantation owners are not white but black big burly black men who stand no nonsense from their obstreperous white charges.'

She paused. There were little gasps of excitement. Evidently Sabhu's change of the scenario was going down well.

'Traditionally, of course,' she went on, 'on all slave plantations, the breeding of slaves and the provision of well-run breeding and rearing pens was very important. But now the main purpose of a slave plantation is to produce an annual crop of little children who can be sold to dealers to meet the incessant demand for beautiful little children for adoption in America and Europe and for . . . shall we say . . . certain other types of progeny . . . for the Middle East. It is a very profitable business and every slave girl has to produce her quota.'

Once again there were little giggles of excitement.

'So ladies, our first scene will be a *Tableau vivant*, a still life of this vital part of life on our plantation.'

Suddenly the curtains parted, whilst the rest of the room remained in darkness.

'Keep still!' again warned Sabhu. Emma had a glimpse of a dozen well-dressed and sophisticated-looking women. Among them she noticed the Baroness. Oh no! How embarrassing to be seen by her wearing this absurd outfit. Then, with a pang of jealousy, she saw Daisy looking very smug as she stood in attendance behind Ursula's chair.

But what really caught her eye, was the huge African woman dressed in brightly coloured African robes who was sitting next to Ursula. The woman turned and Emma saw that she was the horribly cruel woman whom she had had to please the other night. Oh no!

'Firstly,' came the voice of Ursula, 'we will see a representation of one of the rearing pens with a pretty little baby slave girl in it, tended to by one of the plantation nursemaids; all under the control of the breeding overseer.'

Emma blinked as a spotight suddenly lit up by the playpen with Bluebell inside it. There were cries of admiration from the balcony and a little round of applause.

Horrified, Emma wanted to turn and run to the door. But she could not move, for Sabhu had put her on a lead which he was holding tightly. She felt utterly idiotic standing there at attention with her huge rubber breasts and her body encased in the tight rubber which left her backside and legs exposed.

Meanwhile the blonde little Bluebell made a very pretty picture, kneeling up in the playpen in her rompers, her body well sprinkled with baby powder. She was making little girlish noises behind the dummy strapped into her mouth as she played with her rattle, her eyes fixed fearfully on Sabhu.

The light suddenly went out again, leaving the arena in darkness. Emma felt Sabhu snap her lead on to the top bar of the playpen. 'Keep still and keep silent,' he quietly warned Emma and Bluebell.

Seconds later another spotlight came on, this time lighting up the highly erotic picture of Cowslip swaying from her hook and crying whilst Sabhu stood behind her, parting the cheeks of her bottom.

'Here,' came the voice of Ursula, 'we see the breeding overseer checking a slightly older girl who is hanging ready from a hook in the mating stall but ready for what? You may well ask!'

Again there was a round of applause from the balcony, together with some excited shrieks of delighted anticipation.

The spotlight went out again and this time the curtains of the balcony also closed, leaving the clients excitedly wondering what was being prepared down below. A shaded light came on in the arena enabling Emma to make out that Sabhu was now standing alongside her and had unlocked her lead from the playpen.

'Quickly!' he whispered to her. 'Get up on the table and kneel down. Move!'

He gave her lead a sharp tug and tapped her naked

buttocks with his whip. Too scared to argue, Emma did as she was told, scrambling awkwardly in the half light.

Sabhu now fastened her lead to a ring at the end of the table which, with its white sheet, now looked more like an operating table than a butcher's table. Then, holding her tight, he slipped a leather mask over her head. It completely covered her face. It was a horrible feeling, for the little slits, through which she should have been able to peep, were closed, and there was a zip fastener across her mouth, effectively muzzling her. At first she was terrified, but then she found she could breathe freely through two little holes in front of her nostrils.

'Now, you other girls,' Emma heard Sabhu warn Bluebell and Cowslip. 'You keep silent and quite still.'

Hooded as she was, Emma did not see the curtains of the balcony being drawn back. Nor did she realise that the table, on which she was kneeling on all fours, was now lit up by a spotlight, leaving the rest of the room, and the other girls, in darkness.

'Ladies,' came the voice of Ursula, 'we are going to start with perhaps one of the more traditional techniques used in the plantation mating pens. Here, for instance, we have a rather recalcitrant slave girl who has had to be chained down ready to be put to the chosen human stallion.'

There was a ripple of excitement from along the balcony.

'You may find this stallion rather unusual,' Ursula's cool voice went on, 'but of course a well-run slave-breeding plantation has to produce progeny of all sizes, shapes and colours to meet the varying demand.'

Oh my God! thought Emma.

There was an expectant hush.

'Stay still!' warned Sabhu, giving her a sharp tap with his whip across her exposed bottom. She gave a muffled cry and heard the women in the balcony laughing. Then she heard Sabhu walk towards the door. She heard him unlock it. He seemed to be letting someone in or was it more than one person? My God! She heard the patter of feet coming towards her, and then more laughter and applause from the balcony. Oh no!

'First,' she heard Ursula say, 'the girl must be introduced to her lover.'

Suddenly Sabhu undid the zip over her mouth.

'Tongue out!' he shouted. It was one of the words of command that Emma had learnt to obey instantly. Horrified she felt another tongue licking hers; it felt like a man's tongue but it seemed suprisingly small.

'Exchange kisses with your little lover!' ordered Sabhu, enforcing his order with another stroke of his whip. Little lover! Emma gasped, not understanding what he meant. It felt strange thrusting her tongue out through the slit and licking and kissing . . . who? She could hear Ursula and the other women laughing at her efforts.

'Now,' came the voice of Ursula, 'it's time for her to be aroused for the stallion whether she likes it or not! And for that, like stud farms for horse breeding, we use the traditional teaser.'

Suddenly, Emma felt another tongue – licking her from behind as she knelt on all fours. Horrified, she gave a jump.

'Keep still!' snarled Sabhu, giving her another stroke of the whip. She felt him part her buttocks to allow the tongue better access to her intimacies. Then he thrust her head down, making her raise her bottom. She felt him turn the table on its castors so that her bottom was now facing the balcony. Oh the shame of it!

'Tongue out and go on licking!' Sabhu shouted. She strained her neck up and again thrust out her tongue, finding that it was again in contact with another small tongue. Both sets of licks grew in intensity. Emma fought against it but she simply could not help becoming more and more aroused. Soon she found herself parting her legs. Then she felt a finger, a rather small but well-greased finger, pressing against her rear orifice. It penetrated her opening her up again.

The second tongue became more active; licking, sucking and stroking her wet beauty lips lubricating her as it explored her most intimate parts. Meanwhile she was still having to exchange licks with the first tongue as Ursula explained in a running commentary to her fascinated clients.

Who was it who was licking and kissing her? Emma wondered anxiously. And why did they seem so small?

'Come on! Come on, little bitch!' came a woman's cry from the balcony. Mortified, Emma recognised the voice of the Baroness. Yes, she was now indeed a little bitch; a very wet little bitch. Through the rubber breasts, she could feel hands, little hands, squeezing her own swelling breasts. She was trying to control her excitement, but in vain. Little drops of dampness were dripping on to the table. The audience was loving it.

'Get ready!' she heard Sabhu whisper, apparently to someone else. He was now standing by the side of the table away from the audience. Both tongues were suddenly withdrawn but there was no respite for Emma, as Sabhu pulled her head up by her hair with one hand and with his other hand brought the whip down across her back.

'Arch your back! Thrust your buttocks up!' he shouted. 'And now, wriggle!'

Appalled at her wanton eagerness to obey him, Emma now wriggled her backside towards the gallery. It must, she realised, be an arousing sight for the audience. She felt Sabhu's hands again part her buttocks and then she felt them guide into her what seemed to be a rather small manhood. What was it, for God's sake? She gave a muffled groan as she was penetrated from behind; a groan that was answered by laughs from the balcony.

She could feel the small creature, whoever it was, kneeling behind her on the table, gripping her by the waist like a dog mounting a bitch. He was pressing down on her back and crushing her, so as to draw himself deeper and deeper into her.

Then she felt Sabhu's hands on her belly thrusting down between her parted legs towards the little manhood. She jumped as he found her beauty lips. She felt as if she was just a plaything – a bitch on display.

'Bark!' ordered Sabhu from her side, giving her back a tap from his whip.

'Woof! Woof!' she obeyed.

'Woof! Woof!' came the response from behind her in what was clearly a male voice.

'Woof! Woof! answered Emma in a frenzy of excitement that was interrupted by a burst of laughter and applause from the gallery.

Then, suddenly, she felt the little manhood spilling itself into her.

Vaguely, she was aware that Sabhu was holding it to make sure it stayed hard   and inside her. Despite herself, and the feeling of quite appalling embarrassment of being on display on the table, she, too, suddenly climaxed. It had been so long!

But it was also so shame-making being treated like a performing animal   and being taken like one too. She loved mixed-up sex. Somehow in ordinary sex she never seemed to climax, never had a proper orgasm, and normally felt little. But this was different; quite different. Hooded, unable to see, and taken like a bitch, she was wildly excited.

As the throes of her climax eased, she thought of how she resented Ursula using her as a showpiece for her rich friends. A little *Hors d'Oeuvre* before the main action.

'You will appreciate that the advantage of keeping the girl hooded,' Emma now heard Ursula explain, 'is that she is unaware of to whom she has just given her favours.'

There was more laughter from the balcony. Then Ursula went on,

'In this way she will not be tempted to form any annoying and irrelevant emotional relationships that would distract from her continuing work on the plantation; hard manual work under the hot sun, chained to other girls all due to produce at about the same time. And, of course, irrespective of their condition and of their valuable little progeny, their overseer's whip will ensure that they all still work hard for their owner.'

Emma was horrified by the matter of fact tone of Ursula's voice. In her mind this mythical stage setting was becoming mixed up with reality. Thank God, she thought, she had been taken from behind. Was it a safe period for her? With no access to calendars, she could not be sure. Of course Sabhu and Doctor Anna knew all right, but they kept it to themselves the cruel swine.

'And, of course, here in real life,' Ursula went on with a chuckle, 'because the girl can't see her mate, she will remain, whether she likes it or not, emotionally attached to her beloved and wonderful dominating Mistress. Her Mistress is indeed the focus of her life. She thinks about pleasing her all day and dreams of being in her arms all night. She will do anything, submit to anything, just to be rewarded by a little pat from her Mistress.'

Emma gave a little gasp. How true that was! How unfair and yet how true!

Emma was now longing to lie down and sleep. But Sabhu jerked her collar chain. 'Wake up! And kneel up properly again.'

'Well, ladies,' once again came Ursula's laughing voice, 'you will appreciate that a good breeding overseer might be rather sceptical of the hit-and-miss aspect of this traditional technique, which is why we shall shortly show you some . . . shall we say? . . . more rigorous methods.'

Mystified by what Ursula meant, the still-hooded Emma once again heard the patter of feet withdrawing. Then, still kneeling on all fours on the table, her head down and her buttocks raised, she felt Sabhu fastening a chain around her waist. There seemed to be something metallic hanging from the front of the chain, something which she now felt being drawn up and over her beauty lips. It was cold and Emma gave a little shiver as it was held tightly over her beauty lips by another chain that went up between her buttocks.

She felt it being drawn taut and heard a click as it was fastened with a strong padlock to the other chain at the small of her back.

'Naturally,' she heard Ursula say, 'after taking such trouble over this slave, the breeding overseer would not want to risk her getting at herself and undoing all his good work.'

She heard Sabhu unfasten her collar lead from the ring at the front of the table. Then he removed the mask from her head. She blinked in the strong light.

'Get off the table,' Sabhu ordered.

Emma slipped off it and stood up. She was now standing facing the balcony, lit up by the spotlight. There was no sign of whoever had just taken her.

'Attention!' shouted Sabhu.

Automatically, as she had been taught, Emma parted her legs, bent her knees, clasped her hands behind her neck and looked straight ahead. To her embarrassment, she noticed that the women in the gallery were pointing to her hips and laughing.

'The breeding overseer will be taking no chances. He's now going to make sure that the breeding belt is firmly fastened,' explained Ursula.

Breeding belt! Emma gave a gasp. Was this for real or was it all just clever playacting   just a bit of fun? Had the audience not realised that Sabhu had ensured that she had been innocuously penetrated from behind?

She could certainly still feel the little manhood's discharges up inside her. But, innocuously placed or not, could she be sure that, in all the excitement, no little mistake had perhaps occurred?

Sabhu bent down and she felt him checking the tightness of something fastened over her beauty lips   the breeding belt!

Greatly daring, she glanced down and gasped in astonishment. A pretty, meshed, triangular-shaped, chromium-plated flexible pouch was now held tightly over her beauty lips by two short chains fastened to the top corners of the pouch.

These little chains were in turn fastened to another chain that went around her waist. She could feel another chain going up between her buttocks. It was obviously fastened to the bottom corner of the pouch and kept tightly secured over her beauty lips. She remembered hearing the click of a padlock. This third chain must be locked to the belt in the small of her back.

'Head up!' shouted Sabhu, angrily, giving her a sharp stroke of his whip across her naked buttocks. The audience laughed. Then he made her turn round so that the audience could see the padlock in the small of her back, and checked that it was securely fastened.

He nodded.

'Prance around the table!' he shouted, and gave her another stroke of his whip.

Obediently, still clasping her hands behind her neck and raising her knees up high in the air, Emma did as she was told, the shiny pouch still fastened tightly over her intimacies. But, being flexible, it was quite comfortable and did not rub.

'Many successful breeders insist on this post-coital exercise to get the seed really well distributed,' she heard Ursula explain to her clients with a cruel laugh.

There was another burst of applause from the balcony as the spotlight went out.

24

Doctor Anna's Treatment

The room was now in half darkness.

The only light came from under the closed curtains of the balcony. Out of breath from being made to prance round, and still feeling the creature's discharges under the breeding belt locked over her intimacies, Emma collapsed over the table.

'Stand up, white slut! You now act as Doctor Anna's assistant and theatre nurse,' whispered Sabhu, thrusting a nurse's green operating theatre apron and cap at her, and then rubber surgical gloves and a white gauze operating mask to strap over her mouth and nostrils.

'You put these on quick! And you then do just as she says, or you'll get the whip!'

He rushed off to the playpen where Bluebell was still happily playing the role of a little girl in the plantation rearing pens. Emma heard him strip off the girl's baby clothes and lift her up out of the playpen.

He carried her over to the 'operating table' covered with the white sheet. He tied her down on her back with a strap across her midriff. Her hands were pulled back over her head, and her feet positioned on the edge of the table with her knees bent. He thrust a gag into her mouth and fastened it with a strap that went round her head. Then he thrust a pillow under her hips so that her powdered, hairless beauty lips would be well displayed to the eagerly watching women.

He drew a small curtain across her body. She would not now be able to see anything below her waist. But her anxious raised face would be well visible to the gallery.

Moments later the curtains of the balcony parted and a spotlight lit up the scene of a naked and gagged Bluebell lying helplessly on her back on the table, with Emma standing alongside her, dressed, very realistically, as a theatre sister.

'Now, ladies, we are looking down into the plantation treatment room. However, this young lady cannot see what is happening. She does not understand why she has been brought here, nor, as she is gagged, can she ask. Unable to see what's going to be done to her, she will not realise the purpose of the treatment – the very special treatment – she is about to be given!'

What did Ursula mean, Emma wondered. She remembered what Ursula had said the day before, but surely if this was for real then Bluebell's friend, Daisy, would tell her afterwards? So why the secrecy? Emma looked up at the balcony. Daisy was no longer standing in attendance behind Ursula. Indeed there was no sign of her.

Emma gave a little gasp as she realised that Daisy must have been deliberately sent out of the balcony so that she would not see, or know about, what was going to be done to Bluebell.

The audience now saw that approaching the table was a woman dressed as a surgeon with a white gown, rubber gloves and a medical mask over her mouth. It was Doctor Anna. She was carrying a tray of instruments which she handed to Emma.

'We find that this advanced technique works best if the girl's body is first stimulated and in a realistic and natural way,' Emma heard Ursula explaining to her clients.

Wondering what Ursula meant, Emma then heard a patter of footsteps. Sabhu, she realised, must be bringing someone up to the table. She turned to look and, to her astonishment, saw that Sabhu was holding by the arm one of the toy boys who had been made to wear costumes for the dog show. Suddenly, memories of this unusual event came flooding back to Emma.

He was wearing his Pomeranian outfit and his small manhood was rapidly becoming erect, as he stepped up on to a stool between Bluebell's hanging legs, and reached forward to grip the girl's waist.

My God! thought Emma, was it he, and perhaps another one like him, who had so shamefully aroused her and then . . .? But her thoughts were cut short.

'Hold it and rub it between her legs while I get everything ready,' ordered Doctor Anna, taking the metal dish from Emma and laying it on the table.

'Go on,' whispered Sabhu. 'Do as you're told!'

Watched by Ursula and her delighted clients, Emma hesitantly reached forward and gripped the little manhood. Gently she began to rub it up and down between the beauty lips. It was appalling, she thought, for the girl was clearly becoming aroused although, because the curtain was drawn across her body, she could not see what was happening.

Meanwhile, the doctor had opened a medical vacuum flask. Out of the corner of her eye, Emma saw that she seemed to be loading a special type of syringe. The doctor now came forward, the syringe in her hand.

Sabhu waved the little creature away. Reluctantly, he stood back.

'What you have just seen,' came the voice of Ursula, 'was a little preliminary. A little old-fashioned warming up or teasing, to make sure that the girl's body is receptive. We don't want to waste the doctor's expensive treatment!'

Appalled, Emma turned her head away as Bluebell uttered another little cry. Was this all a game, a sort of grown up 'doctors and nurses', or was it for real?

Moments later, Emma jumped, as the doctor suddenly called out in a sharp tone of voice: 'Tray!'

Emma held the metal tray up to her. The doctor dropped the now empty syringe on to it.

'Of course,' she heard Ursula laugh, 'we don't want to put all our eggs in one basket – if you will excuse the pun. And what we are going to produce is very valuable in certain parts of the world, so it's important to achieve a left and a right, to use a shooting metaphor!'

The audience joined in the laughter, and Emma saw that

there was even a little smile on the normally grim face of the doctor as she bent down and picked up another syringe. Bluebell gave another little cry as the process was repeated.

There was a pause while Doctor Anna examined the girl. Satisfied, she raised her head and nodded.

Of course, in this case, what you have seen is merely half the treatment,' came Ursula's cruelly laughing voice. 'Useless in itself, but now in position and ready to meet the second half!'

Sabhu now waved the little creature forward again. His manhood was still erect.

'Insert it,' Doctor Anna ordered Emma. 'Now!'

Sabhu was already holding the girl's beauty lips apart. Bluebell gave a little shriek of protest as the dog-boy eagerly pulled her hips towards him, and this time Emma nervously guided the now rock-hard manhood firmly into the girl's body.

The toy boy was panting as he thrust in and out like a copulating animal. Emma longed to pull him away to save poor Bluebell, but Sabhu was standing behind her, his whip raised.

'Hold it inside her!' he shouted, giving Emma a slash with his whip.

Nature was now taking its course as the little creature continued to pump away, and soon Bluebell, too, was panting with excitement and giving little cries of ecstasy. Emma wondered if it was he who had earlier climaxed inside her and, if so, whether this had simply been intended to get rid of his pent-up desire and so enable him to prolong the arousal of Bluebell. Or was he instead the other creature, with whom she had merely had to exchange licks and kisses? If so, had he been deliberately kept fresh for this scene?

Oh, how clever they all were, she thought bitterly: Ursula, Doctor Anna and Sabhu. They had merely used her body to make this scene more effective. Was it really just a scene? Once again she wondered whether it was all merely an erotic game – or was it for real?

Suddenly, the little creature climaxed, his seed flooding into Bluebell. Seconds later, with a cry of pleasure, Bluebell too, climaxed. The dog-boy collapsed over her belly for a moment and then withdrew.

Sabhu now stepped up. In his hand was a shiny breeding belt, just like the one he had already strapped on to Emma. Deftly, he began to fasten it over Bluebell's loins.

'The two halves are now well on their way to meeting each other!' Emma heard Ursula say. 'But once again, we don't want the girl interfering with what is going on – even if she doesn't yet know about it. Last time it was all just natural a hit or miss affair. But this is an expensive use of medical technology. All the more reason for making sure the girl can't interfere with . . . nature!'

Emma was shocked and yet could not also help being fascinated. Poor Bluebell, being used in this way. Ursula and her clients were laughing and applauding as the curtain was drawn and the lights went out. As for Bluebell herself, Emma saw that she was looking relaxed with a gentle smile on her lovely face, as if ready to sleep.

'The next scene, ladies,' announced Ursula, 'shows another girl being treated in a different way; one I think that will appeal to several of you for there is no male present!'

The spotlight came on again, this time lighting the helpless figure of Cowslip, swaying slightly as she hung from her hook. She had been blindfolded and gagged.

She was watched over, as usual, by the dreaded figure of Sabhu, whip in hand. It made an erotic and dramatic tableau.

'This position is, of course, an ideal one for giving a slave the desired treatment. She can't interfere with what is being done to her and, in any case, being blindfolded and gagged, she does not even realise just what is being done!'

There was a pause and then, slowly, Sabhu raised his whip. There was another pause and then he brought it down across the unsuspecting woman's exposed buttocks, which were gleaming white and shining in the bright light.

There was a muffled scream of pain from Cowslip. The audience laughed.

'The overseer usually finds, in these cases, that a little preliminary thrashing gets the blood going and makes the girl's body more . . . receptive.'

A burst of cruel laughter greeted Ursula's explanation, as Sabhu raised his whip again.

'And therefore,' continued Ursula, 'improves the chances of a successful outcome to the treatment.'

Four times Sabhu brought his dressage whip down, and four times the watching ladies heard Cowslip's muffled screams as she writhed helplessly on her hook. Then Sabhu put his hand between her legs, looked up at the balcony and nodded. Out of the darkness stepped Doctor Anna, followed once again by Emma, still dressed as a nurse and carrying another tray of sterilised instruments and a large medical vacuum flask.

The doctor parted Cowslip's hanging legs. 'Tray!' she commanded.

Once again, an appalled Emma held up the tray and watched in horror as the doctor picked up first one and then another of the already carefully prepared syringes.

Little muffled cries from behind Cowslip's gag were greeted with laughter from the gallery.

Doctor Anna bent forward again to examine what had been done. Moments later, evidently satisfied, she stepped back and began to busy herself with the vacuum flask.

'You will remember,' again came the voice of Ursula, 'that in the last scene, after the girl had been prepared, she was mounted by a delightful little creature.'

There was now complete silence in the gallery. What was coming next?

'However,' Ursula went on, 'many Mistresses, whilst wanting to experience the thrill, and feeling of power, of having a girl put into an interesting condition, ready to produce two exceptionally valuable progeny, nevertheless, do not want her to be mounted, as we have just witnessed, by a male.'

There were murmurs of agreement in the gallery. Not all had found the previous scene to their taste.

'Well, these days, we can arrange things so that the girl

is indeed not touched by any male – large or small. Instead it is her own Mistress who plays the male role!'

Their curiosity aroused, the women were now eagerly whispering to one another.

Ursula paused for a moment before continuing: 'In this case, I must thank one of my clients for agreeing to take on the . . . shall we say . . . paternal role?'

The astonished watchers in the gallery now saw that the doctor appeared to be loading not a syringe but a dildo, complete with realistically hanging testicles. The substance was quite innocuous but would feel just like the real thing.

There were gasps from the gallery and then again came Ursula's voice in a cold matter of fact tone: 'Fortunately, our doctor friend has a good stock of suitable male and female . . . material. These two materials, of course, only need to meet each other in the right environment for our objective to be achieved and by what better way than by what you are about to witness?'

There were laughs and claps as Doctor Anna held up the now loaded dildo.

'And now comes our paternal lady!' laughed Ursula as, into the spotlight down below, walked Her Excellency!

Emma gave a gasp of horror at seeing her again. She must, Emma realised, have been quietly led down from the gallery whilst the rest of the audience was watching the preliminaries. She was still wearing her brightly coloured robes over her huge body. But, as the doctor holding the dildo approached her, Sabhu gripped Emma and thrust her down on to her knees at Her Excellency's feet.

'Get under and lick!' he ordered, giving Emma a smart tap with his whip across her buttocks to make certain she obeyed – and with alacrity.

With a yelp of pain, Emma quickly put her head under the woman's robe. Immediately, she felt the woman's hands pressing her head to her already moist intimacies. Fear of Sabhu's whip overcame Emma's repulsion and she applied her tongue.

Suddenly, she was thrust out of the way by Sabhu as the doctor, discreetly parting Her Excellency's robes, deftly strapped the dildo on to her now well-aroused loins. Meanwhile, Sabhu had gripped Emma by the hair and now pushed her face down between Cowslip's legs and on to her intimacies.

'Lick!' he again ordered.

Soon, an aroused Cowslip was moaning with pleasure and then, once again, Emma was thrust out of the way as Her Excellency, her robe parted, advanced on Cowslip. There was a ripple of laughter along the balcony, as she now thrust deeply and repeatedly down into the madly wriggling Cowslip.

'Take it, you white bitch,' Her Excellency suddenly screamed ecstatically, as she reached down and squeezed the hollow rubber testicles. There was a muffled scream from Cowslip as she felt a strange liquid shoot into her, and then the spotlight was extinguished.

25

Daisy Disappears

Down below in the arena, Sabhu called Emma over. She was still shaken by all that she had seen.

'Now you listen to me, white girl,' he muttered menacingly, 'and you listen carefully. The Mistress, she not want Bluebell and Cowslip to guess what was done to them here, nor what Doctor is planning to do to bring on their milk. Nor does she want Daisy to learn what will happen when she goes to North Africa. They only know truth if you tell them. So one word from you, one little hint, and you get the biggest thrashing of your life!'

Terrified, Emma saw him raise his long dressage whip and bend it back with both hands.

'I shall enjoy beating you, you stuck up girl, but by God you'd better not talk! Remember, one word, one little hint from you or one from them that they know what happened and why, and this whip will be waiting for you. Understand? Answer me!'

Scared out of her wits, Emma could only whisper, 'Yes, Mr Sabhu, sir!'

'Right!' replied Sabhu. Then, carefully locking the door of the arena after him, he went up to the balcony to bid the clients goodbye, or rather as he would suggest, *au revoir* – and to collect the generous tips that the thrilled women would be only too keen to thrust into his hand.

Left alone with the other women in the half-darkened arena, Emma saw that Bluebell was struggling to get off the table. Oh, how she pitied the beautiful young girl. She longed to tell her what had happened and to console her but Sabhu's terrifying threats were still ringing in her ears.

No, she knew she would never dare to say one word to her nor to Cowslip either.

Looking at Bluebell, Emma almost felt as though she loved her. She longed to put her arms around her. But she did not dare to do as Bluebell, she knew, was Ursula's prize pet.

Back at her house again, Ursula had instructed Sabhu to clean the girls up and put them back in their cages, having first put their wrist and ankle manacles on again.

'And we'd better put them back into their proper Bikini-belts. Those shiny metal pouches look good at the display but I'd rather have them back in their electronically-controlled devices. Doctor Anna's bill for that performance is going to be pretty high, so I don't want those sluts getting at themselves and giving themselves pleasure. They're to be kept frustrated.'

'Of course, Madam,' Sabhu said with conviction. 'You can rely on me for that.'

'Good,' said Ursula, frowning. 'Now several of this afternoon's audience will be coming here over the next few days to enjoy one or more of the girls. So just make sure you put the fear of God into them so that they really try to please clients.'

Sabhu smiled. 'That's just why I always carry my whip, Madam. It keeps them all really scared and on their toes.'

'Good!' laughed Ursula. 'But in particular I want Emma to please the African lady, Madame M'tout Korema, when she comes here this evening.'

Indeed, it was a petrified Emma, struggling hard to hide her revulsion, who was put through the full gambit of the words of command printed on the little card that Ursula had handed to Her Excellency; she held the little card in one hand while lying back and enjoying Emma's attentions.

So delighted was she, in fact, that she was now determined to persuade Ursula to let her take Emma back to Africa for a spell in her palace, for a little discipline, and to show her off as her servant girl to her friends.

Ursula had been delighted with Her Excellency's reaction but did not say yes – not yet! Her plans for getting her picture back were indeed coming into shape.

It was time, Ursula decided, to test Emma's state of training herself and to have her brought to her bed.

Emma was beside herself with joy. Thrilled, she strained every nerve to please her beloved Mistress as Ursula put her through the standard words of command, delighted to see how well Sabhu had trained her.

Twice, Emma raised the vibrating little rubber knobs of her belt and wriggled madly to bring her Mistress to an exciting climax whilst feeling nothing herself. Indeed, Ursula was so pleased with Emma's performance that, strapping on her dildo, she sent for Sabhu to take off the girl's belt. Overcome with gratitude, Emma flung herself at the feet of her adorable and wonderful Mistress, kissing them abjectly, whilst Ursula stood over her, her little cane in her hand and her dildo jutting out masterfully.

Ursula smiled as she looked down at the grovelling Emma. How well Emma, like all her girls, responded to the excitement of strict discipline and of being kept frustrated. It really was a very simple and yet highly effective regime for young women – and, remembering Cowslip, for not such young ones too!

Holding Emma down beneath her, Ursula used her dildo to take her as a man would, making the girl cry out with a mixture of pain and pleasure. She thrust in and out of the wriggling little creature until she felt her own climax approaching again.

Still holding the girl down with one hand, she lowered the other and then, at just the right moment, squeezed the dildo's testicles. A jet of sticky warm cream shot into Emma, making her give a sudden jolt of surprise and then a violent wriggle of sudden protest and horror as she remembered how Her Excellency had used a loaded dildo to give Cowslip the secret 'treatment'. They were movements, however, that brought Ursula to the very heights of pleasure.

But horrified or not, Emma could not now control her own arousal. 'May I come for my Mistress?' she pleaded in abandoned excitement.

'Yes, little girl, yes,' grunted Ursula as she felt another climax upon her. 'Now!'

Both women collapsed in each other's arms.

For Emma it was her first climax time since she had been abducted from her home and brought back to Ursula. Oh the relief! Oh the excitement! Oh how she loved her Mistress!

It was indeed a satiated and exhausted Emma, once again locked into her Bikini-belt who, an hour later, crawled, under Sabhu's supervision, back into her cage, watched jealously by the other silent women.

A few weeks had passed since the highly successful performance in the strange arena behind the picture gallery. Not only had the actual spectators been impressed, but the word had got around. A steady stream of new lady clients had come to buy Ursula's pictures and to enjoy her girls. Several had also made arrangements for Doctor Anna to 'treat' their own girls.

It was decided that the girls who had been subjected to the staged mating display should start a course of pills that, to both women's surprise, would quickly bring on a production of milk. Ursula smiled to herself as she imagined how her girls would react, thinking that they were in such a condition. Ursula was thrilled with the exciting new games she had developed with the ingenious Doctor Anna. She decided that it was time to rest her girls for a couple of days whilst she herself went off abroad on some rather special business taking Sabhu with her.

She wanted to reward her girls by giving them a change from keeping them locked up in their cages and, when a horrified Sabhu protested, she cut him short. 'No, Sabhu, you're wrong. You may now be earning much more in tips, but to modify the old proverb, "all work and no play, makes my girls dull and boring for the clients!" Don't worry, you'll earn even more when you come back,' she assured him.

But Ursula was worried about Cowslip who had, of course, realised that she had been mounted in the arena by someone strange. Was she now beginning to suspect it was all a ruse to earn Ursula more money? Certainly she seemed to be in a very irritable state and Sabhu had reported that he had seen her, on the monitoring television that covered the cages, looking sullen and muttering to herself.

Ursula thought carefully. If Cowslip was already beginning to suspect the truth about what had been done to her then she might, in her halting English, try to warn Bluebell that perhaps something similar had been done to her too, or even try to escape. So Ursula agreed to a compromise with Sabhu.

Cowslip was to remain locked in her cage while they were away. The other girls, however, were to be allowed to relax under the more friendly supervision of her Caribbean maid, Babindu, in what Ursula called her nursery wing. This was a comfortable girls' playroom, complete with a row of little cot beds and a bathroom. Babindu would also, of course, be responsible for feeding and watering Cowslip.

Emma was thrilled when she and Bluebell, together with Daisy, were taken out of their cages and put in the playroom. There was still an electronic lock on the door and bars on the windows, but the regime was much more relaxed. Sabhu had allowed them to take their baby dolls with them, and there was even a video on which they could play a selection of children's tapes – and a telephone. No outgoing calls could be made from it, but the girls were thrilled when Babindu explained that their adored Mistress would be able to ring them while she was away.

They still did not, of course, have newspapers, calendars, radios or television. But, Emma realised, they would at last be free to talk.

Indeed, as they played with their baby dolls, the three girls were soon chattering together – or rather struggling to do so, for although Daisy spoke a little English, Bluebell's command of the language was minimal.

Emma, of course, was wondering whether she should, using a mixture of mime, drawings and simple English, tell Bluebell what had apparently been done to her. How could Ursula have allowed the doctor and Sabhu to do such dreadful things to this lovely girl whilst she was gagged, chained down and unable to see what was happening to her? Would it, perhaps, be kinder to say nothing, and just let nature take its course? Emma, in her typically naive way, did not, for one moment, suspect it was all a staged pretence by the ever-cunning Ursula.

Anyway, she kept remembering not only Sabhu's threats about what he would do to her if she said one word to Bluebell about what had happened, but also what Ursula had said, taking her aside, just before she left.

'Now Emma, you're the only girl who actually saw what happened to Bluebell and Cowslip in the arena, and I'm trusting you, whilst you're allowed to rest in the playroom, not to tell Bluebell. Although she's going to be very excited when she realises the truth, she'll only start to fret and anyway it's much more exciting for the clients if she doesn't know. So I want her to be kept quite ignorant about it all for as long as possible just as Daisy will be. So woebetide you if you spill the beans!'

Scared of talking to Bluebell, as she was longing to do, Emma instead had to listen in silence as Bluebell, delighted at last at being able to talk, described in her broken English her surprise when she suddenly noticed that her breasts were slightly swollen.

Sabhu had pacified her, saying that there was nothing to worry about and Doctor Anna had given her some strange pills to take.

Bluebell also described her astonishment two days earlier when Sabhu had, as usual, strapped the exciting cups of the milking machine on to her nipples and little jets of milk had started to spurt into the bottle marked '1'. Indeed, very strangely, milk had mysteriously begun to flow – much to the delight of Ursula and of her clients.

Haltingly, she explained how thrilling it was. Moreover, being in milk had meant being taken out of her cage and presented to her Mistress at least once a day. It had been so exciting giving her milk to her Mistress who was now treating her more than ever as her favourite girl and the clients had loved it too.

Moreover, Bluebell haltingly went on, the Mistress had told her that when in future Doctor Anna came to the attic to make her weekly inspection of the girls, she and Cowslip would be taken downstairs to be paraded in front of a line of seated and admiring clients who would have come specially to see her. The idea made her feel very special and important.

But she still did not understand the reason for all the interest in her, nor for how she was in milk. When, greatly daring, she had asked Sabhu about it, he had angrily replied that it was none of her business. He had even beaten her for asking a question without permission.

But, locked in her cage when not taken out to give pleasure to Ursula or her clients, and prevented by her Bikini-belt from getting at herself, she had had to admit that she was finding it all increasingly, and strangely, exciting.

Emma smiled as she looked at the way Bluebell was innocently holding her baby doll to herself with a much increased passion.

Again Emma could not help smiling as she looked at the increasingly prominent blue veins on the girl's already swelling breasts. Doctor Anna's treatment had been very effective. She felt quite jealous.

Daisy had been listening to what her friends had been describing.

'Ah, yes,' she said. 'It all reminds me of two of the Mistresses favourite sayings: "Life is stranger than fiction!" And the . . . how you say it? . . . Ah yes: "The maternal instinct, once aroused, is very strong!" '

She paused, collecting her thoughts and then went on, speaking in English slowly and with difficulty: 'Many things in life we start off hating. School and then working. Soon you start to enjoy them. I not understand, but I now love being my Mistress's slave.'

Daisy was now telling them how Ursula had just told her

that she had arranged for Sabhu to take her out to the Saudi Arabian Princess's special residence in North Africa. And, she added proudly, Doctor Anna would specially come out to look after her in a strange land.

'It all shows how the Mistress really cares about me,' she said proudly, adding: 'More than about you two!'

Poor kid, thought Emma. How she would be shocked when she learnt the truth about life in the harem! But thank God that horrible German doctor would be away for a while, too. It was her influence over Ursula, and her desire to continue the experiments she had made in prison camps for young women in Eastern Germany, that had caused so much trouble.

That night, Babindu, taking pity on Daisy and Bluebell and thinking it no harm, just for one night, unlocked their belts. They were thrilled. 'Me too! Me too!' Emma had begged. But Babindu had ignored her. The two Eastern European girls were nicely submissive but Emma, she knew, spelt trouble.

Daisy and Bluebell slept together and Emma felt utterly excluded. All night she could hear them, in the bunk below hers, kissing, licking, making love to one another, laughing and crying. Her own cot vibrated with their love making. Driven half mad with frustration, she tore at her own belt in vain. It was so cruel of Babindu!

She now longed for Bluebell so much. But she would have to hide her love from Ursula, for Bluebell was a special favourite.

It was strange, she thought; she had often been present with a man and a woman making love and had never felt jealous. But she felt sick with jealousy whenever Ursula chose another girl for her bed, or when she had to watch or hear other girls making love. Perhaps it was because, basically, other girls excited her more than men. Envy of a manhood was something that Emma did not suffer from.

The following morning, Babindu carefully locked Bluebell and Daisy back into their Bikini-belts. Then, with Ursula and Sabhu still away, the girls were left to themselves in the equally carefully locked nursery. Bluebell helped Daisy pack for her forthcoming journey and Emma just lazed about. It was, she thought, a lovely feeling just relaxing and talking, or trying to talk, to kindred spirits. Despite her belt and the locked door, Emma was feeling as free as a bird. In this circle she felt accepted. These girls were her friends now.

She felt closer and closer to Bluebell and she was thrilled at the thought that when Daisy left she would have Bluebell to herself. Indeed, that very afternoon, Daisy was suddenly collected by a grim-faced Doctor Anna to be prepared for her journey. She came into the room, gripped Daisy's arm and led her out, ignoring Bluebell and Emma.

Poor Daisy had not time even to kiss her friends goodbye. She gave them a rather sad little look and then was just whisked away. The door was locked behind her.

26

While the Cat's Away

Emma put her arms around Bluebell. 'Don't be sad,' she soothed. 'I'll look after you.'

Bluebell, missing her friend, Daisy, was not at first very responsive, but Emma continued to kiss her.

'Now lie down and rest,' she said.

The pink had now returned to Bluebell's cheeks and she looked quite beautiful. Emma felt madly guilty that she had been forced to help Doctor Anna give the treatment and then to hold the little creature's manhood inside her. It was a shocking thing that had been done to innocent little Bluebell.

The girl was now lying on her cot with her beautiful large bosom in full display. The blue veins were now certainly very visible, thanks to Doctor Anna's special treatment.

Emma could not help jealously thinking how wonderful it would be if she herself could be in milk too. How delighted Ursula would be and how she, too, would be in great demand with the clients. With Cowslip also now coming into milk, she herself would be the only one not in milk. It was unfair! She wanted to be in milk, too.

Emma kissed the girl's nipples and they began to grow hard. Bluebell was only nineteen, so her breasts were beautifully ripe and wonderfully firm. The more Emma played with the girl's nipples, the more she could see her lovely breasts swelling.

Soon, Bluebell was very aroused. She was indeed an excitable little girl, which was probably why Ursula had chosen her in the first place. Ursula, Emma knew, had an uncanny knack of recognising girls who were submissive and over sexed: girls who, like herself, longed to be dominated and who needed sex not just once a day but as often as possible; girls who would become her love slaves; girls who became frantic with desire when kept frustrated by their Bikini-belts.

Emma put her mouth down to suck one of Bluebell's erect little nipples. Soon she was rewarded with a little sweet tasting liquid, for Bluebell was now in milk! Eagerly she sucked at both nipples and soon achieved a little regular flow – whilst Bluebell called out with pleasure and astonishment. It was thrilling for them both. No wonder that the clients would pay extra for a girl in milk!

Emma was delighted with the effect that she was having on Bluebell; her legs were now spread wide apart and she was rolling her hips in frustration and squeezing her breasts and pulling in vain at the belt that so effectively covered her intimacies.

Suddenly, Emma saw something lying in the corner of the room. She could not believe her eyes. It was the key to their Bikini-belts! It must have fallen out of Babindu's pocket when she had bent down to pick up Daisy's little suitcase. Eagerly, Emma picked it up.

Soon, both girls were stepping out of their hated belts, laughing excitedly as they did so. They were both now stark naked. They kissed and fell into each other's arms before collapsing on to the cot bed. Emma put her hand down on to Bluebell's exposed and hairless beauty lips. They were wet with arousal.

'Please, Emma,' Bluebell cried, 'please lick me. Lick me hard!'

Emma longed to use a vibrator but, of course, these were forbidden in the nursery. Instead she tantalisingly used her fingers, touching the little beauty bud and then withdrawing again.

She watched fascinated as Bluebell's eyes glazed over and her breasts grew more sensitive, whilst her body heaved in eager anticipation. She was crying all sorts of obscenities and begging for Emma to take her. But Emma wanted to get Bluebell thinking only of her – so she would prolong the pleasure and anticipation.

Bluebell was screaming with frustrated excitement when suddenly the phone rang. Emma started like a little girl found doing something naughty. Hesitatingly she picked up the phone.

'So, Emma darling,' came the well-known voice, 'this is Ursula. I am ringing from Rome where Sabhu and I have just taken delivery of a very interesting piece of merchandise, which you'll meet very soon. Well, how are you? Are you being a good girl? Are you and Bluebell thinking just of me as you sit about strapped into your little belts? Now can I speak to Bluebell?'

Emma could see that Bluebell was in no way fit to talk. She could hardly speak herself. She wanted to say that Bluebell was in the loo, but in fact Bluebell was gasping with excitement – and Emma simply could not stop her. Ursula must have heard!

'So Emma,' came her cold voice, 'you're having fun, are you? With my little Bluebell! So you've both got your belts off have you? It's a case of while the cat is away the mice will play, is it? Well, I shall be looking into all this when I get back tomorrow, but meantime tell me out loud, just what you're doing. Go on! Go on, little girl!'

Too terrified to speak, Emma put her hand down again on to Bluebell's beauty lips, making her cry out in ecstasy.

'There, there, little Emma, you are a clever girl, aren't you! But have you beaten Bluebell yet? She adores the cane when she's coming. You'll find one in the cupboard. Use it and make her wet herself! I want to hear her scream. Plug in the tape recorder to the telephone and put it on "Extra Hearing" so that I will be able to hear it all properly – and then you can keep the tape for me.'

Bluebell was looking so flushed and so carried away that Emma wasn't sure whether beating her would be such a good idea or not.

'Emma!' shouted Ursula down the telephone. 'Beat her! Beat her, but make sure that you don't come yourself. Do you understand?'

Emma found the cane and gave Bluebell a terrific beating on her bare bottom. The red marks made Emma very excited herself. She did it again and this time also put her fingers between her own wet beauty lips. Gosh, this was exciting!

'Pull my nipples! Gently! Suck them!' she heard herself crying to Bluebell, who was herself about to explode in a multiple climax. The beating had indeed been just what she needed. Emma, too, was making herself come. She thought about Ursula on the phone. She could hear her Mistress shouting on the telephone loudspeaker, 'Emma! Emma! What are you doing?'

But Emma didn't care by now. She gave Bluebell another two strokes. Bluebell was in ecstasy, her face bright red and her eyes bulging. The sight of her, together with the physical release of thrashing her, made Emma explode. She cried out in her ecstasy.

'You'll pay for this, you bitch!' came the furious voice of Ursula. 'I told you you were not to come!'

But Emma and Bluebell had fallen upon each other. They were about to lick off each other's wetness, when suddenly Emma remembered the telephone. 'Oh, Ursula! Sorry! What did you want?' she said in a cocksure voice, now feeling thoroughly satiated.

'Just you wait until I get back, you little trollop! I might have known that you couldn't take your sticky hands off my Bluebell while Sabhu and I were away. You'll both pay for this and although I don't know how you got out of your belts, I'm going to ring Babindu straight away to tell her to put you both back into them pretty damn fast – and back in your separate cages!'

Emma caught her breath, scared by the angry tone of Ursula's voice.

'And as you seem to be so keen on being unfaithful to me, I shan't now have any qualms about sending you off to Africa to be lent to Her Excellency for a spell. You'll like that won't you, you ungrateful little bitch!'

'No! No!' screamed Emma. 'Not that awful woman. You can't do that to me! No, please no! And anyway, what about my husband?'

'Ha! I've already told him you've got a chance to go and learn about African artifacts, and he's agreed that it would be a wonderful opportunity for you.'

'Oh, no please, please, no!'

'Oh, yes, Emma, oh yes! And if you ever want to see London again, you'd better do something useful for me while you're there.'

'What do you mean?' cried Emma.

But Ursula had already put the phone down.

27

Ursula Returns

It was the following afternoon.

Ursula and Sabhu had returned early that morning. Emma, together with Bluebell and Cowslip, was now kneeling at Ursula's feet in the drawing room. Sabhu, dressed in black as a butler, stood behind them holding the leads to their collars in one hand and his dressage whip in the other.

Emma and Bluebell were shivering with fear at the thought of their forthcoming punishment. In addition, Bluebell, like Cowslip, was holding a silver bowl of milk in her manacled hands. All the girls had lowered their heads respectfully and submissively.

The doctor's pills never failed, Sabhu ruminated, but what a pity that they only worked properly on girls who had first been given the doctor's 'treatment'. He had brought the milk machine up to the cages earlier and soon the pulsating cups had brought on a regular flow. Before long, first one astonished woman and then the other had filled a little glass bowl marked with her number. Only Emma had failed to respond to the pulsating and exciting cups. Oh, she found herself jealously thinking, if only she too had been treated by the doctor, she too could now be in milk.

Would Ursula have her done at the next little show behind the gallery? Oh, she hoped so. She looked longingly at her baby doll. How thrilling it would be to hold a real little baby to her breasts – a baby of her own! Oh how lovely!

But when the exciting machine was switched off, realism

set in. There would never, of course, be a real baby, never mind one she could hold to her breasts. She was just being brainwashed into thinking like that. Oh she felt so confused by it all!

Sabhu had laughed to himself as he saw her first throw her baby doll away and shake the bars of her cage in anger, and then quietly pick it up again and hold it to her breast. He recognised her symptoms. He had seen it all before!

Now was the moment of retribution as Emma knelt before the angry Ursula. What a fool she had been to seduce Bluebell behind Ursula's back. Ursula pointed at Cowslip and snapped her fingers. The older woman blushingly held up her small bowl of milk. Ursula took it and began to sip the milk.

'Umm . . . Umm,' she said. 'It's rather nice and strong tasting. I think the clients are going to like this. You're going to earn lots of money for your Mistress, Cowslip. And if you're a good girl you'll be allowed to come down and offer your milk to your Mistress as well.'

Emma saw Cowslip blush with pleasure. She felt a pang of jealousy. If only she was in milk, and able to come and offer it to her Mistress.

'And you'll love feeling your Mistress sucking your milk, won't you, Cowslip?' asked Ursula.

'Oh, yes, Madam, oh yes,' replied Cowslip with genuine fervour, her eyes glistening with delight.

Goodness, thought Emma, I'm not the only one who's been brainwashed. She heard an angry little gasp from Bluebell kneeling down beside her. Nor the only one who's jealous!

Ursula again snapped her fingers imperiously. 'Now let's try my little Bluebell's milk,' she said.

Eagerly, the girl held up her bowl.

'Oh, yes, very nice and sweet.'

It was Bluebell's turn to blush with pleasure and again Emma felt a pang of jealousy and anger that her breasts were still dry.

'Indeed it's so delicious that I'm going to let you off

being punished for being naughty with Emma. I'm sure she was the instigator of it all – and she's going to be severely punished.'

Oh, how unfair, thought Emma desperately. It takes two to tango!

'Indeed, Her Excellency has offered to pay a large sum just for the pleasure of beating you this evening, Emma. She wants to use one of the special rattan canes, like a carpet beater, that they use in her country on young women. Apparently it leaves no mark. She says it's called a 'girl warmer'. I shall enjoy watching her and you'll be earning your Mistress a handsome fee by being beaten. A fee of which you will not receive one penny. You're going to love that, aren't you Emma? And what a lovely revenge for me.'

Oh, my God, thought Emma. What a fool I've been to have ever thought I could get away with seducing Bluebell. Her fear of forthcoming pain was suddenly interrupted by Ursula ringing a little silver bell.

Instantly, a door opened and into the room danced a very pretty slim young girl, her eyes sparkling. She was olive skinned, like an Arab girl, and her long dark hair hung down her back in bejewelled and interwoven tresses.

There were no manacles on her wrists and ankles, Emma noticed jealously. She was wearing a long, transparent Arab caftan through which her otherwise naked body gleamed enticingly. Her pert little breasts pushed up suggestively but there was no sign of a belt – nor of any body hair.

Emma and the two other girls watched jealously as, with a confident laugh, the young girl, who could not have been more than seventeen, jumped up on to Ursula's lap and put her arms round her Mistress's neck. Never, thought the astonished Emma, had she dared to behave like that – Ursula would have been furious. But, instead of angrily pushing the girl away, Ursula hugged her like a new plaything.

The still kneeling girls, their feelings of jealousy at fever pitch, looked up in open-mouthed astonishment and anger.

Only Sabhu's warning jerks on their leads stopped them from rushing at the girl and scratching her eyes out.

'Oh, Leisha, my lovely little pet,' murmured Ursula, eagerly running her hands over the girl's caftan. 'And what do you think of my other little girls?'

The beautiful young girl looked down contemptuously at those chained and kneeling humbly at their Mistress's feet. She pouted, and then spoke slowly in a strong Arab accent. 'They're so big and ugly.' She pointed at Emma and Cowslip. 'And those two are so old!'

Big and ugly! Old! The little bitch! Emma could hardly restrain herself, as she felt Sabhu give her collar another warning jerk.

'Yes, I agree,' laughed Ursula then, to further stoke up the jealousy her new girl was provoking, she added, 'Oh, my darling, what a lovely little plaything you are. Quite the prettiest I've ever had. I'm going to keep you for myself and make these other ones work all the harder to please my clients.'

There was an angry intake of breath from the line of kneeling women.

'And, Emma, as well as letting Her Excellency thrash you this evening, I'm now going to punish you for making love to Bluebell without permission, by making love to my little Leisha in front of you.'

'Oh no,' gasped Emma.

But Ursula was already giving her orders to Sabhu. 'Put Bluebell and Cowslip back in their cages and take Emma to my bedroom. Fasten her by her lead so that she's kneeling on all fours by the side of the bed. I don't want her to miss a thing as I enjoy myself with my lovely new girl.'

Ten minutes later, a wild-eyed Emma was kneeling on all fours by the side of Ursula's large bed, her head held down by the lead being fastened to a ring attached to the floor. Emma could not help feeling excited by the idea of being so near Ursula's bed – a bed she had so thrillingly shared only a few days before. Under her belt she felt moist and aroused and very frustrated.

What a slut she was, she reflected. She just loved being dominated and controlled. But she was also a jealous slut and her jealousy hit fever pitch as Sabhu came into the room carrying Leisha, now dressed in a pretty red silken nightdress that was split right up the sides. He placed the Arab girl in the middle of the bed and with a smile put his fingers to his lips. But hardly had he left the room before Leisha turned and whispered contemptuously to the kneeling Emma, 'You now nothing in Mistress's eyes. She only now make love with little Leisha. You just work for her as a whore – and I'll tell her to have you whipped often.'

Emma was about to scream in protest when Ursula, now dressed in a long satin négligée, entered the room and without a word threw herself on to the bed. She took Leisha into her arms, smothering her with kisses. 'Darling!' Emma heard her cry. 'You're going to give me so much pleasure. It was worth trading that stupid Daisy to get you in return. You're quite a little princess.'

After several minutes of mutual kissing and stroking, Ursula knelt up and straddled Leisha, looking down at her lovely body, her buttocks raised just above the girl's now hidden face.

'Lick, darling!' came Ursula's voice. 'Reach up and lick!'

It was, Emma knew of old, one of Ursula's preferred positions one that gave not only exquisite physical pleasure but also, and equally importantly, a strong mental feeling of power. She herself was an expert at satisfying her demanding Mistress in this humiliating position. How could that chit of a stupid young Arab girl begin to rival her own expertise? And was Ursula really swapping or, even worse, buying girls from abroad when, all the while, Emma was ready and willing to serve her Mistress?

Jealousy again coursed through her veins as she heard Ursula cry out in pleasure. 'That's a good girl! Oh yes! . . Yes!'

28

Emma's New Mistress

It was later that evening when Sabhu took Emma out of her cage.

She was still brooding jealously over her Mistress's lovemaking with Leisha. Having to witness it all had been a terrible shock, but it was equally terrible being put back into her cage, still frustrated, whilst the Arab girl continued to lord it about downstairs like an honoured guest.

In her jealous rage, she had completely forgotten about what Ursula had said about Her Excellency. Now, suddenly, as Sabhu took her downstairs, it all came back. She longed to ask what was going to happen. 'Permission to speak, Mr Sabhu, sir?' she asked piteously.

'No!' was the curt reply.

She was taken in to one of the large bedrooms used by clients and told harshly to bend over the end of the bed and to grip the bedclothes. Then Sabhu unlocked her belt and took it off.

Moments later Her Excellency entered. The right hand sleeve of her long voluminous robe was rolled up to display a muscular looking arm. She was carrying what looked like a small carpet beater made of prettily interwoven bamboo with a flexible bamboo handle.

A smiling Ursula followed her into the room. 'Ah, Your Excellency,' she laughed. 'I see that Sabhu has Emma ready for your "girl warmer".'

Smiling, the fat African woman ran one hand over Emma's quivering buttocks and then down between her legs. 'She's excited already.'

'Yes, Your Excellency, these sluts just can't help becoming aroused at the mere thought of a beating!'

There was a sudden whistling noise and Emma screamed as the carpet beater landed painfully on her bottom. She felt a strange warming feeling spread across it.

Ursula clapped her hands with delight as a red rash began to spread across Emma's naked little bottom.

Moments later, the large African woman, her sleeve still rolled up, gave the sobbing girl two more strokes. Emma was now gripping the bedclothes desperately to prevent herself from putting her hand back to ease the pain. Sabhu, she knew only too well, always insisted on a woman who was being thrashed keeping quite still to absorb the pain properly.

There was a pause, and she felt Ursula's hand on her bottom. 'Yes!' she exclaimed, 'it's lovely and warm no wonder it's called the "girl warmer"! There are no ugly marks and it's made the girl soaking wet with excitement. You must let me have one of them before you go.'

Her Excellency's only reply was a grunt as she brought the 'girl warmer' down again.

'Well, we'll leave you now, Your Excellency. Enjoy the girl!'

It was a tear-stained and sobbing little Emma who, two hours later with her Bikini-belt firmly locked back in place, was standing in the attic on the red spot marked '4'. She was looking straight ahead and holding up, with both hands, the rubber pad over her beauty lips. Her legs were apart and her knees bent. Between her ankles she could feel the large brass bowl marked '4'. Like a sergeant major inspecting a recruit, Sabhu walked slowly round the still and silent girl.

He always liked to re-impose his authority on a girl after she had been with a client – and what better way than this? It was indeed a humiliating position for a girl to have to hold in front of her overseer - and one that tested her present state of discipline.

Emma did not dare to move a muscle. She tried to hold

her breath. Only the trembling of her naked breasts gave away her anxiety.

As he went behind her he noticed with a smile that she was clenching her buttocks tightly in the prescribed way and that a reddened flush had spread under the thin leather Bikini. She had indeed been well thrashed.

'Ready!' ordered Sabhu.

Not daring to look down, Emma adjusted the position of her bowl with her ankles and relaxed her muscles. Out of the corner of her eye she could see Sabhu's raised long dressage whip. No more beatings, please, she silently begged, desperately trying to get ready.

'Perform!' at last came the order.

Moments later, watched by the silent Bluebell and Cowslip from behind their bars, Emma was made by Sabhu to crawl back into her cage. As the little barred door slammed shut behind her with a clang, she picked up her baby doll and hugged it to her. She gave a little sob at the thought that the satiated, fat and repulsive Excellency would now be enjoying a glass of champagne with her Mistress – and with that spoilt little Arab bitch, Leisha. And to rub it all in even more, she knew that any minute Sabhu would be summoned to be given a large tip by a delighted Excellency.

Oh, how she hated them all! And yet . . . and yet, how exciting it was being Ursula's slave. It fulfilled her deep-felt need to be dominated. If only . . . if only she could be Ursula's only girl!

29

Emma is Given a Special Secret Task

The soft relaxing music was suddenly switched off. Emma quickly put down her doll and, through the bars of her cage, saw the attic door slowly open. In stepped Ursula, wearing a well-cut business suit.

There was a little gasp of surprise from the caged women, for such a visit was rare. Their Mistress might occasionally take a client up to the little balcony that faced the line of cages, but otherwise she left what went on in the attic to Sabhu.

There was a slight pause as Ursula looked down the line of silent women each gripping the bars of her cage; each smiling up at her Mistess coquettishly; each trying to catch her eye. Oh, the feeling of power! The sheer thrill!

Emma looked adoringly at her Mistress. How wonderful, she thought, that their kind Mistress should bother to come and see them. Then the smile was wiped off her face as the Arab girl, Leisha, stepped into the room. She was wearing a very expensive-looking short dress.

Smirking, she went up to Ursula and took her hand, proudly showing off to these half-naked white women that it was she who was now the Mistress's favourite and, moreover, that she was not subjected to the humiliation of being caged or having to wear a belt and manacles. Emma was overcome with jealousy. Oh, to be free like Leisha! Oh to be her Mistress's favourite girl!

Then she saw Sabhu come through the door. He was dressed in his tight white breeches and gleaming leather boots; his naked oiled black torso gleamed menacingly in the bright light. In his hand, as ever, he held his long dressage whip.

'Show respect!' he shouted.

There was the usual rattle of chains as, like well-drilled automatons, the women dropped on to all fours and lowered their heads to the rubber floors of their cages. Then, they silently thrust their tongues out below the bottom bar, like caged animals begging for titbits. It was a remarkable display of female obedience and discipline that further thrilled Ursula.

Emma had been too well-disciplined by Sabhu, and was too frightened of his whip not to thrust her tongue out, too. But the humiliation of having to do this in front of that smirking chit of an Arab girl was dreadful.

Sabhu smiled proudly. How well-trained and disciplined were the women in his charge. He glanced at Leisha. Doubtless he'd have her too when the Mistress had got over her present infatuation with her. It would be interesting to discipline such an exotic and spoilt creature.

Pleased, Ursula reached into her pocket and handed him a packet of little sweets. 'Give them one each,' she said.

A grinning Sabhu went down the line of cages putting a little sweet on each proffered tongue. Then he looked at Ursula. She nodded.

'Sluts!' he ordered and then paused. At last came the order they were so eagerly awaiting. 'Eat!'

Thrilled, the women all sucked and chewed their little sweets. Oh, how kind their Mistress was! Not like their cruel overseer, Sabhu, who hardly ever allowed them anything sweet – saying he liked to keep them slim and fit.

Ursula laughed as she saw the women all watching anxiously as Sabhu handed her back the little bag of sweets. How easy it was to train and discipline young women. Punishment and reward. Just as with little dogs. But it was time to get on with the purpose of her visit. She and Leisha went over to Emma's cage and sat down on comfortable little chairs that Sabhu hastened to draw up for them. Then he stood back behind them, his whip still at the ready.

'Numbers One . . . Two . . . and Three! Relax! he shouted. There was a rattle of chains as the girls sat up on their haunches, their manacled wrists meekly folded in their laps.

'Number Four! Breasts!' Sabhu commanded.

Surprised, Emma automatically obeyed the well-rehearsed order. Her eyes on Sabhu's whip, she hastily straightened up, clasped her manacled wrists behind her neck, and thrust her naked breasts through the bars of her cage.

'Well, little Emma, it's time that you and I had a little talk,' said Ursula reaching forward and stroking the proffered breasts as if trying to bring down her milk.

It was such a pity, she thought, that this girl, too, was not in milk. The trouble was that it was all just too complicated at present to let Doctor Anna put her into an interesting condition, like the other girls. Not only was the girl married, but Ursula wanted to use her for a special task.

Emma soon found herself giving little gasps of pleasure. She could not help thrusting her breasts forward. She wanted to cry out and beg her Mistress to go on, but with the sight of Sabhu's whip in front of her, she did not dare to break the strict rule of silence in the cages.

Ursula now began to rub the girl's nipples between her fingers and thumbs. Sabhu, she reflected, had done a good job in elongating them. They were now much more prominent – something that both she and her clients liked.

She heard Emma give a little moan of pleasure. How clever these belts of hers were, she thought. By leaving the breasts bare but covering the beauty bud, a modest level of arousal could always be induced, but not enough to make the girl climax. Of course, the television cameras would show if a girl was illicitly playing with her nipples in her cage, but even if she did, she would still remain frustrated.

'Now, Emma, you do love your Mistress, don't you?' she said, giving the girl's nipples an extra little rub with her fingers.

'Oh, yes, Madam, little Emma loves her Mistress.'

Overcoming the humiliation of Leisha's presence, the thrilled Emma lisped in the little girlish voice that Sabhu insisted on them using when allowed to speak to Ursula or a client.

'Well, your Mistress is pleased at the way you've settled down since you were brought here and caged.'

'Oh Madam!' lisped Emma, thrilled that her Mistress was pleased with her.

'Yes, you've been a good little girl and you've earned your Mistress a lot of money and Sabhu lots in tips.'

Yes, indeed, thought Sabhu thanks to fear of my whip!

'And you've nearly made up for all your naughty behaviour when you thought you could do what you like and ignore your Mistress. But your Mistress had you caught and brought back like a runaway slave for punishment didn't she?'

'Yes, Madam!' whispered Emma, contritely. Indeed, what a fool she had been.

'And now you know you'll never be able to get away from your Mistress's control, don't you?'

Emma nodded her head.

'And anyway, you love being under her control and having to do whatever she says, don't you?'

'Oh yes, Madam,' Emma cried. How true that was. Being controlled by her Mistress was the most exciting thing in the world.

'Good! And now you're to be able to show your love for your Mistress in a new way. You're going to earn your Mistress a lot of money and, at the same time, help her get back her famous stolen picture.'

'But how, Madam?'

'Well, I've told you I'm hiring you out as a maid servant, for a large sum, to Her Excellency for a few weeks.'

Emma gave a gasp of horror. She had almost forgotten about being sent to Africa. As nothing more had been said by Ursula she had assumed, to her relief, that the idea was dead.

'No! No! Not that! You've no right,' she cried out.

There was a sudden crack as Ursula angrily slapped

Emma's exposed breasts. 'How dare you speak to me like that you stupid little chit of girl! You'll damn well do as I say and you'll address me as "Madam" or you'll get another taste of Sabhu's whip!'

'I'm sorry, Madam,' whispered Emma, overcome by Ursula's anger and with the pain in her breasts. Oh, how she longed to rub away the pain, but she did not dare to unclasp her hands from behind her neck.

'I should think so!' answered Ursula. 'Now don't be a stupid little girl, Emma. You're going to do as you're told and as I want. And if you ever want to see England again, you'd better listen carefully. Just remember that it will be easy for you to just disappear without trace, once you're there and then I shall get an even larger sum for you! We'll just tell your husband you died of fever. Her Excellency could easily arrange for a false death certificate to be issued.'

'Oh my God!' gasped Emma.

'However, I don't suppose Her Excellency would appreciate the publication of certain photographs she knows I've had taken of her here. Call it blackmail if you like, but provided you do as I say, then I will use the threat of publishing them to ensure your safe return. But, as I say, only if you succeed in finding my missing picture which she has got somewhere in one of her palaces.'

Ursula paused for a moment.

'Well Emma, what is it to be: do I sell you permanently or do I just hire you out for a month?'

'Oh please, Madam, please . . . don't sell me. I want to come back. Back to you.'

'Very well, Emma,' said Ursula in a brisk tone of voice. 'Sabhu will show you pictures of the painting so that you can recognise it. As you will be out there as Her Excellency's white maid servant, you'll be taking out suitable maid's uniforms that will underline your subservient status to Her Excellency's friends. For instance, she says you'll have to wear a white maid's cap and white gloves at all times – and never touch her, or hand her anything, with your dirty little bare hands.'

Again Ursula paused while Emma took in what she had

been saying. A white maid! Maid's uniforms! A white cap and gloves! A subservient status!

Ursula laughed and turned to Sabhu. 'I think Her Excellency's idea of a white cap and gloves is something we might copy here – if not in the cages, then certainly when they're paraded in front of the clients.'

'Certainly, Madam,' smiled Sabhu. Another little humiliation for these stuck-up white sluts; 'I'll see to it.'

Ursula turned back to Emma. 'But your white cap's going to be rather special. A tiny little 'spy camera' will be sewn into it and Sabhu will teach you how to use it. It will then be up to you to find the picture and photograph it *in situ*, so that, when you return, I have proof that she has it.'

'But how long will I have to stay there?' wailed Emma.

'Until you've reported that you've found the picture and photographed it, of course,' replied Ursula, harshly.

'But how will I be able to do that?'

'I've arranged with Her Excellency to let you send post cards back to me to say that you are well. You're not, of course, to mention the word "picture" but, when you've found and photographed it, then you're to put the word "Eureka!", meaning "I've found it", in the text of a card. Then I'll make arrangements for you to come back straight away. Understand?'

Emma nodded. Her head was in a whirl.

Ursula stood up, still holding Leisha by the hand.

'And don't think of cheating by writing the word "Eureka" until you've found my picture. If you do, then not only will Sabhu thrash the living daylights out of you when you come back empty-handed, but it'll also be straight back to Africa for you, my girl and this time for ever!'

30

Africa!

Emma was sitting in a window seat of a big aircraft. She was dressed in a simple white blouse and blue skirt, as befitted a maidservant. She was also wearing the white gloves that Her Excellency insisted that a white maid-servant should always wear when serving her Mistress.

Between her and the aisle sat Sabhu. A little chain discreetly linked her left wrist to his right one. There was to be no escape.

Free from the overwhelming presence of Ursula, her thoughts turned to Henry – what would he think if he could see her now? Probably he'd just say it served her right for playing around with that bitch Ursula. Perhaps he was right. But the mental link that kept her tied to Ursula was so strong.

'She'll just have a little soup and a glass of water,' she suddenly heard Sabhu say to the air hostess, as he himself accepted a large tray of delicious food and fine wine. It was the first such food she had seen since being abducted from her home – and she wasn't being allowed any of it. Oh, how cruel!

Up in the front of the plane, and being treated as a VIP in the first class section, sat Her Excellency.

When they arrived at the airport, Her Excellency was whisked off in a large Citröen car. Two uniformed black guards took over charge of Emma from a grinning Sabhu, handing him a receipt and taking over her wrist chain. Emma could barely understand their heavily accented French. They led her to a van in to which Her Excellency's baggage was being loaded. They bundled her unceremoniously into the van as well and slammed the doors shut.

The President's country palace was several miles outside the town, surrounded by a high wall with one heavily guarded gate. Peering out through a little window in the back of the van, Emma sat crestfallen as she saw the iron gates being shut behind the van by gun-toting guards. Clearly there would be no escape here, either.

Bud did she want to escape? Did she dare to try? She remembered Ursula's warning about how she must first obtain information about the missing picture or risk being sold, disappearing for ever, apparently dead. No, she must go through with it all. She had no choice.

'Now, white slut . . .' came Her Excellency's harsh voice from the spacious bathroom next door to the luxurious bedroom. 'Come and wash me!'

It was the following day. Emma, dressed in just her white gloves, her white maid's cap, and a little white frilly pinafore that left her otherwise naked, was servicing her new Mistress.

From under the bedclothes Emma could hear several voices – men's voices. They were talking politics; the politics of ensuring that all opposition of Her Excellency's husband, the dictator, was ruthlessly crushed almost before it was mooted. Her Excellency enjoyed receiving her underlings in the secret police while relaxing in bed especially when a pretty white servant girl was pleasuring her under the bedclothes.

Emma had now been in Her Excellency's service for several days; days in which Her Excellency had thoroughly enjoyed showing off her half-naked white servant girl to her friends. It had been a humiliating time for Emma but also a frustrating one, for she'd seen no sign of the picture. However, the tiny camera sewn into her maid's cap remained undetected.

Emma felt Her Excellency adjust the loose bedclothes in the air-conditioned room. She felt cool air on her feet. She blushed as she realised that Her Excellency was deliberately, if apparently accidentally, displaying her white feet to the gaze of the much impressed, if astonished, men standing around her bed.

Moments later she was even more embarrassed when she felt Her Excellency's hand grip her hair under the bedclothes and firmly guide her head down over her huge belly to the spot where, she knew, her duty lay. Overcoming her disgust, Emma began to apply her tongue. The voices continued.

After a time, Emma was aware that the voices had stopped. She was alone with Her Excellency. Her hair was still tightly gripped, holding her down. Her face was wet with Her Excellency's juices. She could hear Her Excellency groaning with pleasure.

Her new Mistress lifted up the bed clothes to look down at the little white body that was giving her so much pleasure. To have a white woman in her power! To make her pleasure her! Oh the excitement!

'Lick, white woman!' she called out as her ecstasy approached. 'Lick, you white slut. Lick!'

It was minutes later. Her Excellency was lying back resting for a moment. But she knew she was still not satiated.

'Come up, slut, and lie on your back!' she ordered. The powerful woman knelt over Emma. 'Lick, white slut, lick!' she called out in a hoarse voice. This was her favourite position. Oh, the ecstasy was mounting again. She ground her body down on to the face of the woman lying helpless beneath her. Then, she turned around so that she was facing the girl's legs and the entire slender white body was laid out in front of her. She gripped the girl's arms. The soft little body was now wriggling in protest as she pressed down but she could still feel the obedient little tongue was active behind her. Oh the excitement!

'Lick, white girl, lick!' she cried out, as another climax went through her body like an electric shock.

Oh, there was just nothing like using and dominating a white slave woman!

Later, after a long session of vigorous love-making, Her Excellency allowed Emma the luxury of writing to Ursula.

Emma held out the postcard she had written to Ursula for Her Excellency's approval.

The large woman took it and read it suspiciously. '*I am well and having a lovely time and Her Excellency is being very kind.*' was all it said. No harm in that.

'I'll have it sent by our special diplomatic mail,' she said.

Three days later Ursula smiled as she read the card. She could imagine the sort of kindness that Emma was experiencing. But Her Excellency was paying a large fee!

Emma moved the heavy fan to and fro over Her Excellency's head. A pretty black girl, Emma's fellow servant girl, was doing the same from the other side of the chair in which Her Excellency was sitting talking to two African women friends. As usual, Emma found it almost impossible to understand their sing-song French.

Both Emma and the other servant girl were identically dressed like French maids on the stage, with frilly little short black dresses, stockings and high heel shoes, white caps and pinafores and, in the case of Emma, white gloves. The short black dresses flared out at the back displaying the girls' naked behinds.

There was, however, one rather strange difference in their dress, the significance of which Emma did not understand: sticking out from between the glossy black cheeks of the other girl's bottom was a bunch of long white feathers that curved over prettily behind her like the tail plumage of a cockerel. She seemed to be strangely proud of them as they swayed with her every movement, as if they denoted some sort of status. They seemed to be secured to a little silver plug thrust up the girl's behind. Thank Heavens, Emma had thought, I don't have to wear anything like that!

The two visitors kept glancing up jealously at Emma, as if thinking what fun it must be to have a pretty white servant girl. They could not help noticing the red patches on her bottom – clear signs of a recent encounter with Her Excellency's 'girl warmer'. Oh how exciting it would be to beat a white woman!

'His Excellency,' announced a servant.

Smiling, Her Excellency got up and greeted her husband. They lived separate lives now, for she was fat and ugly, but they were still too dependent, politically, on each other and on each other's families to split up. And anyway, what would be the point of doing so? Neither objected to the girls that the other kept and used – on the contrary, they often swapped them.

The dictator was a tall, brisk, severe-looking man with unsmiling eyes. He was dressed in a well-cut blue suit with a white shirt and a dark blue tie. He looked, for all the world, like a successful businessman – as indeed he was. He greeted his wife and then turned to her guests, who curtsied each in turn, and then left the room.

Emma looked at him as if hypnotised. With his cold, pig-like eyes and expressionless face, he was the most terrifying man she had ever seen – except perhaps for Sabhu.

He turned and pointed at Emma, saying something incomprehensible to his wife. Emma blushed.

'Put down your fan and come and stand here in front of His Excellency,' she ordered.

Nervously, Emma did as she was told. The contrast between her own skimpy dress and the formal suit of the dictator made her blush yet more. Then, following the example of the other women, she gave a little curtsey. The dictator for once gave a slight smile and said something to his wife.

'Bare your breasts!' ordered Her Excellency.

Appalled, Emma hesitated.

'Do as you're told – or I'll fetch the "girl warmer".'

Hastily, Emma pulled her skimpy dress down over her shoulders. Expressionless, the dictator reached forward to feel Emma's extended nipples. Then he stood back and sat down alongside his wife, again murmuring something to her.

'Lift up the front of your dress,' she ordered. 'Properly!'

Again, Emma blushed as she displayed her hairless beauty lips to the seated dictator. But he seemed to shake his head disparagingly, and made Emma turn round and bend over.

Emma felt his hands stroke her soft bottom and then part the cheeks. Horrified, she gave a little gasp as she felt him testing the tightness of her sphincter muscles.

He grunted and said something to Her Excellency. Then she felt his hands withdraw.

'Pick up your fan, and fan His Excellency! And do it properly, as you've been taught,' ordered Her Excellency.

Whilst the black girl continued to fan the woman, and Emma concentrated on the dictator, husband and wife were soon deep in conversation.

Suddenly, Her Excellency pointed at a little footstool in front of the dictator's chair. 'Kneel down and show His Excellency what a well-trained whore you are. Go on!'

Emma knelt down on the stool. Nervously, she lowered her head, the threat of the 'girl warmer' still ringing in her ears. The dictator and his wife had resumed their conversation. She wondered what she should do next.

Slowly, without interrupting his conversation, the dictator parted the bottom of his robes. Emma found herself now kneeling between his parted knees. Then, he parted his robes higher up and, not bothering to look down at Emma, simply pointed downwards.

Emma gasped at the sheer size of him. She had witnessed Africans before, but this one was exceptional. Still talking he snapped his fingers and again pointed at his groin. Obediently, Emma lowered here head. She almost choked as she took his huge manhood into her mouth.

A feeling of natural and utter submission flowed through her and she found herself applying herself diligently to her task.

Suddenly the dictator kicked her away. He got up and turned to go. He said something to Her Excellency, who smiled.

As Emma grovelled on the floor, trying to pick herself up, she thought she caught the word *élargissement*, or stretching. But she did not understand what he meant.

31

His Excellency's Helpless Plaything

Emma was attending on Her Excellency in her bath when later, four black pageboys came for her. They had often come for her companion, the black servant girl, taking her away rather mysteriously with the approval of Her Excellency, and then bringing her back two hours later looking rather chastened.

On this occasion, both girls were attending on Her Excellency in her bath. Emma was holding her soap and the black girl, naked except for her tail feathers proudly sticking out behind her, was holding her towel.

Emma had assumed that, as usual, the pageboys had come for her companion. She was very startled when she saw that it was at her that they were pointing.

Her Excellency smiled knowingly and nodded in approval. The four boys gripped her and led her away to another part of the palace. She tried to struggle free, but they were surprisingly strong.

They led her to a bathroom and made her kneel down on all fours. Two held her down and another parted her buttocks. Horrified, she saw that the fourth boy was holding the well-greased plastic end of a long rubber tube fitted with a small tap.

The tube led down from a large bottle on a shelf above her. The bottle had graduations on the side and contained a soapy-looking, green-coloured liquid.

Moments later, a horrified Emma gave a little cry. She tried to struggle free but her hands were firmly gripped.

There was nothing she could do. She felt a boy reaching down to put his hand on her belly. Then he grinned at his companion who was operating the tap and nodded.

Ten minutes later and the discomfort was all over. Oh, the relief! But, oh, the shame of having it done by these grinning page boys.

And they had not yet finished.

They now produced a pretty plume of white tail feathers, just like the ones the black girl wore. They were attached to a curiously shaped silver plug with an indentation round it so that, once inserted, her stretched muscles would grip it and hold it in place.

She could feel it stretching her. It was a horrible feeling. Horrified, she remembered what the dictator had said about *élargissement*. She was being deliberately stretched!

She tried to pull it out but the boys had fastened a tight chain through a little ring at the end of the plug – a chain that went round her hips, down between her legs, through the ring, and up between her beauty lips. It was then fastened back to the chain by a little padlock on her belly.

The boys laughed as Emma tried ineffectually to ease the plug. They laughed again as the white plumes of her tail feathers dipped and swayed with every movement of her loins as she tried to ease the discomfort.

Her Excellency also laughed when they brought Emma back to her with her tail feathers swaying prettily behind her.

Twice a day the four pageboys would come for her and take her back to the bathroom with the dreaded bottle of green soapy water and the long tube. There they would unlock the padlock on her belly, remove the plug, and insert the tube again.

But each time, after the tube had been removed and she had been judged to be sufficiently washed out, a slightly larger plug was then inserted, and the stretching process continued.

Finally, after three days, the boys seemed satisfied with her progress.

* * *

It was a huge, low-level bed that Emma was led towards later that evening by the four grinning pageboys. She was naked except for her white maid's cap and her white gloves. Her bottom was still red from a special application of Her Excellency's 'girl warmer', applied by her when the pageboys had come for her.

'You'll get it again if he's not satisfied,' she had said mysteriously.

Once again the pageboys had taken her to a bathroom next door and given her an enema, holding her down so that she had to accept a full ration.

Then, afterwards, they had carefully greased her and replaced the plug and plumage, but this time without the restraining chain.

Now, she saw, there was a large leather bolster lying across the foot of the bed and, half way up it, the lower half of a sort of leather-padded wooden stocks with one large half circle and two smaller ones. Above the bolster hung a steel hook linked by chains to a pulley.

Silently the boys motioned to her to kneel across the bolster.

Dumbly, too scared not to obey, Emma climbed up on to the low bed. The boys then silently thrust her head forward so that her neck was lying in the larger cutaway half circle. One of them held her head still and two of them held her wrists in the smaller cutaway half circles.

The fourth boy now lifted up the hinged matching half of the stocks. It was also leather-padded. He lowered it across the back of her neck and across the back of her wrists, before fastening the two ends together with a little catch.

The other boys now released her head and wrists and, equally silently, fastened a little pole behind her knees. The ends of the pole fitted into little slots on either side of the bed.

Then they fastened a leather strap tightly around her hips. It must have had a ring in the small of her back for she heard the pulley being turned and the hook pulled down until it slotted into the ring in the belt. Satisfied, they nodded to each other. One of them dimmed the lights and each retired to a different corner of the now darkened room.

Emma was now held rigidly kneeling on all fours on the edge of the bed with her buttocks and the pretty white plumes of her tail feathers raised high in the air. Her head and shoulders were held down on the bed by the leather-padded stocks.

Whether she liked it or not, she realised, she was now offering herself completely and helplessly. She must look a very erotic sight, she thought, with the long white feathers sticking up from between her buttocks. She felt utterly debased and extraordinarily sensual.

There was a long and silent pause. Then, Emma heard the door open. She tried to look round but with her neck tightly gripped by the two halves of the stocks she could only see the wall ahead of her and the top of the bed.

She heard heavy footsteps approaching the bed behind her. There was the noise of robes being cast off and one of the pageboys slipped forward to pick up and carefully fold the discarded clothing.

A man, she realised, a naked man must be standing at the foot of the bed immediately behind her buttocks. It must be the dictator. She was going to be taken by the dictator. How awful!

But the dictator himself was enjoying the feeling of power and authority that was surging through his loins as he surveyed the beautiful European woman chained helpless for his enjoyment. His wife might now be unattractive, but he could forgive her anything while she produced such gorgeous creatures as this one for his enjoyment.

As for Emma, she could not help a feeling of pride and arousal flowing through her at the thought of all the preparations that had been made to her body to make her ready for the all-powerful and ruthless dictator. She recognised her weakness: power and ruthlessness in any man are indeed a heady cocktail for a woman.

There was indeed something very attractive about such a man, especially as she had been cleaned and stretched especially for him. She simply could not help proudly giving her buttocks a little coquettish wiggle, so that her pretty tail feathers shook attractively.

She heard the dictator laugh sardonically at her movement. She knew he was thinking that white women were such sluts at heart!

Then, Emma jumped as she felt a man's hard hands on her buttocks, stroking them and then pulling them apart. She jumped again as she felt the plug being removed. But she jumped even more when she felt something hard pressing against her a manhood, the dictator's manhood, she suddenly realised. She began to protest.

But no attention was paid to her cries. Indeed they seemed to excite him all the more. She heard the chains and pulley being adjusted and felt her hips being slightly raised so that the manhood was now pressing exactly on her well-greased rear entrance.

Again she yelled and tried to writhe in protest, but the hook on her hip band, the bar behind her knees and the stocks holding her neck and wrists, all combined to hold her quite still - and now, she realised with a sob, exactly in position.

There was a long pause. Emma held her breath. She simply could not believe what was happening. Then suddenly the man thrust forward and entered her.

He was huge. No wonder they had stretched her for three whole days! Once again she shouted out and tried to wriggle, but the more she screamed and the more she tried ineffectually to wriggle, the deeper the dictator penetrated and the greater the pleasure she gave.

It was a performance that she was often called on to repeat over the coming weeks - much to the delight of Her Excellency whose hold over her husband was much strengthened by it all.

Poor Emma never knew when Her Excellency was going to summon her to her bed, nor when the four pageboys would grinningly come to collect her for yet another trip to the bathroom and on to kneel across the foot of the dictator's special bed.

It seemed so strange that Her Excellency was interested in her tongue and her beauty lips, whilst the dictator was only interested in her backside. Between them, they certainly kept her busy and exhausted and, of the two, at least the dictator stimulated her to reach climax and showed a curious interest when she did.

Her Excellency was giving a party for her favourite women friends. Delicious food and champagne were being handed round by girls dressed in traditional costume and decked in heavily-beaded jewellery.

This costume went back to the days when the country villages had just consisted of clusters of crudely-thatched mud huts and girls went naked except for rows of beads around their necks, and wore over their intimacies a little embroidered flap that hung down from a string round their waists. The exposed black skins and pert breasts of the native girls were an arousing sight. But a sight that was being particularly discussed by the chattering crowd of well-dressed African women was an even more arousing young woman.

This young creature was dressed identically to the other serving girls, except for white gloves and a maid's white cap. But what was really attracting attention was her equally exposed white skin which contrasted sharply with the black skin of her companions as she blushingly handed round a tray of champagne.

Poor Emma could hardly believe it when she was just given a little native flap to wear for Her Excellency's party. It scarcely hid her hairless beauty lips quite apart from leaving her bare-breasted in public. Now she was so ashamed that she scarcely knew where to look. Oh, how she longed to hide from all these leering men and sneering women!

She saw that a door leading into another room was ajar. Emma was intrigued for it was a door that was normally kept locked. She had never had a chance to look inside, for Her Excellency insisted on her waiting on her day and night and following her about like a little lamb. And when she had gone in to it, she had made Emma wait outside.

But now Her Excellency was busy with her guests. She would not notice if Emma slipped into this other room for a few minutes to hide her nakedness. Quietly, Emma opened the door, entered the room and closed the door behind her.

Then she gasped, for she was in a picture gallery; a gallery of modern art. Astonished, she looked around her. Their Excellencies must be secret collectors of modern abstract pictures. It was a collection that even the Tate Gallery would have been proud to own.

She started to explore and then gave another gasp. There, hanging on the wall in front of her, specially lit up, was Ursula's missing picture. She rushed up to take a closer look. Yes, there was no doubting it really was identical to the photos that Sabhu had showed her. There wasn't a moment to lose! At any moment Her Excellency might notice she was missing or a guest might walk through the door.

Thank heavens she had been allowed to wear her cap and not been made to put her hair into African plaited locks to make her look more like the black serving girls as Her Excellency had at first wanted.

Quickly she took off her cap and pointed the tiny camera at the picture. She took several pictures of it and, while she was about it, some of the other paintings as well.

'*Their Excellencies are now both being very kind to me.*' Ursula read from a pretty post card three days later. '*So I'm a very lucky girl, Eureka!*'

'Eureka!' cried Ursula. She picked up the phone to arrange for Emma's immediate return.

32

Back in Her Cage

It was a week later that Emma returned to London and handed to the delighted Ursula the photographic proof that the stolen picture was hanging up in a secret picture gallery in Her Excellency's palace.

Ursula was so pleased with Emma that, to Emma's own delight, Ursula kept Emma with her in her room for three whole days.

They were three wonderful and thrilling days for Emma – a second honeymoon. Just like our old times together, she thought, before the awful Sabhu, and before those awful cages, belts and manacles and awful clients.

Even more wonderful was that there was no sign of that chit of an Arab girl, Leisha, whom Ursula had been so besotted about. Emma had Ursula all to herself.

Emma fell more in love again with Ursula than ever. Ursula was her wonderful and clever Mistress and the source of so much pleasure and delight. She even allowed Emma to reach peaks of arousal and excitement that made her forget all about Her Excellency and the dictator – and all the humiliations she had suffered earlier from Sabhu.

Indeed, there was no mention of Sabhu, nor of any clients, nor of having to return to the attic. It all seemed a new world for Emma. She even persuaded herself that Ursula would now keep her for herself. She would be her Mistress's pampered favourite, allowed to come and go as she liked. She would be free - free as a bird!

But all good things must come to an end and on the third morning Sabhu suddenly entered Ursula's bedroom in response to a secret summons. In one hand he held his long dressage whip – the whip that Emma had so dreaded. In the other he held a collar and lead.

'Put her back in her cage!' Ursula ordered brusquely.

'No! No!' Emma cried.

But Sabhu pointed to the carpet in front of him and raised his whip. 'Number Four!' he shouted. 'Here!'

The sight of Sabhu and his whip, and his shouted calling of her former number, brought back all Emma's training. With a little sob, she found herself instinctively crawling to his feet and offering her neck to be collared. Then, with tears running down her cheeks, she turned and looked pleadingly at Ursula as Sabhu led her away, crawling on all fours at his feet.

But Ursula was already busy telephoning a client to say that Emma, Number Four, was now available again if she wished to make an appointment to use her.

Back in her cage, Emma was again put into one of the awful belts and had her wrists and ankles manacled again. It was all a terrible shock after a month of freedom from the cage, the belt and the manacles. Her short, but wonderful second honeymoon with Ursula was over.

However, she was delighted to see that an equally crestfallen Leisha, now renamed more humbly Pansy or simply Number Five, was in the cage next to hers. Not only was Pansy now belted and manacled like the other girls, but Sabhu seemed to be taking a particular delight in humiliating her as he broke her, like a circus animal, into performing his tricks.

Perhaps, in fact, his strict attitude to Pansy was in part a reaction to the proud care with which he was handling both Bluebell and Cowslip, and indeed Daisy, who had returned after her trip to the Princess's harem in North Africa. Emma was longing to tell them of her experiences in Africa and of hearing about what had happened to Daisy when Doctor Anna had taken her out to the Saudi Princess.

But, of course, no talking was allowed in the cages. It was a rule that, thanks to the microphone hanging down in front of the cages, was now even more strictly enforced than ever so as to keep the other girls in a quandary as to what might be happening to them under thir belts.

Emma was given her old doll to play with in her cage. But she was surprised to see that, whilst Pansy also had a doll like hers, Sabhu had now given two dolls to each of the other three girls – identical twin dolls. Indeed, Sabhu would quietly watch them playing with their twin dolls, a curious smile on his face.

The twice daily encounters with the milking machine soon had their old effect on Emma and, with her maternal instincts also being brought on by her doll, she found herself being very jealous of the three girls now in milk – and of what she suspected was their true state.

Oh how she wished that she, too, had been given Doctor Anna's treatment. Then she remembered that she was, in fact, a married woman, shortly due to be returned to her husband.

Soon, however, like the other girls, she was back to just concentrating on attracting and pleasing Ursula's clients. It had been a terrible shock when a rather slack performance with a client, on her first day back in the cages, had resulted in her being thrashed by a furious Sabhu. To make it worse, she had been thrashed in front of the smirking Pansy.

Emma found that one change had been made while she was in Africa. Ursula had borrowed the idea from Her Excellency and now, for the selection parades, the girls were naked except for their Bikini-belts – and, to heighten their half nudity, they had to wear white gloves and white maid's caps.

Emma found herself once again being madly jealous of the young Arab girl – not this time over Ursula, but because, being so young and exotic looking, clients sometimes chose Pansy in preference to herself.

Indeed, with five girls to choose from, and three of them being excitingly in milk, it was much harder now to be chosen at all. While Sabhu welcomed the increased jealousy and competition among his charges, Emma soon realised that it was now a serious matter if she was to avoid the end-of-week thrashing for the girl who had pleased the least number of clients.

Soon she was again desperately counting the ticks against her name on the board and waiting, tense and on tenterhooks, for the phone to ring to tell Sabhu just how pleased or disappointed her latest client had been with her performance. As before, it was on these that Sabhu's tips depended and consequently whether he gave her a little sweet or a thrashing.

She never, now, had a chance for a private word with her Mistress, and her success in locating the missing picture seemed to have been forgotten. As before, her life revolved around avoiding Sabhu's whip, and spending long periods gripping the bars of her cage as she desperately thought up ways of outdoing her companions in attracting the attention of clients and of providing them with unforgettable pleasure. All this was, of course, just what Sabhu intended.

So the days passed with poor Emma becoming more jealous and receiving more than her fair share of Sabhu's frightening whip.

But, unknown to her, a new factor had entered her life as one of Ursula's girls. Her oceanographer husband was at last returning from several months of scientific study on a remote Pacific atoll.

33

Home Again – But it's Not the Same Now!

Emma's husband, John, might be quite well off and well connected, but he was also a serious-minded scientist who lived for his work as an oceanographer. He had always been delighted when Ursula, often unknown to Emma, had asked for his agreement, whilst he was away, for her to give 'young Emma' what she would describe as 'an intersting job in the art world that will keep her out of mischief'.

Indeed he had a high opinion of Ursula and of her intelligence and understanding. But he had no idea of her preoccupation with submissive young women of her own sex.

Ursula had, of course, intercepted his letters to Emma. She had not even told her what they said; she did not want the girl being distracted from her job of pleasing the clients. Nor did she want to disturb Emma's acceptance of her subservient role by getting any ideas above her station. Instead she herself used to reply to his letters, saying that Emma was away on a course, but sent her love.

On one occasion, to allay any suspicions, she had dictated a letter for Emma to sign, saying what a wonderful and interesting time she was having, how kind Ursula was being to her, and how she was looking forward to his return. When Emma had then tried to ask Ursula about him, she had had her beaten by Sabhu for impertinence.

When John wrote to Emma saying that at last he was on his way back home, his letter was immediately forwarded to Ursula by the housekeeper she had put into Emma's house. Ursula did not say anything about this to Emma. She would first have to earn a lot more from the clients!

So, it was a greatly surprised Emma who, one day, was taken out of her cage by Sabhu and told to put on the pretty dress that Ursula had specially bought for her.

Emma was thrilled, thinking that Ursula was going to keep her downstairs for another honeymoon. Still wearing her manacles, she proudly paraded up and down in front of the other girls, who were all looking at her jealously from behind the bars of their cages.

Her manacles and Bikini-belt were left on but Sabhu did not put on the usual lead before taking her downstairs. Emma glanced back at the other girls in their cages, and gave a superior little toss of her head. She was special!

To her surprise, Sabhu took her to the garage. Ursula was already sitting in the back of her private car, busy reading some business papers, her brief case open. She did not even look up as Sabhu told Emma to sit beside him in the front and to keep quiet. Like a servant, Emma thought.

Sabhu drove off. Emma did not dare to open her mouth. But how exciting it was to be out of her cage and away from the house. She saw that Ursula was packed as for a journey. She did not dare to ask where they were going. Perhaps to Venice for a second honeymoon? Oh how exciting!

But instead of heading for the airport, they started to drive northwards.

'I'm taking you back to your home where your husband has just arrived,' called out Ursula from the back. 'He's asked me to stay for a few days while you settle down again to domestic bliss. The housekeeper I put in, whilst you were away, has got everything ready and you can leave everything to her.'

'John's back. Oh, how lovely!' cried Emma, like a little girl. Then she looked down at her manacled wrists and ankles. 'But . . .'

'Sabhu will take those off before we arrive, but the belt remains on. I'm not going to have you rushing around looking for men like a bitch on heat, just because you've been let out from my house for a few weeks before your husband goes off abroad again.'

'But my husband . . . surely he'll . . .'

Ursula laughed and pulled a letter out from her bag.

'This is a copy of the letter that Doctor Anna sent him saying that you caught a rather nasty illness, and a possibly contagious little rash, while you were in Africa studying native art and so you won't be fit to perform your conjugal duties for some time. I've told the housekeeper to put you in separate rooms.'

'Oh!' gasped Emma. Ursula always thought of everything. But how embarrassing to have to wear a chastity belt in her own home – and have to spend a penny through the grill and . . .

'Your new housekeeper is also trained as a child's nurse and will be keeping an eye on you,' Ursula went on. 'Sabhu will be briefing her about the belt, but he'll keep the key himself – in London. Otherwise you'll be free to entertain and live your normal life, at least for the time being until John goes off again. Then it will be back to the cages again for you, my girl. Doctor Anna and I have got some special new plans for you – and that's another reason why meanwhile you're going to be kept locked up in the belt!'

Emma gasped and put her manacled hands up to her breasts. Oh no! 'What do you mean . . . Madam?' whispered Emma anxiously. 'What plans?'

'Ah! You'll have to wait and see!' Ursula laughed. 'I don't like inquisitive little girls. But, anyway, I shall be calling you back to London for your weekly inspection by Doctor Anna, and for Sabhu to make sure you're still nice and smooth under the belt. Of course, doubtless, whilst you're there, we'll be able to find a client or two for you – or, who knows, I might even use you myself!

Emma's brain was in a whirl, not knowing whether to be appalled or thrilled at the thought of serving her Mistress again.

'And Sabhu will be weighing and measuring you to make sure you haven't put on any weight. So if you want to avoid his whip you'd better make sure you don't touch a single sweet! Doctor Anna's letter says you're to be kept on a strict diet and the housekeeper has been told. She's also been told to hide all chocolates.'

Emma did not know whether to be sad or excited. On the one hand her hopes of being free again in her own house had been dashed, on the other she had to admit that the idea of appearing to be free but really being under Ursula's secret control sounded very exciting.

But there was more to come.

'And, of course, every morning you're to ring Sabhu and make a formal report to him about your natural functions – and again at mid-day and in the evening, so that he can keep his record book up to date. He'll tell me if you fail to make a single call. And I shall expect a call from you last thing at night in which you can tell me what you've been up to and how much you miss your Mistress!'

How horrible, thought Emma, to have to report to Sabhu. But at least she would be able to speak to her Mistress as well.

'But we shall still be seeing quite a lot of each other as John seems keen for me to come down at weekends. I've asked him if I could perhaps bring the odd interesting lady friend and he was delighted. So, unknown to him, you'll still be earning money for me, Emma – it'll pay for the housekeeper.'

Emma gasped again. Bring a friend? A client? To my own home? Under the nose of my husband? My God!

'Yes, it will be a rather piquant situation. Real country house romances with little footsteps creeping along the passages at night! Of course, I shall be charging a good deal extra for it all!'

That evening Mrs Maunder, the housekeeper, served a delicious dinner. She was a typical former nanny, and delighted to have another young lady, Emma, to look after.

'Don't you worry, my dear,' she had whispered to the embarrassed Emma, 'Mr Sabhu has told me all about you and I'm sure that we'll all get on very well, and Miss de Vere . . . well! Isn't she a charming lady? She's been so kind and generous while I've been looking after the house while you and your husband have been away. You're lucky to have a friend like her.'

Ursula had picked out a low-cut shimmering lime silk caftan for Emma to wear. Like nearly all of Emma's dresses, it had originally been Ursula's, but Ursula had adjusted it so that Emma's nipples were only just concealed and a matching flowing silk scarf hid the tell tale collar of her Bikini-belt.

'But no underwear, Emma!' she had ordered. 'Just your Bikini-belt.'

As Emma sat there, wearing a real evening dress for the first time in months and toying with the first real meal she had eaten since she had been abducted, she was more aware of the belt than ever.

But what a situation! She could hardly bear to meet John's eyes. Clearly he was longing to bed her and had been bitterly disappointed to read Doctor Anna's letter.

'Well, we must get you better soon,' he had said hopefully.

As they went in to dinner, Ursula had gently pinched her bottom. 'I want my little puppy dog to come to my room at midnight sharp,' she whispered, whilst John busied himself lighting the candles. 'She's to crawl in as the clock strikes twelve and then I want to hear three little woofs. And she's to make sure she's wearing the little dog mask I shall ask Mrs Maunder to put on her bed. And if she's a good little puppy dog, I might even let her out of her belt for the night!'

Emma could hardly believe her ears!

But then, as they sat down, Ursula deliberately tossed a little key up into the air.

Emma, now nearly overcome with anticipation and excitement, recognised it instantly. It was the key to her Bikini-belt; her horrible combined chastity belt, purity belt and control belt – the belt that perhaps her Mistress might be unlocking later that night.

'What's that the key of?' asked John jokingly. 'Your jewel box?'

'Ah! That would be telling! Just something I rather like to keep locked up for my pleasure from time to time,' replied Ursula enigmatically, putting the key down on the table beside her place and picking up her evening bag to take out a pretty embroidered hankie.

Emma simply could not take her eyes off the key. She could feel herself becoming more and more aroused under her belt at the thought of being controlled like this. It was terribly exciting and terribly frustrating. Would Ursula really take off her belt at midnight? Oh, the thrill of it all! Oh, how she longed for relief!'

Whilst Ursula and John were talking she could not resist slyly putting her hands down to her lap. Through her dress she could feel the belt locked around her loins. She simply could not help gently lifting up the velcro fastenings. But then, of course, her fingers touched the hard unyielding plastic grill. Oh the frustration of it all!

Then suddenly she jumped and gave a little cry as she felt a nasty little shock between her legs. Ursula, she saw, was quietly putting her hankie away into her bag.

My God, Emma thought, Ursula must have one of those little control boxes in her bag! She must have noticed what Emma was doing and had deliberately given her a shock to remind her that she was still under her Mistress's control even if she was now in her own house and sitting down opposite her unsuspecting husband.

'Are you all right, darling?' asked John, solicitously.

'Oh, yes, thank you,' murmured Emma. What explanation could she give? She lowered her eyes and continued: 'It must have been the sudden shock of being back here again.'

'A nice shock, I hope, Emma,' laughed Ursula. Then she turned to John. 'I'm afraid that, as my friend Doctor Anna wrote and told you, our little Emma is still rather weak from her illness. It's her nerves, you see. She keeps imagining these little shocks.'

Imagining, thought Emma! But John was already nodding

understandingly and Ursula turned to Emma. 'No more little shocks, Emma?'

Emma was staring at her like a rabbit hypnotised by a stoat. 'No! No! Please no!' she cried.

'What do you mean, Emma?' asked Ursula innocently, and then adding, apparently concerned: 'You brought the shock on yourself, didn't you?'

'Yes!' whispered Emma, contritely.

Ursula turned to John again. 'Remember what Doctor Anna said in her letter? Emma just needs a little quiet rest.'

'Yes, so I see,' replied John. 'I'm very grateful to you and Doctor Anna for your help.'

'Oh we're all very fond of little Emma,' said Ursula. 'She's very popular with my friends!'

Then, as John turned to fetch another bottle of wine from the sideboard, she turned to Emma and whispered angrily: 'Just you keep your hands on the table, you dirty little slut! Where I can see them!'

'Are you all right again now, Emma?' teased Ursula in her normal voice as John sat down again.

'Yes,' murmured Emma, demurely. In fact, she could hardly stop herself from falling to her knees at her Mistress's feet and then, looking up at her adoringly to lisp humbly, like a little girl, 'Oh yes, Madam, oh yes!'

Ursula was in sparkling form over dinner, making John laugh and keeping him entertained. But Emma was quietly pensive.

Here she was, she kept thinking, sitting at her own dining room table with her husband and, unknown to him, with the woman who was her strict and adored Mistress: a woman who had such control over her that she had secretly punished her, in front of her husband, for trying to touch herself, and who had locked her up in a chastity belt to keep her for herself and her clients.

It was an explosive and yet highly arousing situation. Oh, how she longed to be able to touch herself to relieve the tension. But of course she couldn't do so nor would she dare to try.

John now wanted to know what she had been up to while studying art with Ursula. Fortunately, Ursula diverted the conversation away to his own adventures in the Pacific.

What, she wondered, would he have said if she had told him about the cages, about Sabhu and the clients, about Their Excellencies and the picture, about . . . Of course, she told herself, he would dismiss it all as another of Emma's little fantasies! But the truth was that she had had a far more exciting time than he – far more!

That night, a pretty young woman crawled quietly down the darkened corridor. She was naked except for her Bikini-belt and over her face was a plastic dog mask.

The house was in complete silence.

Suddenly, she heard the clock in the tower of the village church strike twelve. She scuttled along to the door of Ursula's bedroom and waited on her knees until the last chime of midnight.

Then she reached up, quietly opened the door, and crept into the darkened room. She paused, uncertain as what to do next. Suddenly she felt a sharp shock between her legs. She had forgotten to bark!

'Woof! Woof! Woof!'

'Good little dog! Now come and please your Mistress, and if you use your tongue really nicely, then perhaps I will think about . . .'

34

An Unexpected Guest

It was three weeks later and soon John would be leaving again for several months, posted to another remote atoll in the Pacific.

Every day, three times a day, Emma had had to make, on her private telephone in her bedroom, a humiliating report to Sabhu – and answer his embarrassingly intimate questions. It was, she realised, all a clever way of making her feel that she was still one of Ursula's girls, and still under Sabhu's control, even if she was now living back at home.

Indeed all day she could not help thinking longingly about Ursula; a longing that was made even more poignant by her frustration at being kept locked up in her belt. Every night on the telephone she would pour out her love to Ursula – madly jealous because she could hear one of the other girls licking and stroking her beloved Mistress.

Every week, a shamefaced Emma had reported to Sabhu in London and had stood stark naked on the red spot in the attic marked '4'. Then, watched from behind their bars by the other four girls, Emma had had to stand quite still, her hands clasped behind her neck, her legs apart and her knees bent, while Sabhu had rubbed his special potion over her mound and down between her legs.

Then he had taken her, still stark naked and smooth down to the drawing room where Ursula and Doctor Anna were waiting. She was made to lie on her back on a couch while Doctor Anna, talking in incomprehensible German to Ursula, had examined her intimately. How Emma longed to know what they were discussing. It couldn't just be the weather. She remembered with dread, Ursula's remark that they had special plans for her.

Then Sabhu would take her back to the attic, lock her Bikini-belt back on her, fasten on her old wrist and ankle manacles, and thrust her back into her cage. There she had to wait in silence either for a client who had specially booked her or to be paraded, with the other girls, to a client who had just come 'on spec'.

As Emma knelt silently in her cage, longing to be able to talk to her former companions and to hear how they were getting on, she could not help thinking how awful it was that she, a married woman, was being treated like this. Awful, yes. But also very thrilling.

Once Ursula had come to stay again for the weekend but without the threatened 'lady friend'. But now she *was* coming with one.

'I'm bringing an old friend of yours, Emma, but I'm not going to spoil the surprise by telling you who she is. However, I'm sure John will find her an interesting guest.'

Who could it be? Emma repeatedly asked herself. Perhaps it was the Baroness? But in any case how humiliating to have to make love to another woman in her own house, almost under the eyes of her unsuspecting husband. She wondered if she would dare to refuse to do so. But the memory of Sabhu's whip was still very strong. No; she would just have to go through with it.

Ursula arrived alone on the Thursday night 'to make sure everything was ready'. John was delighted to see her intelligent conversation was rare in the country. But, as usual, Emma had to crawl to Ursula's room at midnight, this time carrying Ursula's own whippy little cane in her teeth. But this time the belt had not been taken off.

'I want you in good form tomorrow night for my client,' Ursula had said. 'She's paying me a fortune to come here and take you in your own house and you'd better please her! I've told Sabhu to accompany her and to bring his whip. If you show any hesitation to please my client, or she is not entirely satisfied with your performance, then he'll be taking you out for a little walk to the old stables and give you a thorough thrashing. So you've been warned!'

Emma was looking out of her bedroom window when Ursula came back from the station with her mysterious guest.

Before leaving to pick her up, Ursula had told John that Emma had a headache and must rest. Then, just to make sure that Emma did not try to run away, she had secretly locked her in her bedroom.

Emma saw Ursula's car drive up to the house. Her heart was in her mouth as she saw the sinister figure of Sabhu, dressed as a chauffeur, get out and open the back door. First Ursula got out and then . . .

Emma simply could not believe her eyes. But there was no doubting the huge figure dressed in bright coloured robes with a matching turban. It was indeed Her Excellency! Oh no! Not her! Emma ran to the door desperate to get out, to run away, to escape. But the solid door was firmly locked.

Emma beat on it, but no one heard. Mrs Maunder, the housekeeper-cum-nanny was in the kitchen. Emma's husband had gone to the door to greet his distinguished guest – and to apologise for his wife's temporary indisposition.

Running back to the window, Emma saw that Sabhu was now bringing in Her Excellency's luggage and moments later she heard his heavy steps on the staircase. Then she heard voices, Her Excellency's and Ursula's, as the guest was shown to her room.

She also heard John politely inviting Her Excellency to come down for tea in an hour's time, after she had relaxed from her journey. By then, he added, his wife would probably be up and about again.

My God, Emma thought! Sobbing, she flung herself on to her bed.

It was a few minutes later that she heard the door being unlocked and in came Ursula. Following her was Sabhu. As he came into the room, he pulled his long whip out from the waistband of his trousers.

The whip! Crouching up on the bed, Emma could not

take her eyes off it. She really was being threatened with the whip in her own house!

'Now, little Emma,' came Ursula's voice. She was speaking softly and kindly. 'You're going to be a good and obedient little girl, for your Mistress, aren't you? You're going to please Her Excellency aren't you? You don't want Sabhu to take you to the stables do you?

'No! No!' Emma almost screamed, her eyes fixed on the whip.

'So you're going to undress – except for your Bikini-belt, of course, and you're going to run along the passage to Her Excellency's room and you're going to go in and say how pleased you are to see her again – aren't you?'

Emma nodded as if hypnotised.

'And don't say a word about the picture yet.'

Again the terrified Emma nodded.

'Number Four!' came Sabhu's harsh voice. He raised his whip. 'Move!'

Emma tore her clothes off like a mad woman. Sabhu opened the door. She ran along the passage, her naked breasts bouncing, and flung open the door to Her Excellency's room.

The hugely fat woman was standing in the middle of the room, with her legs apart. She was obviously expecting Emma. Her robes were half open. Emma had a glimpse of flesh; black mountainous flesh.

'Well, little Emma!' she cried in her strange half French accent. 'My hostess! Now come and give me a kiss . . . no not on those lips . . . on these ones!'

Emma felt her hair being gripped and her face was thrust down. She fell to her knees. She felt Her Excellency part her legs and thrust forward. 'Now let me feel some nice little kisses!' she heard Her Excellency laugh.

There was a sudden knock on the door. Sabhu entered. He saw Emma on her knees at Her Excellency's feet and smiled. 'Forgive the intrusion, Your Excellency,' he said in his Haitian French. 'But Your Excellency will not have had time to unpack the 'girl warmer'. I thought that perhaps Your Excellency might like to use this.'

He handed his whip to Her Excellency who silently took it in one hand whilst holding Emma's face to her body lips with the other.

'Your Excellency will find that the white woman is scared of that whip. It need not be applied very hard.'

He bowed and left the room.

Her Excellency gave Emma a sharp tap with the whip on her naked buttocks. 'Lick, white woman, lick!' she cried hoarsely.

Her Excellency was fascinated.

It was the following afternoon and Emma's African visitor was sitting in one of Emma's comfortable chintz-covered chairs, deep in conversation with John and Ursula, who were sitting opposite her. Sabhu was helping Mrs Maunder, the housekeeper, by acting as a butler, handing round cups of tea and plates of cucumber sandwiches.

To one side, seated in an upright chair, was Emma. She was wearing a tweed skirt and woollen jersey. She was looking flushed and agitated and saying little.

She saw Her Excellency glance at her. Deeply embarrassed, she lowered her eyes. Oh the humiliation! To have had to service a client of Ursula's in her own house – and this one in particular!

But Her Excellency was delighted. To be invited to stay in an English country home was unusual enough. But then secretly to have her pretty hostess at her complete service was thrilling – especially when the hostess had been her own maid servant for a month, and was the very girl she had come back to England to enjoy again.

And the girl's husband was blissfully unaware of what was going on under his very eyes, even when the girl had had to spend all of last night in the bed of an African lady guest!

Ursula had demanded a high price before agreeing to bring her here, saying that otherwise she would not be able to have Emma. But goodness, it was all proving very well worthwhile. Just as Ursula had promised, the mental satisfaction was proving as exciting as the physical.

Ursula had told her that the girl would be at her disposal whenever she wished throughout the weekend – and that was just how it had turned out. And, moreover, to ensure the girl's continual frustration and eagerness, she was kept tightly belted the whole time.

Her Excellency coughed and obediently Emma looked up. Discreetly, Her Excellency pointed upstairs. Emma glanced appealingly at Ursula, and then with a little gasp, excused herself and went out of the room.

'You really must excuse my wife,' John said to Her Excellency, 'but I'm afraid she hasn't been very well. Some bug she apparently picked up somewhere in Africa.'

But Her Excellency was not listening. She knew that in a few minutes time she would again find Emma kneeling naked on the bed in the guest room, eyeing with terror the 'girl warmer' which had been left lying on the bed ready for her. Should she give her four strokes this time or six? Perhaps a nice round five! And which was greater, the present mental satisfaction, or the physical pleasure which was to come?

35

Finale – Now What's Going to Happen?

It was Sunday evening. Ursula and Her Excellency were about to leave Emma's house for London, where Her Excellency was due to catch a plane back to Africa.

Ursula had sent for Emma and humiliatingly told Sabhu to make sure the Bikini-belt was properly locked on her. Oh, the frustration! Oh, the excitement of being under Ursula's complete control!

Emma could hear raised voices coming from Ursula's room. The door had been left slightly ajar. How exciting, she thought. What are Ursula and Her Excellency having a row about? About herself? Gosh! Like a naughty eavesdropping schoolgirl, she crept along the corridor to listen to what her elders and betters were saying.

'Your Excellency,' she heard Ursula say, in a voice she was obviously trying to control, 'how you got the picture is none of my business, nor how much you paid or to whom. But you must have suspected that it was stolen.'

'Bah! So you say!' Her Excellency replied angrily.

'All I know is that I have proof that it is my property, that its theft was reported to the police, and that I have this photographic proof that it is now hanging up in your palace. I want it back – and with as little fuss as possible – or else Interpol will be asking some embarrassing questions and there'll be a great scandal.'

'Interpol! A scandal! Oh no, I don't want that. My husband would never –'

'Then give me back my picture!'

'And if I do, then what do I get – Emma?'

'Emma? Well . . . She earns me a lot of money and Doctor Anna has made rather special plans for her as soon as her husband goes off abroad again. But I suppose we could compromise. Let's see . . . How long would you want her for? Why don't you simply see her on your visits to Europe? Anyway, we can discuss that further on the way to the airport. I'm going off abroad myself for a few days – though I haven't told Emma. Now let's get your baggage down in to the car.'

Emma scuttled away, back to her room, her mind in a turmoil.

They had been talking about using her as if she had no mind of her own – as if she was a mere slave. It was very exciting not knowing what was going to happen to her next, but this was too much!

She hardly knew which was a more frightening prospect: Doctor Anna or Her Excellency? Oh, what did the future hold in store?

Suddenly, the telephone rang. It was her private line – the one she used in the privacy of her bedroom to make her humiliating reports to Sabhu and Ursula. Hardly anyone knew the number. Who could it be? Hesitantly, she picked up the handset.

'Emma?' boomed a man's voice. It seemed familiar.

'Yes,' she said nervously, looking at the door. Ursula would be furious if she learnt that she was taking a call from a man.

'Where the hell have you been? I've been trying to get hold of you for weeks,' boomed Henry's distinctive voice.

Henry! It was Henry, who had been her lover, before he had gone off and got married. Henry! The only man who had ever thrilled and dominated her in the same exciting way as Ursula. She felt a sudden tingling sensation running through her body.

'I suppose you've been off with that bloody bitch Ursula! Has she got her claws into you again? Locked you up in a chastity belt did she?'

How did he know? Henry always seemed to guess everything. 'Yes,' she whispered.

'Yes, what?' boomed the voice again. 'You call me sir and don't forget it.'

'Yes sir!' whispered Emma, giving a frightened look at the still open door. But the tingling feeling was growing stronger. Oh Henry! Why did you disappear? she thought.

'That's better,' came Henry's voice. 'Now listen carefully. I'm in a hurry. Meet at my club in London for lunch next Tuesday. One o'clock sharp!'

'But –' Emma began to wail.

'No ifs or buts, just be there. And look pretty. Don't wear anything under your dress unless you're still locked in that bitch's chastity belt! See you Tuesday!'

The phone went dead.

Emma heard footsteps coming down the corridor. Ursula! Guiltily, she hastily put down the phone, her mind more in a torment than ever. But the exciting tingling feeling was almost overwhelming.

'Now, Emma, come and say goodbye to your Mistress,' she heard Ursula call out.

Her mind in a whirl, Emma rushed out into the corridor and, with a sob, flung herself into her Mistress's arms.

'Oh you are being an affectionate little girl, Emma. Are you going to miss your Mistress very much? Well, we'll meet again very soon and meanwhile, don't forget to make all your daily reports to Sabhu. And remember, no flirting with any man or else!'

Oh my God, Emma was thinking, now what am I to do?'

It seemed another, even more complex, time was just around the corner.

NEW BOOKS

Coming up from Nexus and Black Lace

Pyramid of Delights by Kendal Grahame
November 1996 Price £4.99 ISBN: 0 352 33112 7
Ancient Egypt. Many lascivious diversions are enjoyed in the court of the pharaoh, and into it stumbles a handsome, libidinous young soldier, Aran, who is all but sated by a beautiful Princess and her handmaidens. Then Aran is drawn to the Pyramid of Delights – a forbidden temple where mysterious and supremely erotic rituals are carried out. He determines to discover its secrets, regardless of the risks involved.

Warrior Women by Yvonne Strickland
November 1996 Price £4.99 ISBN: 0 352 33113 5
The land of Manantia is ruled, with a rod of iron, by the leather-uniformed women of the warrior class. Jennar – a young, athletic blonde, captured from the primitive Outworld – is trained to be a warrior and, with the help of Vargan, her lesbian mentor, fights her way to the upper ranks, discovering a taste for domination in the process.

Madam Lydia by Philippa Masters
December 1996 Price £4.99 ISBN: 0 352 33115 1
Victorian London. Lydia is now a fully-fledged working girl. As she assists an increasingly wealthy and hedonistic clientele – both male and female – with the realisation of its kinkiest fantasies, she comes to enjoy the exhibitionism, ritual and role-play involved – and relishes having her own sexuality tested to its very limits.

Eden Unveiled by Maria del Rey
December 1996 Price £4.99 ISBN: 0 352 33116 X
Sex and discipline form the basis of the alternative lifestyle enjoyed in Eden, a small, hi-tech community deep in the British countryside. When Eden's founders suspect that plans to undermine their control are afoot, they recruit a young couple to spy on its other residents, as they are subjected a programme of bizarre sexual training.

Julie at the Reformatory by Angela Elgar
December 1996 Price £4.99 ISBN: 0 352 33134 8
When Julie is sentenced to three years of bondage, discipline and corporal punishment at Roughton Hall Reformatory, she discovers that total submission is demanded by the sadistic mistresses. Behind closed dormitory doors, however, fellow inmates provide comforting relief from the daily humiliation, and revolution is soon in the air.

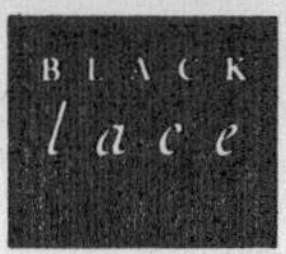

Passion Flowers by Celia Parker
November 1996 Price £4.99 ISBN: 0 352 33118 6
Katherine – a brilliant but stressed-out lawyer – is sent, by her boss, on a well-earned holiday, only to discover that her mystery destination is a revolutionary sex therapy clinic, located on an idyllic Caribbean island. For the first time in her life, Katherine feels free to indulge in the sybaritic pleasures all women deserve. But will she be able to retain this sense of sexual empowerment and liberation when it's time to leave?

Odyssey by Katrina Vincenzi-Thyne
November 1996 Price £4.99 ISBN: 0 352 33111 9
Historian Julia Symonds agrees to join the sexually sophisticated Merise and Rupert in their quest for the lost treasures of Ancient Troy. Using her newly discovered powers of seduction, Julia extracts the necessary information from the leader of a ruthless criminal fraternity, and soon finds herself relishing the ensuing game of sensual deception – as well as the numerous other pleasures to which her new associates introduce her.

Continuum by Portia da Costa
December 1996 Price £4.99 ISBN: 0 352 33120 8
When Joanna takes a well-earned break from work, she also takes her first step into a new continuum of strange experiences and enters a decadent parallel world of pain, perversity and unusual pleasure. Simultaneously exalted and degraded, she explores a secret world of erotic suffering. Will her working life ever be the same again?

The Actress by Vivienne LaFay
December 1996 Price £4.99 ISBN: 0 352 33119 4
1920. Milly Belfort's facade of innocence cannot hide her innate sensuality forever and, when she renounces the life of a bluestocking, in favour of more fleshly pleasures, her adventures in the Jazz Age take her from the risqué fringes of the film industry, to the debauched excesses of the yachting set, to a stint as a Mistress of Correction.

Île de Paradis by Mercedes Kelly
December 1996 Price £4.99 ISBN: 0 352 33121 6
Shipwrecked on a tropical island, the virginal Angeline comes to enjoy the eroticism of local ways. When some of her friends and lovers are captured by a depraved band of pirates and taken to the harem of Jezebel – slave mistress of nearby Dragon Island – she and her handmaidens have a very sensual role to play in the rescue strategy.